# Isabella's Shield

By Kara S. McKenzie

For more information on the Light Romance Quaint Novels, visit Kara's website at: http://www.karasmckenzie.weebly.com

First Edition
ISBN-13: 978-1515127949
ISBN-10: 151512794X

## Other Novels by Kara S. McKenzie:

A Gate Called Beautiful, TJT Designs & Publications

Kalista's Hope

A New Dance

# Dedication

To my family and friends.

# Isabella's Shield

## By Kara S. McKenzie

"…I am your shield, and your very great
reward." Genesis 15:1, KJV

# Chapter 1

Matheu set his goblet on the table, and his jaw opened slightly as he eyed the fair young woman seated in the great hall across the room from him. She turned to adjust the ribbons on a little girl who sat beside her and put a finger to her lips to shush a small boy, then pushed a stray, wheat-colored ringlet of her own hair over her shoulder. She smoothed out the folds of her silken gown and took a drink from her goblet, then placed her hands back in her lap, keeping a close eye on the two children next to her.

Matheu's friend, Dante nudged him in the ribs chuckling. "I wouldn't think too much on Alward London's daughter. A knight's salary will never be enough for him."

Matheu didn't take his eyes off the young woman. "She's lovely though, isn't she?"

Dante grinned. "From this distance. Yet, you cannot be sure of what you might find, if you were to cross the room."

Matheu took a bite from a piece of meat on his platter. He gave his friend a sidelong glance and then smiled. "I'm sure there's nothing wrong with my eyes, or with her for that matter. And by the looks of it, it seems her beauty goes beyond what you are seeing."

He marveled at the way she fussed over the children sitting next to her on the wide bench, clearly too old to be her own, maybe her brother and sister? There was something considerate in her behavior toward them, and her concern for them was apparent, because she never took her eyes from them.

When he began to get up, Dante pulled him back to his seat. "You must at least wait for the dancing. You cannot introduce yourself to her, without speaking to her father, first. He's the host in this place."

This time Matheu grinned, sidelong. "I suppose you're right." He resignedly took his seat. "I'll wait. But, it will not be easy."

\*\*\*\*\*

Isabella winced at the sound of her siblings arguing. "Henry, Anabel. Put that down," she whispered to them. "You'll make father angry."

Her younger brother and sister turned, both dropping the piece of carved sugar sculpture that they'd been feuding over, from their small fingers. It fell onto a plate between them, spraying sweet crystals all over the table.

Anabel giggled. "Aw, Isabella, he won't care what we do. You see, Cook made a special treat for us."

Henry nodded. "Anabel's right. He never gets angry with us."

Isabella shook her head. "Well, I think father should make you behave. But, if you keep it up, you could end up like Hastulf, thinking he can do anything he wants and get away with it."

All three of them turned to the head of the table.

Isabella sighed. Hastulf, their older cousin, was seated next to his father dressed in his usual fanciful attire. She couldn't help noticing the rapt attention that was directed toward him, by those around him and how he seemed to delight in it immensely.

Henry laughed. "Ha! Hastulf's a silly fool, and everyone knows it."

"Henry! It is not becoming of you to be saying such things." Isabella frowned. "You must be kind to your cousin."

Anabel patted Isabella's arm and smiled. "Aw, sister. Hastulf cannot help it. But, I suppose we should to listen to you, so we do not draw the wrong kind of attention to ourselves."

Henry looked down. "Anabel's right. We should listen."

Isabella smiled. "Well, I'm glad you'll change your ways. I'm sure father will notice it, and not in a good way. He will see to it you are not misbehaving."

They began eating their food.

Isabella eyed the ornate room, flickering with lanterns. Servants in brown, woolen tunics and hose scurried past, attempting to delight the lords and ladies. Social events were not something she relished in, and without her twin, whom she had been so abruptly torn from, the meal seemed unbearable. She wished Blysse were still with them, but couldn't blame her sister for abandoning them when she did. Blysse had good reason to run away.

Blysse and Isabella were identical by date of birth, yet not by looks, nor fashion of personalities. In most aspects, they couldn't have been more different. Isabella wasn't exactly considered plain, and yet without the rosy glow and lively personality her sister possessed, she went virtually unnoticed within the confines of family and among the social circles. And while Blysse relished in the limelight of festive occasions, Isabella found isolation and quiet her solace.

She looked around the room, not surprised at the great amount of people attending the party. Her mother always made sure there was a crowd at every dinner she hosted. Ladies in woven gowns of bright colors, wearing tall, peaked hats, draped with flowing cloth, filled the room, and gentlemen from all walks of life, in their dark, silken tunics, woolen hose and leather boots, conversed easily amongst themselves.

Her father and mother sat at the end of the table she was at, along with the most influential guests. Other slabs of wooden tables filled the spacious room with peasants and Londoners alike. In the far corner of the room, there was one, usually reserved for the knights.

Isabella's brow winkled, when she realized two men at the knight's table seemed to be regarding her with interest. She looked quickly away. Her father wouldn't appreciate any attention given to her by a knight, especially those passing through on their way to the tournaments. And if they were anything like the knights at Godfrey Hall, she wanted nothing to do with them. She didn't dare look back at them again, especially in her father's presence.

She turned her attention to Anabel and Henry instead.

*****

Alward London shook his head, the lines in his jaw tight. "I don't know how I ever raised such an obstinate witch, running off with a shoemaker of all things. And for what purpose? So she could live with a man who cuts leather for a living?" He turned to the servants scowling. "The music! Where are the lutes and harps?"

A chill hung over the dark, cavernous hall. Sounds crackled in the stone fireplace at the far side of the room where a dirty, wool clad man with dark, green hose stooped and tossed two heavy logs on the fire. He bowed and backed out of the room beneath an arched doorway. A servant woman motioned to others, and immediately the room was livened with stringed instruments and tambourines.

Isabella lowered her head and looked down at her bread trencher, which held large pieces of roasted lamb. She lifted a thick slice, nibbling at the corner. She couldn't understand why her father treated Blysse the way he did. Her sister might've been unruly at times, but was certainly not a witch.

And what other choice did Blysse have but to run off with Alan? Marriage to Wolfhart? Even she would've chosen a peasant's life, working morning to night as a shoemaker's wife, over marriage to that man. Someone said he whipped his servants and was suspected of lacing his brother's wine with poison, so he could have his family's wealthy estate.

Lord London sniffed and turned to Wolfhart. He pulled his woven brown surcoat tighter around him and drew a thick-rimmed goblet of wine to his lips. "I still don't understand why that blasted girl chose a peasant over you, Wolfhart. She would have been well set, with all your riches."

Wolfhart reached out a wrinkled hand and drew a slice of bread and cheese to his lips, jowls sagging as he took a bite. His other hand rested on an extended belly threatening to tear the seam on his shirt. "Tis a shame it's come to this. 1349's been distressing, and it'll be worse without Blysse as my wife."

"Blysse will pay dearly for what she's done. You can count on that. But, at least with the truce in this troublesome war, England might rally again."

Wolfhart nodded. "We've spent too much money on this conquest. France is worn down, but not broken by any means. I don't see any end to it."

Alward of London leaned back in his chair. "It could be years before it's over, but with this lull in it, I intend to enjoy what we peace we have."

# Isabella's Shield

Isabella glanced down the thick, wooden table, past earthenware platters piled with food. Her eyes rested on Wolfhart. He was wiping his mouth with the back of his hand, a sour expression on his face. She shuddered at the thought of him, and was glad such a disagreeable man wasn't her sister's husband.

\*\*\*\*\*

Isabella looked up when Angnes Small, a tiny fair-haired servant with light brown freckles bridging her nose, came bustling through the arched doorway. Her brown, woolen tunic covered her feet, which were barely showing underneath her long skirt. She held her tattered shawl tightly around her, twisting the end.

Angnes hesitantly approached Isabella's father at the end of the table. Her face was pained as she stopped short at his feet. She curtsied. "Sir. I've news. I'm sure you'll want to hear it."

Isabella's mother, Muriolda, scolded, "This cannot wait, Angnes?" Her green eyes narrowed. She lifted a hand to secure a piece of thick, brown hair, which slipped from the netted covering, holding coiled plaits at the back of her head.

Angnes drew a breath. She scuffed the floor with her soft leather shoes and shook her head. "No, Madame. There's a vile force afoot, some are saying it's the work of accursed fairies."

Muriolda's glittering jewels slid to one side of her neck against her fair skin, as she turned to her husband. "Alward? Maybe we should listen to her."

Lord London waved his hand impatiently. He shot Angnes an impatient look. "If you think it's important, then say it. We've matters to attend and can't wait all night."

Angnes looked him square in the eye. "It's Eustace, the baker, Lord London. He's dead, sir, with the most dreadful sickness!"

Lord London's square jaw jerked slightly. He lifted a dark brow. "But it was merely days ago that he got sick?"

"Yes, Lord London, it was the black spots that got him." She shivered, as if she recalled something terrible. "And his neck popped out the size of a fist. He had chills and a fever and was dead before he knew what took him over. It happened fast, but he suffered horribly."

Muriolda's eyes registered alarm. She took her husband's hand. "Do you think it's some type of curse set upon us?"

Isabella shivered in the cold draft of the spacious stone room, despite the fire along the opposite wall. She could barely feel the heat from it. She watched for her father's response.

"Not anything to concern ourselves with I'm sure, other than we may have to go without bread for a time with the baker dead and gone. I suppose we'll need to hire a new one."

Angnes sighed. "I'll speak to the bailiff. He'll have this done, m'lord. And how do you want us to be dealing with Eustace's carcass?"

Alward snorted, a look of displeasure on his face. "Go and find someone to bury it, of course."

"I will, sir."

Isabella's father waved his hand impatiently. "Go! We're having a meal and party! We're not even close to speaking the ending prayer!"

Angnes curtsied. "Yes, m'lord." She turned and went back out through the stone archway taking short, clipped steps.

Isabella watched Angnes disappear. She felt a gnawing in her stomach, as she took a bite of the spicy pottage set on the table by one of the cooks. She swallowed hard.

Before her sister left, she hadn't given much thought to the commoners' lives and how people treated them, but because her twin was gone, things were different. Her sister *was* a commoner. An ache settled deep inside her, when she thought of how her father spoke of prayers, after so callously dismissing the whole incident of the baker's death.

Anabel looked alarmed. "Isabella, do you know anything about this? They're saying there are black spots and swellings?"

Isabella reached over and patted her little sister's arm. "Don't worry, dear. We're living in the manor away from it all."

Anabel smiled, her expression softening. "So it won't affect us?"

Isabella smiled back. "No. Don't be afraid."

# Isabella's Shield

Anabel leaned over her plate of food, eyeing other dishes being passed around. She sighed. "It's hard not to be, when so many things are happening."

Isabella looked around. The servants moved to a separate table at the far side of the great room, eating the left over food bits and throwing used bread trenchers to the dogs who impatiently waited under the tables. Three of the wolfish animals ripped into a piece of meat, snarling and snapping at each other. The people around them leaned back laughing.

She wondered. Would the walls of the manor hold this sickness from them? Or was it already among them, in the company of Eustace's friends? Sickness was not selective between the rich or poor. It didn't play favorites. She hoped the walls, were a great enough barrier.

Her eyes were drawn to a small amount of light which filtered in from outside the tall, ornate windows on the side of the building. Some of the servants circulated, re-lighting candles in the lanterns hanging from the walls. They stoked the roaring flames in the great fireplace and waited on her father's guests. Isabella lived a privileged life, but understood there were other people who were not so lucky. Blysse was one of them, now. How would her twin fare beyond the manor walls?

She caught her own name being dropped in a conversation at the end of the table and looked to where her father was sitting. His eyes were intent and riveted to Wolfhart Butler, who suddenly cocked his head to the side.

"You say there's another daughter, Blysse's twin? I had no knowledge of this." His small, black eyes scanned the room impatiently. "Where is she? I might want to be making a deal for her." He laid his cloth napkin on the table, one wrinkled hand reaching up and scratching the top of his balding head.

Isabella shuddered. Were they speaking of her?

"What is the lady's name?"

Her father's eyes glinted. He drew a goblet to his lips and took a sip. "Isabella, and she's every bit the woman that Blysse was. You might even find her even more well suited to you."

Isabella suddenly felt sick to her stomach and set her wine goblet on the table. They *were* talking about her. She heard it again, her name being passed between them at the end of the table. She closed her eyes, breathing deeply. Her father couldn't do this, not to her. The matter was closed. Wolfhart had eyes for her sister.

Her heart beat wildly in her chest. She clenched her fists under the table. Did they trade women like cattle? Were there no feelings involved with men?

From the tales circulating among the servants, Wolfhart was a heartless snake. Why couldn't a father take pity on his daughter and make a match in love for her?

She sighed. In her case, the suitor's money was the only thing that mattered, and Wolfhart was rich. A daughter's value was in the marriage deal. This is what Isabella heard so often as a child, and this is what she knew she meant to Alward of London.

And Lord London, her father, considered her the same as Blysse and all other women for that matter, including her own mother. They were the gate of the Devil, or the sting of the serpent as her cousin, Hastulf would whisper in her ear so often, along with so many other men she knew.

She wouldn't look up, sensing all eyes at the table suddenly on her. She knew Hastulf wore that pleased grin on his lips beneath a slightly crooked, hawk-like nose, so similar to her uncle who sat beside him. Both of them looked her way, smiling.

She ached to run from the room and escape, as her sister Blysse had done, but knew it wasn't possible. She had nowhere to go, and no one to help her, not as her sister had.

"She's the flaxen maid on the end of the table." Alward of London turned his head toward her. "She looks nothing like her twin, yet Isabella's as worthy a prize as Blysse. I wouldn't take less in money for her."

Isabella sucked in her breath. No. She cringed. She prayed a quick prayer, hoping God would hear her pleading heart. She imagined Wolfhart, the cruel old man, wringing his hands and contemplating the price. Her head remained bent and still.

"From where I sit, she doesn't compare. She's not the dark beauty Blysse was." Wolfhart muttered something underneath his breath.

Isabella gritted her teeth, suddenly nauseous. As if *he* were a prize.

"Isabella!" Her father summoned her. "Wolfhart wants to take a look at you! Come!"

Her voice croaked. "Father? Must I?"

"Come here!" He motioned to her.

Isabella's head bolted upright, and she shivered. She rose and went to her father, tipping her head down, her hair hanging in her face.

***** 

Matheu glanced across the room, when he heard Lord London's voice. He watched the young woman get up and take wary steps to her father and stop short of him, her lovely, flaxen hair spilling over her bent shoulders. She lifted a hand to her distressed face, wiping back a tear that threatened to drop.

"What are they saying?" he asked Dante. The room was silent, but from the far corner of the room, the words were still muffled. Matheu could guess what was happening.

When he made a move to get up, Dante pulled him back down. "Matheu, leave it alone. It's not your business. You can do nothing."

Matheu sat back down, agitated. "It appears an agreement's being made." He let out a breath.

Dante shook his head. "It certainly does appear so. I'm sure we'll know soon enough."

***** 

Isabella's father reached out and lifted her chin, and then pushed her hair away from her face. She shook, as she held herself upright. Her eyes filled with tears.

The sagging jowls around Wolfhart Butler's mouth turned up slightly. "Her eyes are odd. Is that blue or purple?" He rubbed his hands together and then stilled them.

Isabella's father looked pleased. "A trait you're likely not to see, a rare, dark violet. She'll draw a good price for me, this one."

9

Wolfhart let out a breath of disgust in a mock display of annoyance. "It may be a worthy trait, but she's not worth the money of Blysse, not so handsome. I like spirit in a woman, and don't see a lot in this one. Yet, we could bargain for a price."

Isabella gritted her teeth again. They were bartering for the best deal. At least it might buy her a week or two before the amount was set.

She felt a tear slip out of her eye and trail down her cheek. She wiped it away with the back of her hand.

Alward of London's eyes narrowed. "I'm not taking any less than what I offered for Blysse." He let out a breath with a dismissive air.

Wolfhart extended a thick, wrinkled hand and stroked the sleeve of Isabella's dark blue, damask gown.

*****

Matheu groaned. "*Wolfhart's* the one her father's betrothing her to? That snake? How could the man do such a thing?"

Dante let out a breath. "I, too, feel for the young lady. But, it's obvious Lord London will make a great deal of money in the process. From what I've heard, Wolfhart has a fortune."

Matheu shook his head. "But, it isn't right. It doesn't make sense."

Dante shrugged. "Yet, he can do as he pleases when it comes to his daughter." He eyed Matheu warily. "And as I told you before, you can do nothing."

Matheu bristled. He watched the proceedings, the lines in his face hard. "But, Wolfhart doesn't deserve her, and someone must at least see to it, that her father understands this."

*****

Isabella endured Wolfhart's touch, fearing her father's wrath, if she didn't. She regarded her mother with a pleading look in her eye.

Muriolda remained quiet, her face indifferent. She began to eat.

"You think on it Wolfhart, and we'll speak of it later." Lord London smiled. "There's no need to make a quick decision. There's time to decide."

Wolfhart seemed somewhat put out, answering reluctantly. "Next week, I'll be coming back through London, and we'll speak then. I'll be needing to leave for my manor in the country, as there's trouble brewing between the serfs."

Lord London nodded. "I look forward to seeing you again. At some time, I think we'll be reaching an agreement." He had a pleased expression on his face.

Isabella shivered.

Isabella's cousin's eyes gleamed, the mousy brown cowlick on his forehead falling forward, as he tipped his head to her. His mouth drew into a thin, self-righteous smile. Piercing gray eyes, ran coldly through her. Isabella realized, he believed what he was taught since birth, that she and the rest of her family were tainted and not worth a farthing.

She lifted her head. "May I leave, Father?" Her knees shook, and she was no longer hungry. She drew back from Wolfhart's hand, still clutching her gown. The flaring, blue skirt was wedged between his two fingers, and she yanked it away in an unladylike gesture. In this moment, she chose to ignore the impropriety.

Wolfhart's grin twisted into what appeared to be a scowl.

There was a pleading look in Isabella's eyes directed at her father.

Alward sneered. "Not staying to be offering the ending prayer, Isabella?"

Isabella didn't respond, biting her lip.

Her father's eyebrow rose, and he waved her off. "Go! Get out of here! But, in the future, I expect you to be paying off in gold."

Isabella made smooth, slow strides toward the doorway in an effort not to trip over her gown. Her long, leather shoes made soft sounds against the floor. She wished to run, and yet knew it was impossible with the ridiculous length of her tunic, the sign of a true lady. Oh, how she ached to be a peasant in a time like this, a young girl marrying for love!

She heard Hastulf chuckle behind her and the other men break out into laughter.

\*\*\*\*\*

It took all Matheu had not to go after the delicate, young woman, who fled from the room, as if markedly upset by what had transpired. He knew what he'd surmised all along had to be true. There were negotiations in the works for the young woman to be wed to that villainous dog, Wolfhart. He must at least speak to her father and try to dissuade the man from making such a deal.

This time, when Dante tried to deter him from making a move, he didn't heed his friend's warning. He strode purposefully across the room, asking to speak privately with Alward London himself.

\*\*\*\*\*

"You wish for a private meeting?" Alward London, eyed the imposing young man curiously. And then he got up. "I suppose I can spare a moment. Come."

Matheu followed the older man to an inner chamber of the castle and into a private room.

Alward gestured to a small table and chair. "Here, take a seat and tell me why your look is one of grave concern."

Matheu preferred to be eye to eye with the man, so declined the offer. Although Alward London wasn't a short man, Matheu had the advantage and tipped his head slightly downward to meet Alward's eyes. "Lord London, I apologize for the inconvenience, but I felt it necessary to speak with you."

Alward let out a breath. "Concerning a knight's position? Do you wish to sign on at Godfrey Hall?" And then his brow wrinkled. "Or is this about that blasted plague?"

Matheu didn't waste time. He gestured to the great hall. "The matter involves your daughter, sir."

Alward London looked surprised. And then he laughed. "Isabella?" His eyes danced. "I suppose you think me a fiend for marrying her off to Wolfhart? Is that it?"

Matheu was taken back a moment. "Well, sir. I do believe he's beneath a woman of her standing."

Alward laughed again. "Do you even know the worth of his estate? Wolfhart? Inferior to her? Isabella will be well set. She'll lack nothing, with his money."

He eyed Matheu curiously, rubbing his chin. "You're not wishing to propose a deal for my daughter on a knight's salary? As if that would even come close to what Wolfhart would offer?"

"How could I make a proposal, when I don't even know her, sir? I've never met her. I'm merely asking for you to consider another man, one more worthy in deed for her."

Alward's jaw tightened, and his dark eyes turned hard like flint. "You sir, are coming between two lords with an agreement. Is this the business of a knight to interfere with a gentleman's decision? My daughter is certainly not your affair." He snorted arrogantly.

Matheu held his hands to his side to keep himself from strangling the man. He couldn't understand how anyone could do such a cruel thing to his own daughter. But, it was clear that no one could stop him from carrying out his black deed. Lord London's mind was made up. Matheu wasn't going to talk this high-handed man out of anything.

He took a step back and let out a breath. "I can see my words hold no merit in your eyes, and I will have no way of convincing you otherwise."

Alward looked nonplussed, shrugging casually, a smile tugging at the corner of his mouth. "You're right in saying so, sir. I will not be swayed."

A thread of anger ran through Matheu, as he pushed his hands through his dark hair. He was about to say something else, and then drew back, his jaw clenched and his eyes hard. "Then, it looks as if there's nothing I can do. It pains me to say it, but if I cannot convince you, I'll suppose our time here is finished. I'll let myself out and not bother you again. But, in faith, I'll leave this in the Lord's hands and will surely pray for your daughter. I am certain she'll need his help in the days to come." He bent his head slightly and left the room.

*****

Outside another hall, Isabella hiked up her gown and bolted down the dark passageway lit with lanterns, to her room off the solar room. She lay down on her bed and began to sob. She shivered from the draught in the room, as the warm stones had not been put out yet. She pulled a dark covering around her. The window let in the last rays of sunlight, yet it wasn't enough to warm her through the thick walls.

Blysse was gone, and now this. She couldn't even bear to think of it. She'd pay a high price for her title as lady and for the comforts she'd been afforded growing up at Godfrey Hall, her parent's rich manor house in the country.

*****

Matheu shook his head, as he got onto his horse. "That pompous man wouldn't give heed to any type of reason, so bent upon the riches he'll receive for his consent. All that can be done is to pray for that young lady and conclude that God will see her through."

Dante followed suit and climbed on his horse, his face grim. "It *tis* a sad affair. She'll most likely become the wife of more than one rich old man, before her time is up."

Matheu pulled his shield closer to him. "And yet, the Lord can extinguish all the burning arrows, sent her way, so I'll keep this in mind this, for her sake."

Dante smiled. "And I to, as it will surely be her escape."

Both of them gave a quick sound and dug their heels into their horse's sides. Not far down the road, they took different paths, Matheu on the route to the next town west of them, and Dante following the path home to the north. They planned to meet up again after the tournaments.

# Isabella's Shield

\*\*\*\*\*

Hours later, Isabella heard footsteps outside her room, recognizing the quick, short steps of Angnes Small, the servant woman only a few years older than herself. Angnes laid three large, warm stones on the floor and lit a candle, setting it down on a small table next to her bed.

As the servant crossed the room, Isabella held her arms out and fell into Angne's comforting embrace.

"I came quickly when I heard the news." Angnes held tightly to Isabella, smoothing back the damp, tousled tresses from her lady's forehead.

Isabella peered up at her, wiping the tears that kept falling. She couldn't keep from shaking, partly due to the coldness in the air and partly because of the fear that coursed through her. "I can't marry him, Angnes. How can I bear something so horrible?" She choked out the words and began crying again.

Angnes held Isabella away from her, propping her up. "We don't know what will happen." Her voice was motherly and tender, even at her young age.

Angnes had been friends with Isabella since they were children. She spoke softly, pulling Isabella's wool coverlet around her shoulders, noticing her shaking intensify. "No young lady's deserving of this. That man is a blackheart, if I ever saw one."

Isabella turned and bit her lip. A silence consumed the candlelit room. Her dark eyes widened. "You're saying this, even if I'm a gate of the Devil?"

There was a brief flicker of anger in Angnes' eyes. She reached out and grasped Isabella's shoulder, lifting her chin. "Listen, my dear, and remember the things I say."

Angnes spoke quietly, watching the door furtively. She had a serious look in her eyes. "Your father says you are the gate of the Devil, yet each and every one of us sin. You're no more a gate of the Devil than any of us, for that matter, including the men here. And you do know, sin did enter the world through Adam."

Light from the candle threw shadows on the wall, and the sound of Angnes' voice seemed to echo in Isabella's ear. Isabella's lips parted slightly. "Angnes! What you're saying is blasphemy!" A chord of fear struck deep in her heart.

Angnes quickly shook her head. "No, not blasphemy, but the truth."

Isabella had never heard such a thing. Sin, through Adam? And yet, he was a man? The tears quit running on her cheeks. She sat upright and the wool covering fell from her. She adjusted the sleeves of her gown. "But, you *don't read*, Angnes? You're but a handmaid."

"I'm learning from men who study the Word. They're reading it aloud to me and teaching me to read."

Isabella looked astonished. "The Holy Bible? But they're not monks? And you're a woman?"

Angnes shook her head. A strand of hair slipped out from the plait of woven, coiled blonde braids on her head, and she tucked it behind her ear. "And yet, they listen to God and through this, they understand the Good Book. They want others to know the Holy Scriptures."

"But I thought only the friars and priests should be teaching these things? They can instruct us on what it means."

Angnes sighed. "It's what some of them want us to believe and yet, these men are helping me to understand the scripture by letting me hear what it says. Through them I've learned that God can speak to each one of us."

Isabella took Angnes' arm. "But, they have no authority to do this. We should go through a priest to understand."

Angnes bit the edge of her lip. "We can and if they are godly, they can help. But, the scripture says we have a High Priest we can go directly to with our needs, and that Jesus is this intercessor."

The servant woman looked at the door again. "And if you read the words in the Good Book, there are verses that encourage the study of it. They teach us that we'll grow in our understanding if we do. One of them in the book of Acts says the Berean Jews were more noble, because they studied the scriptures and checked it to see if what Paul said was true."

Isabella drew in a short breath. "Angnes, you're saying the friars and priests don't teach truth?"

Angnes' voice lowered to a whisper. "Not all of them. There are priests who still follow the Word and teach it correctly. Yet, in these days, many of them choose their own way, instead. And how are we to know what is true, unless we read it for ourselves? Do we want to be led astray by men?"

Isabella leaned closer to the small servant woman. Her eyes were suddenly large. She was interested, in a fearful sort of way. Sometimes she felt some of the monks and priests acted unscrupulously, and she wondered why they did. But, she still trusted them to tell the truth.

"Tell me, Angnes. What have these men been teaching you?" She glanced at the stone archway leading from her bedroom into the empty space beyond. The heavy, wooden door was open on its great bronze hinges. There were no footsteps or sounds close by. The flame on the table was growing dimmer. Time was getting short for them to be talking of such matters. Others would be coming down the hallway soon. "Quick, I want to know."

Angnes leaned closer. "When I said the sin came to the world through Adam, I meant it. Eve was deceived."

Isabella looked shocked. "So you're saying the *men* are the *gates* of the Devil?"

Angnes smiled. "No, Isabella. You've been led to believe wrongly, but it is why we must study the word diligently to know what truth is, so no one will deceive us."

"Truly? Then, what does the Good Book say?"

Angnes grew serious. "That none of us are without sin, and we're all destined to destruction. Truly, if there is any sin in us, it's not possible to approach a Holy God, not even to be entering heaven when we're dead."

A sudden fearfulness overtook Isabella for she knew on this very day she'd sinned against the Lord with the anger she felt in her heart for her family and for that loathsome man, Wolfhart.

Angnes was more insistent. "Isabella? Do you understand what I'm imparting to you?"

Isabella looked down and fidgeted with the hands in her lap. "But it's not possible, to not sin, Angnes. You said it yourself. Who is able to keep every law?"

Angnes sighed. "Not a one, I fear."

Isabella tugged on the brown, wool shawl Angnes draped about her neck. "Then, how is anyone redeemed? Is there a way for us?"

Angnes patted her shoulder. "There is."

"But, Angnes?" The tears were gone from Isabella's eyes.

Angnes took Isabella's hands in her own. "You must plead for forgiveness, dear, for all you've done wrong, and he will save you."

Isabella quickly bowed her head, praying fervently. Not long after, she looked up with a curious expression. "I've done what you said and prayed for this."

"Good." Angnes smiled. "Now, you must know that Christ took your sins to the cross and paid for them there with his life."

Isabella's eyes widened. "All of them?"

Angnes nodded. "Even the ones you haven't committed. He's clothed you with his righteousness." Angnes patted Isabella's arm. "Now, he'll guide you on the paths you'll be taking all your days. Just pray and listen to him."

Isabella bowed her head again, the soft light of the candle casting a glow upon her. She spoke in quiet, gentle whispers, while a peace pervaded her heart. When she finished, she lifted her head and smiled.

The warmth from the stones radiated throughout the room. Angnes got up and closed the long, reddish-purple panels that covered the windows and then sat back down beside Isabella. She shook her head, and tears misted her eyes. "You're one of his, and will no longer carry the weight of sin any longer. You can be assured you'll be with the Lord when you pass to the other life. Speak your prayers everyday for him to lead you through your darkest times, even what may come of Wolfhart Butler. God will be your place of strength in trials, and he'll be there for you through anything. No one can take the Lord from you."

## Isabella's Shield

Isabella was solemn, yet a spark of hope lit inside her. With the knowledge that she'd someday be with her Lord forever, she felt less afraid.

After Angnes left, Isabella settled down to a deep slumber. Tomorrow would be a new day, and she'd face the path chosen for her. And with this new understanding, God would be her shield. She determined faith would take the place of fear.

*****

The next morning, Isabella got dressed, choosing a lesser gown of dark brown and slipped into a green jacket. She walked out onto the grounds to meet Henry. He was waiting for her under a tree on top of a hill. Anabel was with him.

There was a warm breeze this day. The grounds were turning green, and spring blossoms budded in the gardens set around the house. Serfs had been up early working the land, and house peasants stepped in and out of the great manor going about their chores.

Before Isabella reached the tree, she turned to the sound of footsteps behind her.

One of the squires from the manor came to her, the scar on his cheek bright red. He chuckled to himself. "I hear Wolfhart's set a bid for you."

Isabella eyed him with disdain. The man was in training to become a knight. As she understood, all of them took vows of virtue and care for others. This one sure wasn't taking them to heart. "It's not any of your business, Roldan."

The squire scowled. "You think you're better than I, yet your family's selling you off like a lowly cow. I'll be running a manor in time, and you'll be no more than a menial wife."

Isabella shivered and turned away.

Roldan laughed again. "A time will come when I'll show your high and mighty family. I'll have riches too, as they do."

"But, money can't make a person happy." Isabella sighed. She thought of what it would be like when she was married to Wolfhart.

Roldan nodded. "Yet, there's power that comes with it."

"Which I want none of." She tossed her hair over her shoulder and walked away. She drew in a long breath and followed the path leading to where her younger brother and sister were waiting for her. Her brother was the only one her father allowed to be versed in schooling, so Henry was secretly teaching her and Anabel what he had learned.

\*\*\*\*\*

Anabel laughed and tapped her long, pointed leather shoe from beneath her satin gown, as she watched her brother prepare a lesson for her sister.

"What's the matter, Henry?" Isabella got down next to him.

He looked up. "Nothing."

Anabel held her hand to her mouth, as if to hold back a giggle. "He can't find a long enough stick to write in the dirt with." She danced around the tree, peeking out, laughing.

"Anabel! Leave him alone." Isabella shook her head.

Henry took a stick in his hand and wrote the word, 'greetings' in the dirt.

Anabel giggled again. "*Greetings* to *you*, brother."

Henry quickly turned. "It was supposed to be for Isabella." He tossed an acorn at Anabel.

Isabella smiled, watching them.

Then, suddenly, a hollow ache settled deep inside her. She looked over at the home she grew up in, the colossal stone manor with tall, arched windows and massive towers placed strategically on each end. She could see her bedroom window from where she stood and knew every stone beneath. She wondered what it would be like leaving the only home she ever knew, hoping with all her heart Wolfhart's plans would fail.

"What's the matter, Isabella?" Henry eyed her curiously.

Her eyes misted over. "I'll be leaving soon, so Anabel will have to be your student. But don't let Father know you're teaching her."

Henry's looked away agitated, the tone of his voice, suddenly bitter. "He'll not marry you off to that old man, Isabella. It can't happen."

"But, I don't have a choice. I'm a woman."

Both Henry and Anabel were silent.

Anabel came over and took her sister's hand. "But, I don't want you to go to another manor."

Isabella smiled, a strength welling up inside her in the wake of her newfound faith. "All will be well. You'll see. God will care for me."

Isabella eyed their anxious faces. She'd felt the same dark, inescapable fear the previous night and knew the hopelessness of it. She wondered whether her little brother and sister would respond to what Angnes told her? It was worth a try; for to see these two children in heaven someday with her, would be a beautiful thing. And if she denied them the message…well…that was something she couldn't do.

She leaned closely to them and whispered in their ear. "Do you want to know a secret?"

Both nodded. Their eyes were wide, as they bent their heads to listen.

Isabella's heart swelled with happiness, when both children willingly listened in acceptance of what she was saying and acted upon it. She was unaware it would be a lesson, which would prove to be most valuable and necessary, and decidedly so, for the coming days ahead.

*****

"Where were you this morning, Isabella?"

Isabella's father stood with there his feet planted apart on the floor, bulky arms crossed. His long, brown tunic of tight woven cloth was tied with a wide, leather belt. His legs beneath were covered in green hose. "She backed away from the door."

"Your mother was angry. She said you might try to escape as your devil twin did."

Isabella smoothed out the folds in her dark brown tunic and tugged on the sleeves of her jacket. She sighed. If she answered her father, he'd only twist her words against her. He was no different than most men she knew, having believed women were deceptive and conniving from birth. Even when she tried to show kindness to him, somehow the meaning got confused, and her heart was exposed as villainous.

"Just as I thought." He sneered. "You aren't answering. It shows you're up to no good. You will stay here now, with the door locked."

"Father, please," Isabella pleaded. "You're not being fair. I met with Henry and Anabel by the tree. It's where we always go."

Her father sniffed. "Covering for another misdeed? I knew it."

Their mother appeared at the door. The brows over her green eyes rose, as she swept into the room sashaying past in her lengthy, purple gown.

She turned somewhat sharply. "Lock the door, Alward! It looks as if Wolfhart's ready to pay. I'm sure of it. We can't have her run off as her sister did. At least Blysse was a charming little thing. Isabella, I'm sure will have no other prospects."

Isabella looked away, her eyes downcast. "Mother."

Muriolda's expression was one of scorn, the green veil on the back of her head slipping over her shoulder. "You'll stay in here from now on. Wolfhart seems to be willing to pay a good deal of money for you."

Isabella's father's eyes sparkled. He took the key and slid it around a ring, holding it up for Isabella to see, his thick fingers curling over the end of it.

Isabella went to her bed and sat down. Her shoulders slumped with the realization there was little she could do to ward off the inevitable. Marriage to Wolfhart was already being arranged, and she could do nothing to stop it.

Her father and her mother left the room, their voices ringing in the corridor. She covered her ears, to drown out the sadness she felt because of it.

A key turned in the massive, oak door, and the heavy lock clicked. There was nothing she could do now. Only an act of God would keep her from Wolfhart's clutches, now. Her faith was weak, and her situation hopeless.

She lay on the straw mattress beneath her, and placed her head on a pillow at the end of the bed. It was cold as a tomb in the room. How long would it be before someone came with a hot stone to set under her bed?

Isabella shivered, her body chilled. She reached out and pulled the dark, wool covering tightly around her. In spite of it, she could still feel the draughty, London air beneath the heavy, scratchy fabric.

If Blysse were here, she'd know what to do.

Her sister had a way of handling hardship better than she did. When Blysse was faced with a difficult situation such as this, she threw up her hands and laughed, all the while secretly plotting her escape. She endeared herself to people who shared their ale and music, replacing the emptiness in her heart with life around her.

If she were only like her sister, unafraid and fearless in the face of danger, living a life of uncertainty and relishing in it.

She, on the other hand, weighed every situation carefully and shied away from anything that threatened harm, including most people, which she was reticent to trust.

She pulled the covers tighter around her. Life had given her some turns, and may have given her reason to behave the way she did. Yet, sometimes dodging safely out of harm's way, rather than charging head on into it, had its advantages.

Evading taunts and scorn became a game, of which she'd grown accustomed. If it weren't the knights on the manor grounds casting boorish slurs her way, or her cousin, Hastulf weaving yarns to get her into trouble, she'd find herself distressed by the constant disregard for her at the manor by the servants.

Anabel and Henry, as rascally as they were, for the most part, received praise at the manor. And since Isabella had practically raised them from birth, she considered them dear to her own heart, and overlooked the way they used their devilish charm to weave their way into her parent's hearts.

Blysse got a share of praise from the village people and grounds workers, for her engaging manner and captivating beauty. Other than the fact that her outgoing ways, sometimes landed her into trouble, for the most part, she flourished, at least outside the manor walls.

And, when Hastulf, her cousin was visiting, it didn't seem fair that he was doted on the way he was, coddled and cherished, whether he deserved it or not by his own family and hers. Yet, when he stared down his nose, and treated her like dirt under his feet, chastisement was rarely considered. And Isabella quite often felt the brunt of it.

And even though she knew it to be wrong, Isabella's heart was turned against all of them. She wanted to forgive them, but couldn't find it in her heart to do so.

She sighed. She sank deeper into her pillow. Her eyes rested on the locked, wooden door. She stared at it long and hard.

In her lonely cell, awaiting her fate, she allowed her mind to dwell on the cruelness of her family, Wolfhart, and what awaited her in his cold dark castle devoid of friendships. Her heart was like ice and shuddered with each thump.

A mouse scurried across the floor and into a crack. It's small feet made scraping sounds between the walls. Very little light came in through the window, as the sun was on the other side of the building by now. It would have been a good thing if they'd left her a lit candle.

She got up and undressed. She hung her gown in the wardrobe and then reached in and pulled out a thick, warm tunic for sleeping in and put it on. Angnes hadn't come to help her dress. Maybe she'd show up later.

Someone would eventually be there to allow her time outside of her room under close supervision. They'd want her to wash, eat, and take some air, to keep her in the best condition for Wolfhart. There were enough servants to oblige them with this.

She crossed the room, the cold stones chilling her feet through her woolen stockings. She quickly got back up onto her bed and pulled the covers over her.

She reached out and touched the rich, purple folds of fabric hanging from the golden canopy above her bed, the color of kings.

The softness and shine of the fabric drew her thoughts to her true Father, the King of Kings, the one Angnes led her to.

Isabella's Shield

Suddenly, she remembered that there was one who loved her. Her lips parted and then drew into a smile, a Father to her, loving her in spite of her sin. No matter what the others said about her, she knew that *he* was the only one who really mattered.

Her eyes closed. Her heart slowed in rhythm, and her breath came heavy and long. Soon she was fast asleep, content in the knowledge that her heavenly Father was with her.

*****

And as she slept, this Father looked down upon her with a grace the world couldn't begin to understand. He saw her heart and loved her, not for anything she had done or would do for him, but for the mere fact that she was his child.

*****

# Chapter 2

The sky was a deep purple color, and a chill was settling in, while a low fog spread over the hills and valleys of a narrow stretch of the king's highway where two, lone male figures were traveling.

Matheu shook the hair out of his face so he could see. He turned squarely, his gaze resting on his squire ahead of him, a well-built boy of about sixteen, riding on a mare. He'd caught up with Gawain after coming from London only weeks ago. He was glad to be out of that place, with the plague at its peak and devastation at every turn. He'd said many prayers for the young lady he'd seen at Godfrey Hall, hoping her father would reconsider. He wanted to believe she was faring well.

His squire's horse suddenly halted. He looked ahead. "What is it, Gawain? An inn?"

Gawain obediently turned in his seat, revealing a crooked nose acquired through a hard fought battle, conspicuous in the light of the low moon appearing on the horizon. "Sir Matheu, it's not easy to see through this thick fog." His eyebrows lifted slightly beneath a bright shock of red hair.

Matheu's smile was slight, revealing humor, yet the firm grip on his own black horse, and his quiet, watchful expression presented a different image to others who were not so familiar with him, that of a knight with business to attend, and one they'd not likely cross.

A lance hung from his saddle, in addition to a smaller dagger attached to his side. Heavy, gray chain mail armor draped his body, covered with a dark blue tunic, displaying the symbol of a stone gate on the front. "Look again. There's a worthy inn right beyond that next hill, if my eyes aren't deceiving me."

Gawain took another look and turned back around. "Well done, sir. It's a warm looking place up ahead."

Matheu grinned, revealing straight, white teeth. "Yes, I see it through the fog."

Gawain smiled back.

As they neared the tall, narrow inn overshadowed by a heavily thatched roof, they saw a sign with the etching of a candlestick on it. The place was inviting with its light, brown walls slatted with dark beams and tan bricks trimming the edges. The colors created a warm look, snug and quiet. A shuttered window up near the peak was open, and they could see into a cozy bedroom above.

Gawain eyed it curiously. "It is looking sufficient."

Matheu nodded. He turned in the direction of the town that rose out of the mist in the distance. "I thought we were getting nearer the village of Hertford. I'm glad it won't be long before we're back at the manor. It'll be good to see Dante again."

"Yes, sir. Maybe six to seven more days north, if we're riding hard. I'll be glad to be done with the tournament path. It'll feel good to be back home."

Matheu eyed the village in the distance and sighed. He was also glad to be almost finished with the tournaments and couldn't wait to get back to Thorneton Le Dale. He looked forward to seeing his place again and caring for the serfs who worked the land. Efforts to unseat knights from their horses, time and time again, grew wearisome.

As the youngest brother of a family with expectations, he was born into knighthood with little choice. His eldest brother was to receive the inheritance of his parent's manor, and for this reason, Matheu was given into training for a knightly position at the young age of seven.

He was relieved for the lull in the war, knowing otherwise he'd be gone fighting for the cause. Despite his distaste for battle, his honor bound him to his obligations to the king, honed into him at a very young age through training, discipline and tests of loyalty.

Gawain's familiar voice jarred his thoughts and brought him back to the present.

"At least we're escaping that dreadful disease, sir."

"Yes, hopefully, we'll be far north before it's in the country."

Gawain nodded. "And being we're headed in another direction, we should be able to avoid it."

"Yes." Matheu patted the side of his mare and nodded. "When I went through London, there were few cases of it. Now, I wonder what the future holds for the city."

Gawain got down off of his horse and guided the gray mare into a stable next to the inn. He limped back to where his friend waited, an old injury clearly giving him pain. He helped Matheu down from his horse, letting up on his foot to lessen the suffering.

Matheu stood next to him, impatient to free himself of the heavy metal suit.

Gawain obediently lifted the armor off Matheu's shoulders.

"Thanks. There's a day coming when you'll make a worthy knight." Matheu stretched.

Gawain's brown eyes sparked, yet he remained quiet. He hoisted the armor over his own shoulder and carried it into the inn.

Matheu reached out and took the lance hanging from the saddle, waiting for Gawain to come back out and help him care for the horses before they went inside.

Tomorrow, they'd push the horses as fast as was comfortable and maybe find themselves in a town past Bedford by the end of the day. They could possibly be landing themselves in Thorneton Le Dale in a week, if all went well.

Matheu looked forward to the day that he was back at his property, resuming his duties there.

\*\*\*\*\*

A week passed. Isabella was still locked inside her room, which was beginning to feel more like a prison. She grew tired of the thick, dull walls of her bedroom and was irritable, not being able to stroll about the manor alone.

She paced the floor, counting the gray, stone slabs beneath her feet, memorizing the cracks and peculiar markings etched upon its hard, cold surface.

Upon hearing footsteps and a click in the lock, her head whirled at the sound. The door of her room heaved open, and Angnes Small poked her blonde head around the corner. Her freckled nose turned up. She beckoned to Isabella, holding out her hand. "Isabella! Your cousin is here and needs you. Hurry and follow me."

"What is it, Angnes? Tell me. Why has Hastulf come on this day?"

Angnes sighed long and shook her head from side to side. "Not now, dear. You'll have to see this for yourself. Come down the hall. Your parents summoned your cousin for a reason."

Isabella followed the small servant woman through the dark quiet corridors of the castle, surprised no lanterns lit the walls, and there were no sign of servants along the way.

Angnes' footsteps echoed hollowly through the chambers, leading straightway to the end where Isabella's mother and father's bedroom was.

"Angnes? Why are we stopping here?" Isabella stared at the door, apprehensive. A sick feeling crept over her.

Angnes put her finger to her lips. "Shush, m'lady." Her voice was a whisper. She pushed the door open, motioning for Isabella to step around it.

Isabella shivered, reluctantly following Angnes inside. Something raw churned in her and she drew back, reticent to know what was happening in her parent's bedchambers.

Upon entering, she was hit with a rancid smell. She immediately coughed at the wretchedness of it. The drapes that hung from a tall window next to the bed were closed. Isabella waited for her eyes to adjust to the darkness. Something was terribly wrong.

When she could see into the shadowy room, her eyes widened in disbelief. Bile rose to her throat, and she gagged, holding her hand to her mouth.

Lying on the massive bed in the middle of the room were her parents in their nightclothes, drenched in sweat. Even from across the room, she felt an intense heat radiating from them, most likely from a raging fever. Dreadful swellings and black spots covered their arms, legs, face and neck. They lay half-delirious on the bed in the spacious, dark room, their cheeks red with the heat, both coughing and retching into wooden pails. The horror of the disease they bore was incomprehensible.

The smell inside was overpowering from the vomit and the stench of death, along with the scents of the vials of potions resting on a stand nearby. The lighting was low, other than a couple glowing candlesticks on the mantle of the stone fireplace, against the wall.

Hastulf, her cousin, stood on the furthest side of the room. He had a stony look on his face.

"Angnes?" Isabella choked on her words. "Are they going to be all right?"

At the sound of Isabella's voice, Muriolda's sunken eyes narrowed, and she looked up at Isabella. The red in her cheeks turned bright. "What is *she* doing here? Why is she standing there gawking at us?"

A sick feeling welled up inside Isabella, as if she'd swallowed poison. Her voice came in gulps. "I'm here to help."

Muriolda put her hand to her forehead. Her green eyes were filled with hate. "I didn't ask for you." She pointed to the door. "Get out! Out of my room at once!"

Isabella felt the blood draining from her face. "But, mother..."

Muriolda's eyes narrowed again. She began to scream. "I told you to get out! I don't want you here!"

Isabella opened her mouth to speak, but nothing came out. It was as if her feet were rooted to the floor, and she was unable to move.

"Leave this room at once, witch!" Muriolda screamed again.

Angnes tugged gently on Isabella's arm. "M'lady, it's not what I thought it would be. We should go."

"But, they could die, and my father's here, too. I can help him." Tears began to fill her eyes.

Muriolda tried to stand up, but fell to the floor instead, ranting. "If your father wasn't sick, he'd beat you for this!" Her eyes were blazing. "I said to get out!"

Her father kept retching violently into a pail, not looking up.

Hastulf turned, his eyes deadly. He uttered a sharp, piercing cry. "Don't you hear her? Do you even care? You're parents have bequeathed the manor to me! I'm in charge now! I make the rules, and your parents don't wish for you to be here!"

# Isabella's Shield

A sudden breathlessness overtook Isabella, and her voice came out in a whisper. "But, she's my mother, Hastulf. I want to help." She drew her hand over her heart.

"But, it's not possible! They do not want it! Be gone witch! Get away from them!" Hastulf's face was red with anger.

"But, cousin."

Angnes took her by the arm. "Isabella. Let's go, dear. I'm sorry I brought you."

Hastulf's eyes were dark, and the veins in his neck swelled. In a fit of anger, he grabbed a vase and held it up as if he planned to throw it at them.

Isabella put out her hand. "Hastulf! There's no need for this violent action." She backed out of the room, tears streaming down her cheeks. "I'll go."

Hastulf put down the vase, a merciless glint in his eye.

Isabella took a couple more steps out of the room and into the hallway.

When the door shut behind her, she sunk down onto the cold floor of the corridor. She held her hands to her mouth and rocked back and forth. "Oh, Angnes! God have mercy on me."

Angnes reached down and touched her shoulder.

Isabella looked up at her with tear-filled eyes. "Why do they hate me so?" She stared at the closed door. "I may never see them again, and my own cousin won't let me stay."

"It's not your fault, dear. You've done nothing." Angnes wrapped her arms around Isabella and gave her a gentle squeeze.

Isabella looked at the closed door. "I never meant to cause any harm. Not to anyone, especially not my parents."

"It's true, m'lady. You wouldn't do such a thing. It isn't in your nature."

Angnes took Isabella's chin in her hand and lifted it. "M'lady, if I knew how they were going to treat you, I wouldn't have brought you here. I thought in their condition, they'd see things differently, but I was wrong." There was a pained look in her eyes. "They're not right in their thinking. It's not you who's done wrong."

Isabella tipped her head to the side. "Oh, Angnes, I merely wanted to help."

Angnes nodded. "It's a mystery why your sweetness is not apparent to them." The young servant woman pulled Isabella to her feet. She let out a weary breath. "People have a difficult time seeing the heart, as God does. We see what we wish to see."

Angnes lifted Isabella's chin with her hand. "The Lord loves us as we are. You need never do anything to impress him."

Isabella's cheeks deepened in color. She looked at the floor. "But, what if I'm not as you imagine. What if in that room…for the briefest of moments, I wanted something bad to happen to my cousin. I'm angry Hastulf is telling me what to do, in a time as this, and I've felt such bitterness toward my own parents."

"Isabella, we cannot undo what Christ did. If you truly believe he took all your sin, then he has taken that one, too."

Isabella put her hand on Angnes' arm. Something in her heart stirred.

Angnes smiled, a solemn look in her eyes. "He cares for you very much and has covered every sin. And you must remember, m'lady, that he's your father now, and is faithful and will see you through this."

Isabella nodded, wiping tears from her cheeks. "Even when I've wronged my parents and my cousin?"

Something lit in Angnes' eyes. "Even when we have nothing to give to him, he continues to extend his grace and will love us anyway."

Isabella turned to leave, but Angnes took her by the shoulders.

"Wait. You mustn't go yet." The young servant fidgeted with her hands.

Isabella eyed the servant with a puzzled expression. "But, why? Why would you need me, after what just happened?"

Angnes looked weary. "I did not wish to tell you this, but you must know it. And it's difficult to tell you in the very hour of your distress, that I need you for your help."

Isabella studied Angnes' work-worn face and concerned expression. She shivered, wondering what the matter was. "What is it? Tell me, Angnes?"

Angnes bit her lower lip. "I am having great difficulty caring for all those suffering from the Black Death in the manor. I must stay with your mother and father. All the servants have left the grounds, and I've no one to help nurse those who are sick. There's Hastulf, yet he is little help to me."

Isabella looked around. "But, you told me that all the servants are gone? So, who else is there in need of assistance?"

Angnes looked pained. She took a deep breath and tightened her grip on Isabella's shoulders. "I'm sorry, my dear. I'm reticent to discuss the matter with you, but fear I must."

"Angnes? What has happened? How can I help?" Isabella took her by the shoulders.

Angnes face turned a pale shade. She swallowed as if something dry was in her throat. "You'll not wish to hear it. But, there is nothing I can do. I'm sorry."

Isabella couldn't imagine why Angnes was hesitating. "Please. I can endure…"

And then, as if she suddenly realized what is was Angnes was keeping from her, her eyes widened, and her voice began to quaver. "Angnes? It's not Anabel? Or Henry? Surely, it cannot be them?"

Angnes' expression sobered. She reached up and wiped a tear from her eye. "Oh dear. My poor one. I didn't want to be the one to tell you, but it is true. They have contracted it. I'm sorry."

Isabella was suddenly faint. She shook her head slowly from side to side. "Henry? Anabel? Both of them?"

Angnes held tightly to her and nodded.

Isabella sucked in a breath, her fingers digging into Angnes' arm. "But, it's not possible."

Angnes looked down.

A gust of cold, drafty air suddenly swept through the long hallway. Any other day, it would have been considered ordinary, but on this day a great chill crept deep into Isabella's bones, shaking her from head to toe.

"They're in the green room. I need you to go to them." Angnes sighed deeply.

Isabella clutched her chest. It was as if the devil himself had reached for her heart and was twisting it inside her. The pain was almost more than she could bear.

"But, I can't see them this way. It'll break my heart."

Angnes continued to clutch her arm. "Get ahold of yourself, Isabella. I know you wouldn't wish for them to suffer with this dreadful disease with no one at their side. They may be dying, and I must care for your mother and father. I cannot be with all of them at the same time. It's impossible. Would you leave Anabel and Henry to suffer alone in a time like this?"

Isabella couldn't imagine her brother and sister lying in that dark room without her. Her shoulders sunk, and she was filled with dread. "I cannot bear to see them with this dreadful illness, yet I believe that you are correct in saying I should tend to them. They must not be left alone, and I'm the only one who'll see them through it."

She reached down and took the flickering lantern Angnes set in the hallway, gave her servant a sorrowful glance, and left quickly following the corridor that would lead to the bedroom her young brother and sister were housed in. She dreaded the time she'd be spending with them, loathe to watch them in their suffering.

*****

Isabella lifted her hand to her chest in the shape of the cross. The newly dug graves of both her parents and her little brother and sister were a cold reminder of their recent death. She prayed God would lessen the overwhelming sorrow that had took hold of her heart and crushed her inside.

Angnes Small walked over to where she stood and took her arm, silent.

Isabella turned, her eyes swollen. Tears ran in streaks down her cheek.

"Oh, dear lady...I'm sorry for your grief. I'm also sorry to have come to you in a time such as this."

"Angnes?"

Angnes shushed her. "Be still. Listen." And then in the slightest whisper, she relayed her message. "Isabella, you're going to have to leave the manor tonight." Her voice was barely audible, and she looked at the grave.

Isabella took her hand.

Angnes' voice dropped even lower. "I know it's a very difficult time for you, but you must hear this."

"What is it, Angnes?"

Angnes squeezed her hand. "When the sun slips over the horizon this evening, put on the woolen garments I've placed on your bed, and be ready to leave."

"But, Angnes."

"No, do not speak." She sighed. "Your cousin has taken charge now and fixed a deal with Wolfhart. The old man's taking you with him, tomorrow. The money gained from it is surely what he is after."

Isabella gasped and bent her head to listen.

"You must go with us to your sister's place in Cropton. Men we can trust can take us there."

Isabella's violet eyes widened. She didn't know much about trusting men, but she would trust Angnes' words.

Angnes' voice was barely above a whisper. "I cannot tell you anything else. But, I'll be there later and tap your door twice. Come quietly with me then."

Isabella bent her head forward slightly.

After Angnes left, Isabella went back to her room. She dressed in the clothes that were lying on her bed set out for her for this occasion, a commoner's shapeless, brown woolen tunic along with a rope-like, leather belt she tied about her waist. She pulled a fur-lined shawl over her shoulders and sat down on the bed to wait. It seemed a dangerously long time until the first hour of darkness and yet it came, and very suddenly was upon her.

*****

Getting away from the manor was not as difficult as Isabella imagined it would be, beneath the watchful eyes of Hastulf. Since her parents died, and he'd inherited the manor, he'd been

35

unpredictable in his behavior, and she was uncertain as to what he might do, if he caught her leaving.

And yet, because of the plague, the guards had all run off, and only a few animals remained. The dogs were familiar with Isabella, so it took little time for her to quiet them. Her escape with Angnes and her friends was accomplished quite easily, in less than an hour.

The men Angnes chose to form an alliance with, were different than what Isabella expected them to be. Despite the fact that all three men were well on in years and not exactly possessing great physical strength, they revealed sharp wits, devotion to her cause and kindness.

As the group left London on darkened streets, eerie cries and strangled coughs of those stricken with the Black Death littered the shadowy paths. The stench of death invaded the cobblestone streets and homes of both commoners and the wealthy. And it didn't stop with the people. Animals also lay bloated in the lanes. A strong, gruesome stench rose over the land.

Isabella stopped, the pain of the last couple days searing her chest. She looked out into the darkness. "Oh, Angnes, they're dying. It's horrible. Can't we stop to help?"

Angnes grabbed her hand and pulled her along, her jawline taut. "No. We have to get out of here. They're beyond help. And we must hurry, dear. Wolfhart will be on our heels. There are too many of them, and we can't care for them all."

"Angnes?" Isabella clutched her chest, tears springing to her eyes.

"I said there are too many. Even the doctors are dying from this accursed sickness." Angnes gave Isabella a gentle shove. "We have to get out of here."

Isabella carefully watched the ground beneath her as she walked, shuddering at the thought of tripping over a dead carcass, be it man or beast, lying in the path in the darkness. With so many people dying so quickly, the caretakers were not able to clear the streets of the bodies, and it seemed this disease was placing its mark upon each and every area of the city.

Isabella crossed herself and held back a sob forming in her throat. She couldn't cry. Her own hysteria would only add to the misery around them.

Many people were escaping en route to the countryside where it was said to be safe from the plague. Who could have guessed such a thing would be happening in these times?

Isabella trudged along on the wide, crude trail that led deep into the countryside. Her feet were sore and bruised, as she wasn't accustomed to such distress. She ached with the pain she carried from the death of her family, along with her physical pain and felt little hope for the future ahead. She fought to stay awake, as the group she was with took her further from her home and the things she was familiar with.

Yet, enduring the scratchy, wool fabric of her tattered tunic and uncomfortable, leather shoes that graced her swollen feet, along with the hunger pains she felt from the bits of unappetizing food the men doled out at intervals, was nothing compared to the sounds of death around her.

Now, all but her and Blysse were gone, and there was nothing left to do but to find her sister. She began to pray, despite the fact that her faith seemed to be wearing thin. Regardless of the fact that God was wholly able to carry through with any plan he orchestrated, deep down she believed there was really nothing he would to do to help her.

And if there was, by some small chance, something that could be done, she wondered if she was worth it. She could never quite shake the feeling that she was tarnished, and God wouldn't want to waste time with someone so terribly flawed. Now, she wished her faith were larger. She turned to Angnes who was walking by her side.

"Remember, we must keep moving, dear. We can't rest yet." Angnes tugged on her arm.

Isabella sighed. "I know. I only wanted to ask you a question. We can keep up with them as we speak."

Angnes turned her head. Her blonde braids swung freely down her back, contrary to the customary netting, holding them in place. She seemed younger with her hair loose and unattended. "What is it? Does m'lady desire to eat again?"

"No, Angnes." Isabella pulled her wool shawl tighter around her. "I have had difficulty believing that all that has happened could be God's plan. How could he take my family from me and send this awful plague?"

Angnes sighed. "Oh, Isabella, he's known what all your days would be, before he created you. He's always loved you. We must keep our faith in him no matter what happens. He'll care for us. He's taking you far from Wolfhart. Do not try to understand everything that has come to pass."

Isabella swallowed hard, nodding noncommittal. She wrestled inside with her feelings, knowing God's goodness, yet wondering why so many horrible things had happened. She knew the only thing she could do was to cling to the thought of his love and care for those who were his. She had nothing else.

Bedford would be their first stop. There were many days before they reached Blysse's home in Cropton. She wondered what it would be like living with her sister and Alan, the Shoemaker.

Another step. Another day. Soon she'd be seeing for herself the new home she would be privy to. It would be a blessing to finally see her sister again.

*****

Blysse eyed the dirty, brick walls of the tavern, her brows arching at the incongruent sagging roof held in place by two strong, brown wooden beams. She laughed at the thought of it, drawing a ceramic jug of ale to her lips.

Alan was gambling again, sitting at a round, wooden table lit with candles, situated directly behind two, large metal rimmed barrels of drink with spigots attached. Three men in tattered tunics watched a young servant woman walking by, while waiting in line for their turn at the faucet.

On the far end of the hall, a pig roasted over a fire on a giant skewer. Two stout women tended to it, sweat forming under the arms of their shapeless wool tunics, crudely sewn. A minstrel in the corner was playing a melancholy tune on a lute.

Not exactly the kind of life she'd envisioned for herself, but it was a leap above what she would've had with Wolfhart, the ugly toad.

Alan waved her over, his white, linen shirt open, revealing a muscular chest. "Come to me, Blysse. You bring me luck."

She smiled her sauciest grin, revealing a straight row of white teeth and she moved across the slabs of square gray stone on the floor of the room. She took lively steps drawing every eye in the tavern to her.

She laughed again and sat jauntily on a stool next to her husband directly below a huge, wooden wheel suspended from the ceiling with candles on the upper side, shedding light in a large circle around them. Even in ragged, gray wool, her dark plaits wild and out of order, Blysse's dancing eyes full of life and spirit, drew people to her like ale to a drunkard.

"What kind of luck? Greater money, or a greater *time* with your pretty lady?" She winked at him out of the corner of her eye.

The commoners there slammed their wooden cups onto the tables in their merry making, their beverages sloshing out onto the floor.

One of the men waved his glass in the air. "I'd take me home now, if Blysse was me woman! What are you waiting for, Alan?"

Another called out. "You big ox! Are you lame in your thinking? Why are you still sitting there?"

Alan scowled. Then he turned to Blysse who struck a pose, grinning widely and batting her eyes. He couldn't contain his own laughter and joined the group, slapping his mug upon the table. "Me Blysse has got me bound to her same as a knight and his lord. What's making me bow to this one?"

Howls flooded the room as he bent down and took Blysse over his shoulder, carrying her out the doorway, Blysse's rosy cheeks glowing.

She laughed secretly to herself, knowing she had browned two loaves of bread in one oven with her quick thinking. For one, Alan was done throwing his hard-earned money into other people's pockets. She would remember to hide some of it away, while he was still feeling tipsy. And for the other, he was leaving with her, where she could have him all to herself.

*****

"What! She's gone?" Wolfhart choked on his words. He grabbed Hastulf's shirt, looking as if he wanted to reach out and wring his scrawny neck.

Hastulf's forehead was etched with deep lines. Sweat beaded underneath his mousy, brown cowlick, and he wiped it away with the back of his hand. He reached for a chalice on a shelf in the great hall, annoyed at the fact there were no servants. He shakily poured red wine from a bottle into a goblet and extended his arm. "Don't worry. Drink this with me, and I'll tell you what's happened to Isabella, the one of course not worthy of you. She couldn't have traveled far. I'm sure I know where she's gone. Sit down." He pointed to a wooden chair trimmed in gold, padded in thick, red velvet.

Wolfhart let out a breath of disgust, taking the pewter container from Hastulf's hand and drawing it to his lips. He swallowed, the sagging skin folds around his mouth shaking, as he drank the full cup of wine and wiped his mouth with the back of his wrinkled hand.

He set the chalice on a stand next to the chair and sat down, a cruel, twisted frown contorting his lips. He fingered the silk cloth that formed a lump around his large mid-section. "You promised me the young woman, and she's not here. I traveled back to London in the middle of this ghastly plague and all for naught. How will you be paying me back for the trouble I've been through?"

Hastulf eyed Wolfhart wringing his fat hands together. His cousin would pay for the trouble she caused him. To him, Wolfhart looked like a tired, wrinkled dog awaiting his last meal. Hastulf almost laughed, but he knew it was best he refrain. He understood full well the extent of anger that lay beneath the dark heart of this man and wanted rid himself of him.

Hastulf drew his lips into the most hospitable grin he could muster and took another sip from his own cup. "I believe she's on her way to Cropton where her sister resides. If you leave quickly, you'll catch up with her soon enough. I'll give you my best horse, a chestnut stallion. You'll be in Isabella's reach within a fortnight, and you can keep the horse when you're done."

Wolfhart's greed-stricken eyes enlarged slightly and then narrowed. "But, I wanted to marry her when I found her, and we've not agreed on a price."

Hastulf rubbed his chin and let out a snort. "All I want is this manor. I'm aching to wash my hands of this devil cousin of mine. To see her wed to you would be bestowing upon me a great pleasure. If you can find her, you have my blessings to her. I'll write an agreement up for you." He reached out a thin hand toward Wolfhart smiling, his mouth closing into a thin line.

Wolfhart hesitated. Then, when he realized the deal was to his advantage in all ways, he smiled back. A free horse and a young, golden-haired wench, for the cost of a trip to Cropton and a friar's fee, was more than he could ask for.

He reached out his thick, wrinkled hand and grasped Hastulf's thin one in a lopsided shake. The deal was clenched. He'd see to the papers being signed and be on his way to capture his young bride.

*****

# Chapter 3

Isabella accidently bumped into an elderly woman standing next to her in the packed crowd surrounding the village square of Bedford. Briefly their eyes met. She offered a quick apology. "Pardon me, madam."

The woman laughed. "Your proper words aren't necessary in Bedford. You're the first to excuse yourself to me in such a way, for a very long time."

Isabella shifted uneasily. "I've not been here long."

The woman eyed her curiously. "Where were you from?"

"I've been traveling for a time." Isabella turned, feigning interest in the fair entertainment.

Leofwin played a lilting tune with his whistles and bells, while Theobald sang. In blending their musical skills, they complemented each other well.

The older woman next to Isabella, tugged on her sleeve. "You were with this entertaining pair when you came into this village?"

Isabella nodded, fearing she might reveal too much. She turned back to Theobald and Leofwin, watching their act.

"Fighting the battle fair, was Roland,
A worthy man of valor…"

Theobald Gray tipped his conical hat, belting out an epic poem in a low sweet voice, while Leofwin towering above him, played instruments keeping in tune with his friend. Beyond them in the square were the Mayday dancers attached to ribbons around a great pole and animal trainers, handling prancing horses and dancing bears. Tournaments with knights played out further down the street.

Isabella's mother and father didn't allow her to join the activities outside the manor walls. A deep guilt coursed through her for taking part in the fair, despite the fact she had done nothing wrong. She wished to be rid of the deep shame she felt inside, but she realized it wouldn't go away that easily.

# Isabella's Shield

She winced, lifting one foot from the hard, cobblestone street and resting it on her other one, wishing there were a place to sit down. Her feet still hurting, despite the fact the group she traveled with, rode the last half of the day on a farmer's wagon. She'd never walked so far in her life. It felt as if bruises covered the bottom of her feet.

Isabella promised Angnes she'd stay near Leofwin and Theobald. Angnes went to find food and shelter, taking the rust-haired peddler, Godhuwe of Malton, another of Angnes' friends, with her. Scanning the crowd, while waiting for Angnes, Isabella noticed a familiar, chestnut stallion entering the village from the far side of the square. An icy chill ran through her veins. It was her cousin's animal. She could tell by the white marking on its cheek in the shape of a large triangle.

Her eyes shifted quickly to the rider. "Wolfhart."

He sat firmly on the saddle, his eyes slits, while he scanned the crowd. His long, reddish-purple tunic wasn't lost in the sea of gray and brown wools. His brow was furrowed beneath lines on his forehead. He appeared uneasy on the saddle, his cumbersome bulk clumsily rocking from side to side.

No waiting for Angnes now, Isabella thought. A pulse inside her quickened, and she looked around for an escape.

If Wolfhart found her, there'd be no getting away from him this time. The white blonde color of her hair would surely stand out in the crowd and give her away. She slipped deeper into the thronging mass of people and edged closer to the wall of a building, then turned a corner and crept into a passageway between two shops.

Once out of Wolfhart's sight, she ran between the buildings and down a couple streets, eventually slipping into a quiet alley next to a tavern. Her heart was beating wildly within her chest, and her breaths were heavy. She was terrified. Wolfhart was looking for her, and he had Hastulf's horse. What to do?

She sat on an old wheel lying next to her, the wood gritty against her fingers. She put her hands to her face and held them there a moment, dread setting in as to what course she should take. As the sun lowered in the sky, it cast deep shadows against the mud-packed walls.

When she heard the sound of footsteps at the end of the alley, she swung around quickly.

"Who do I see here, a fair one, looking for help? I'll be pleased to offer you comfort."

Isabella jumped at the sound of a man's gravely voice and backed against the cold, sod wall behind her. She wrinkled her nose at the heavy stench of ale and grime coming from end of the passageway and covered her mouth with her hand.

The man was stocky and short in size. Isabella eyed him with distaste. His stringy, unkempt hair covered one eye, and a scar ran down his cheek. He wore a roughly cut, rumpled tunic over his brown and tattered, woolen hose.

He skulked into the alley in a half-swagger, wringing his hands and rubbing his whiskered chin, letting out a loud, unrestrained burst of laughter.

Isabella trembled; looking around furtively, until she realized her only escape was past the man's bulky frame. She sucked in a breath. "Sir, I merely stopped for a short rest, but I'll be leaving now." She took a step to pass to the side of him and drew back, when he blocked her way, leaning his hand against the wall.

He let out a snort and took hold of her arm, laughing.

Isabella tried to loosen herself from his grasp, yet he held her in a firm grip and pushed her against the wall.

"Sir!" She felt his smelly breath upon her face and winced. "Please, I've money."

He grinned, his wide cheeks flushed. "Sir...Bedford, at thy pleasure. But, we'll speak of your money another time."

She worked to wrench her arm free, but to no avail. "Sir." She felt the wall for a loose rock or something she could rain down upon his head, but found none.

"You're my stroke of luck this evening."

She shoved against the man, but he didn't budge. Not again, she thought. Did her troubles never cease to end? She escaped from Wolfhart, only to be thrown into the grip of this repulsive man. Lord, she pleaded inside. Please help me. You've saved me once. Please, act on my behalf again.

# Isabella's Shield

*****

Blysse woke early to the light tap, tapping sound, coming from the room adjacent to where she lay upon her bed. She propped herself up on her straw mattress and listened. Alan must have risen before the crack of dawn, as she hadn't heard him stir.

She dragged herself off the bed and sprinkled her face with water from the small basin on a stand in the room. She ran a comb made from a bone through her dark hair, drawing the silken strands into two, loose plaits dangling down her back, then dressed in a simple, blue tunic with a woolen apron, slipping it over her head. She sat back down and pulled on brown leather shoes, examining their exquisite handy work. At least with a shoemaker as a husband, she could still retain some sense of dignity.

She stepped into the other room of their home, which served more than one purpose, a place for eating and cooking, and for business.

Alan was near the fireplace on a stool, putting the last finishing touches on a pair of shoes, in which a pattern had been cut only days before.

"Is he coming for them soon?" She eyed him curiously.

He nodded, without comment.

Blysse noticed the lit candle on the table, less than a couple inches long, heavy drips around the edges. She'd have to make more, as there were few left in the cupboards. "Have you eaten?" Her voice was edged with concern. Lately, they hadn't brought in a lot of money, and she hoped Alan would make a sale soon.

"Not yet. I thought I should finish this handsome pair of shoes, first. I've only a few seams to do."

He lifted the pair for inspection, his warm gray eyes seemingly pleased. Without his drink, he was a quiet man, introspective. "I'm hungry, now that you speak of it. I could use something to fill that empty spot in me."

Blysse went to the cupboard and pulled out the rye loaf she'd made the day before. It had already begun to harden. She sawed off a large, dark piece for both her and Alan and set them on a wooden platter, which she laid on the table. She grabbed two cups and filled them with some ale from a wooden barrel that was on a stool in the corner. She put them next to the plates and sat down beside him.

Alan stopped what he was doing and scooted his stool closer to Blysse. Then, he reached into his pocket and pulled out a small moneybag and dragged it over the surface of the table.

The money inside made clinking sounds, as he placed it in front of her. "Can you take this to the church for me, before you begin your work? It's our ten percent."

Blysse rolled her eyes. "For them to be using for their fancy provisions, while the serfs in the village are nearly starving. And they're supposed to be humble men of God?"

Her dark eyes flashed, as she looked out one of the windows in the direction of the church. It didn't take her long to learn the unfairness of the class system. A few months of living this life had done the trick. At least Alan wasn't a serf and could provide a fairly adequate income with his shoemaking business. They weren't starving, as some were.

Alan smiled. "It's true most of the monks and priests are wretched persons, yet I believe there are some honorable ones, too. Our own Friar Dixon, who resides in this very village, is a most worthy heart. You cannot be denying it."

Blysse snorted. "There may be one or two respectable ones. But, if God wants these other men to be his servants, then I cannot think he's worth believing in."

Alan's eyes grew large. "Blysse, you cannot say these blasphemous things! I cannot bear it if anything were to happen to you."

Large, thick lashes danced above Blysse's brown eyes. "I merely say what others are thinking in their hearts. Because they do not have the courage to tell others what is truly in their mind, does not mean they do not think the same thoughts I do. How can others believe in a God who places such greedy men above us, a God who's honoring the prayers of wicked people who care a naught for others, and only act as if they do?"

Alan drew in a long breath and put up his hand. "Blysse! Stop this. Do not say these things, or they'll not let you live. They'll call you a witch."

Isabella's Shield

She reached out a slender arm and took his large hand in her much smaller one. "It'll not be the first time." An impish grin appeared on her face. She squeezed his hand gently. "But don't worry, my dear. Because of you, I'll keep quiet."

His shocked looked was replaced with a sigh and a relieved smile, then he shook his head back and forth. "What was I thinking to take you from Wolfhart? You may have been a worthy pair, the two of you."

It was Blysse's turn to be shocked. She shook her braids out behind her, grinning. "What? I cannot believe my ears? My husband is suffering in his mind!"

He laughed and got up from the table, turning back to his shoes. "I'm suffering in my mind, to have fallen so greatly for you."

Blysse laughed and then downed the last chunk of bread, washing the platters and cups in a tub of water and putting them back into the cupboard. "I might agree with you this time."

She took the moneybag, swinging it along her hip as she moved gracefully across the stone floor of her home and opened the door. "I'll be back, after I am done handing our money to those humble priests in that sad, deficient church."

She walked out the door and down the path toward the priest's tower a couple shops away, the moneybag still swinging against her side. She wondered at her own playful comments, edging on bitterness. She knew she played a dangerous game. What if she was wrong? What if God was listening to the things she said?

A pang of fear coursed through her for the briefest second, yet she pushed it deeper inside, focusing on the task at hand. If she were wrong, it was too late at this time to change anything. Her path of wickedness was set out for her a long time ago. She could never be good enough for God.

Her eyes narrowed, and she tightened her fist on the moneybag, quickening her pace, attempting to shake off the anxiousness that stirred in her heart, but to no avail. It was the same foreboding she carried with her as a child, sometimes overtaking her so forcefully she felt she couldn't breathe. Would it never let her go?

She took slow, uneven breaths, her heart thudding against her chest rapidly. Why would it never leave her? The insidious pounding inside gripped her like a vice.

Quickly, she lifted her skirts and began to run along the cobblestone path in efforts to rid her of the devil who haunted her. She was unconcerned with the unevenness of the surface, not affected by the fact that she could stumble and hurt herself.

She lifted her hand to her chest, willing it to stop pounding, her mouth set in a grim line. Her eyes narrowed. Soon she'd reach the door of the church and hand the greedy priest the scot she and Alan owed, and be done with it. Once home, she'd busy herself with her chores and fill her day with real things, ones that mattered and helped her forget those that brought her distress.

She'd beat this evil, this snare upon her heart. She would fight it and conquer it, winning this last battle waging a war deep within her soul. One thing she knew how to do, was to fight a good battle and win.

*****

Matheu peered into the ally from which he heard a scuffling sound. Against the wall, he spied a young village woman seemingly in distress, struggling to right herself. An older peasant man had his hands about her neck.

Gawain snorted. "We need to leave, Matheu. We haven't time to spend recklessly. They're likely sweethearts quarreling."

Matheu's eyes narrowed. He stopped his horse and got down. His chain mail armor beneath the dark blue tunic belted around his waist made soft, clinking sounds, while his leather shoes were quiet against the cobblestone street.

"We've taken a vow to defend the weak, Gawain. I think the lady needs our hand. Stay with the horses. I'll take care of this." He started in long strides down the narrow passageway.

*****

# Isabella's Shield

Isabella kicked the vile man hard in the calf, breaking free from his grasp and then took off in a sprint down the alley, her heart thumping wildly. Yet, in her attempt to escape, her ankle turned beneath her on the uneven cobblestone, and she fell down onto the hard path. She tried to get back onto her feet, but gave a quick cry of pain and reached down to tend to her injured foot. Tears spilled onto her cheeks.

She felt someone grip her hand and then grab hold of her arm and lift her to her feet. She tried to pull herself free, but wasn't able to, so she backed up against the wall of the alley and held herself there. Her eyes widened when she turned and realized the man who held onto her, was not her attacker. She wondered where she'd seen this man before.

"What's this? Is this man causing injury to you?"

His grim expression unnerved her. She grasped the wall tighter. The smelly man of Bedford wouldn't stand a chance against this broad-shouldered man, possessing a hard glint in his eye.

Let him try, she thought. She only hoped this knight honored his vows of chivalry, and she wouldn't fall victim a third time. She nodded, tears finding their way over her cheeks. She quickly wiped them away.

*****

Matheu took a step backward, his eyebrow lifting slightly. The oversized, woolen clothes the young woman wore, rubbed her skin raw in spots, and she seemed unaccustomed to the ill-fitting shoes on her tiny feet. Her hands were soft and unmarked and her skin fair. Something about her was familiar to him, yet he couldn't recall where he'd seen her before.

Blacwin of Bedford scowled. "Leave her alone. I found her before you did."

Matheu moved in front of the young woman. "I believe the lady was not desiring your company."

Blacwin spat on the ground. "It matters not what she wants."

The young women took a hold of the wall and stood up. It was apparent the pain in her foot was lessening. She looked down her slender nose. "Pardon? I merely came upon you moments ago. You prey upon those who cannot defend themselves!" She lifted her chin a notch regally and pushed her hair behind her, her back straight.

Both men turned, their eyes widening at her boldness.

She tilted her head. And then as if realizing she'd made a grave mistake, she looked away and uttered her next words in a meek tone, much more subdued. "It is true. I have never seen this man who threatened me, and could use your help, sir."

Matheu bowed slightly. "Matheu of Thorneton Le Dale, miss. I was passing through when, my squire and I saw you in the alley, I thought I might be of service."

The color returned to Isabella's cheeks, at the suggestion that she use his given name. She met his eyes briefly and then curtsied. "I'd appreciate it, sir."

Matheu stole another glance at the young woman, eyeing her straight back and graceful movements. Who was she? What game was she playing? Where did he see her before? He felt a tug from behind and turned, facing the man causing all the trouble.

Blacwin gulped when Matheu turned around. He seemed to realize immediately the disadvantage between them and quickly backed off. "Awe, she's not worthy of my time. I'll leave, and rid myself of her bad luck."

Matheu moved to the side to let him pass.

*****

Blacwin scurried down the passageway, as Isabella watched him turn the corner and disappear.

She scuffed the ground with her feet and looked up. Next to this knight in the alley, she felt small. The walls seemed as if they were closing in on her, as she tried to quell the uneasiness she felt in the company of a knight. Her heart thumped wildly, and she put her hand to her chest, holding it there. Too many of the knights at her father's manor were not to be trusted, and she was afraid this one would be no different.

She curtsied again. "I appreciate what you've done, sir. I wish there were more time to thank you properly, but I must quickly take my leave, so that my friends do not worry."

He gave her a puzzled look. He lifted his hand to stop her. "Wait, m'lady. Do not be going, just yet. I must question you further."

Isabella's eyes grew wide, and she backed away "No, sir. I'm sorry, but I cannot tell you anything in regards to my situation. Please, I must get back to my friends."

She turned and started down the alley.

He took her arm gently and pulled her back around to face him. He seemed to study her with a quizzical expression. "Who are you? I'd very much like to know."

Isabella felt a chill run through her. No one must know anything. This knight might turn her over to Hastulf, or worse yet, Wolfhart. She'd traveled too for such a thing to happen.

Matheu met the guarded look in her eyes. "You can trust in me. I cannot help, if I do not know who you are."

Isabella shook her head. "No, I cannot trust anyone. You might be a worthy sort, yet the knights I have known are not."

He looked surprised.

"I'm merely a humble serf's daughter, and I regret I cannot disclose more to you than this."

Matheu's mouth curved up slightly. He crossed his arms. "You are not a serf's daughter. It is plain to see. You've not disguised yourself well, m'lady."

A chill ran through Isabella. Would others be able to detect what he saw so easily? "You cannot be saying this, sir. I'm begging you to keep this information to yourself."

Matheu shook his head from side to side. "M'lady, you can trust me. I'll not repeat anything you tell me."

Isabella hesitated and then turned tearful eyes to him. "But, I cannot trust anyone. I want to think differently of you, yet, it is not so simple." Her wheat colored hair caught a last ray of light streaming down into the alley, and a tear slipped over her cheek. She quickly swept it away with her hand.

Matheu's concern for her was apparent by the expression on his face. He reached out and took her hand in his. "I'll say no more, but make sure you're safe with your friends before I leave you."

She took her hand from his and lowered it to her side. "I commend you for this, sir."

As they neared the end of the passageway, they approached Matheu's squire who was sitting on his gray mare, a weary expression on his face.

"This is Gawain."

Isabella curtsied, and then she looked around the corner and ducked back behind Matheu. "Hide me! It's him!"

Matheu turned, a puzzled expression on his face. "M'lady? You've no need to worry. You are safe now."

Gawain frowned. "Our day's nearly over. We're losing time, and all for a silly woman."

"Wait, Gawain." Matheu placed his hand on the horse's neck to steady it. He eyed Isabella curiously. "The man who was bothering you is gone. He'll not touch you again."

Isabella took hold of his arm. "No." She moved closer to him, her voice a whisper. "Not him! It's Wolfhart. He's after me. You must help me to get away from him. I beg you not to let him see me."

Matheu turned and scanned the street.

Isabella clutched his arm tightly from behind, shielding herself from the lone man riding a chestnut stallion toward them. "Please. Don't let him see me."

His eyebrow lifted. "I know him." He turned to Isabella with a curious stare.

Isabella hoped he hadn't guessed the truth about her. He might decide to turn her in.

"Gawain, give me the other cloak." He put out his hand, keeping one eye on Wolfhart.

Gawain looked annoyed. "I have need of all my cloaks."

"Gawain, now. This is no time to be difficult. I will purchase you a new one."

Gawain snorted, his face reddening. He grabbed a woolen cloak from his saddle and handed it to Matheu, who took it and wrapped it around Isabella, covering her head and pushing her hair beneath it.

*****

The young woman's silky strands were soft to the touch. Matheu's hand lingered on one piece that strayed. He looked down into her sweet face and was drawn to the large pools of dark, violet eyes staring up at him. His expression suddenly changed, and he quickly pulled his hand away.

If the woman was who he thought she was, his prayers had been answered. Although, with the oath Matheu took as a knight, he still could not act dishonorably by coming between two lords with a signed agreement.

He noticed her trembling hands and pale skin, and could see the fear radiating from her dark eyes, and remembered another vow he'd taken to protect this young woman he'd felt a special place for in his heart. He wouldn't interfere with her marriage, yet would do what he could, to allow her the chance to find her own way out of it.

*****

He took her hand in his and led her to his horse, lifting her onto it. "We'll be finding your friends, m'lady. I'll lead you around, until you see them. Don't worry because of Wolfhart. He cannot see you beneath this cloak. Keep it close about your head. He does not know you're with me."

She nodded. "Sir, you do not understand how indebted I feel toward you."

He smiled and winked, his blue eyes intense. "I am happy you feel indebted to me. Maybe someday you'll pay me back some way."

Isabella blushed. "Maybe with some money." She said it, knowing it wasn't what he was speaking of.

He nodded and laughed. "Yes, m'lady."

*****

53

# Chapter 4

Matheu of Thorneton Le Dale provided assistance to Isabella in finding Angnes and the traveling men. Then, he went on his way.

Isabella was relieved to see her friends again and grateful to have escaped Wolfhart.

The group she was with was closing in on the next town, where they planned to stay for the night. Nottingham wouldn't be much further.

With no farmer's wagon, the walking was difficult. Isabella's feet were terribly sore, but she did her best not to complain, as Angnes was not used to such exertions either and was quiet about her own trials.

Isabella was grateful for the hooded cloak she wore, as she'd been able to remain hidden from Wolfhart. She still was watchful to steer clear of this man along the way, hoping over a period of time he'd tire of looking for her and give up.

Keeping up to Leofwin's long strides was difficult. She strained with each step. "How much longer will it be?"

"I'm moving too quickly for you?"

"No, Leofwin, we'll get there faster this way."

He could see her face was flushed and realized it was more difficult for her then she was letting on. He slowed his pace.

She smiled. "Have you been troubadour all your days?"

He tipped his head and smiled as he walked. "Yes, m'lady. My father taught me. He was a great one."

She nodded. "Have you been with Theobald long?"

"No. We began to work as a team shortly after we met you." His eyes grew somber. "Theobald's wife died of the plague."

"Oh." It was all she was able to say. She turned her head to hide tears forming in her eyes.

Leofwin patted her arm. "It's difficult for you to hear this."

She spoke again, in a whisper. "Yes, but it's something that cannot be changed. The Black Death is all around us, and there is no way to escape it." She pushed the trailing tears off her cheeks.

# Isabella's Shield

Leofwin nodded. "I spoke to Theobald when his wife died, and he didn't have the heart to stay in London where the disease was spreading. He's blessed with a good singing voice. So, when he saw his chance to leave, he joined our company."

Isabella nodded. "And I can see why."

"And I, too." Leofwin looked down the path where Angnes was keeping stride with Godhuwe.

Isabella suddenly seemed puzzled. "Where's Godhuwe's cart with his wares? I thought he kept it and his horse with him."

"The new one he purchased is with a friend in Nottingham. He sold his old one in London."

"Oh." She tipped her head to the side. "Will we be able to ride on it?"

"You and Angnes. There'll be enough room for the two of you. I believe you're hurting?" Leofwin smiled tenderly at her, a sparkle in his eye.

Isabella smiled back, but her eyes were somber. "I am, yet I don't see humor in it, Leofwin. It does hurt very much."

He was instantly contrite. "I'd like to see you get rest soon. I would carry you, but it might prove difficult."

Isabella's mouth drew open. "Oh, I wouldn't allow such a thing. You're already too thin and it would not be good for you to lose more. There would be nothing left of you."

Leofwin laughed. "I suppose you're right." Then, he looked to where Theobald was.

Theobald suddenly waved wildly to them. "Nottingham!"

Isabella turned, eying the city in the distance. There was an enormous castle set upon a hill. She wondered who inhabited it.

They crossed a bridge over a silvery stream that ran through a lush valley. The river was surrounded by meadows filled with wooly, black-faced sheep. Ragged shepherds walked alongside them and tended them in the fields. There were homes just over the bridge.

Isabella sighed with relief. Nottingham was the last village she'd have to walk to. After that, she and Angnes could ride on Godhuwe's new cart, and in a very short time, she'd be seeing her sister.

*****

Isabella hobbled over the wide, cobblestone street that led into Nottingham, relieved to see the large, stone monastery on the path ahead of them.

Surrounding a gray, weather-beaten church next to it, were small shack-like homes made of cement, straw and wood, harboring thatched roofs with land around each. Women drew water from wells, and a Smith worked nearby with the sign, 'Bridle Smith', posted out front. Behind other gates were homes of artisans and tradesmen. The ones closer to the castle most likely housed the merchants, physicians and lawyers.

A monk stood in the high arched doorway of the monastery. Although his brown tunic was simple in style, it was clean, without a wrinkle. A cross, exquisite in detail, etched in a golden design, dangled from his neck, and a braided rope hung about his waist.

"It looks as if you'll be needing a place to stay this evening?" He scanned their group, while tapping his fingers against his side. "Well? Is it what you've come for? I've little time to wait on every traveler who comes to our door."

Isabella didn't envision him as the humble, kindly monks she imagined, from talk at dinner tables and gatherings in her home.

Godhuwe, of Malton tipped his head forward. "We do need a bed and a meal for a night."

The monk eyed them warily, but lifted his hand, gesturing to the door. "We've a couple beds for one night."

He took steps on the stone path that led to the doorway, and then opened the door for them to go through. "You may have rest here, tonight."

Angnes cheeks were red and expression was weary. "I look forward to sitting a spell."

Isabella nodded.

"Take the first of the rooms to your right, one for the men, and the other for the women," The monk turned to go and then looked back at them. "I'll tell them you'll need a meal."

"We're thankful." Godhuwe took a fur cloak from his shoulders and held it in his hand.

# Isabella's Shield

The monk stepped into a long hallway. "Wait here. I'll be right back."

Isabella scanned the outer room of the monastery. Her mouth opened slightly, awed by the rich looking room. There was carved, gilt-edged furniture on large, fine-woven rugs. Vases and chalices with intricate patterns painted on their surfaces were placed on marble pedestals. Elegant silk drapery covered the windows.

"I didn't know monks and nuns were in possession of such things. I thought they took vows to live in simple ways? Isn't the ten percent collected to assist the needy?"

Angnes edged closer to her. "Remember what I told you? Some of them are losing sight of what's good and right."

When the monk returned, they collected their provisions and carried them into the rooms. They followed the monk into a simple dining area with a wood table. For each of them there was a bowl of pottage, mostly broth, and a small wooden cup of ale.

In the next room, a group of monks and nuns sat around another table, which was draped with a purple cloth. It held platters of exotic foods, including dark breads and piles of meat. Voices echoed with laughter, and the wine flowed freely.

Isabella nudged Leofwin. "Don't the monks eat in silence and have simple meals?"

Leofwin set down the bowl of soup he held in his hands. "Remember what Angnes said, that many of the monks and nuns are not honoring their vows, but use this place to make money for themselves instead, on the backs of the serfs."

"And that's Christian?" Isabella couldn't contain her look of surprise.

Leofwin shook his head solemnly. "No, Isabella, it's not. It's why so many don't believe in God, when they see others acting as such."

Isabella drank some broth from her bowl. "Then, these nuns and monks are not Christian?"

Leofwin sighed. "Some might be and some, surely are not. How are we to know what's in their hearts?"

"So, it might be good to tell them the things Angnes shared with me?"

Leofwin smiled. "It would, and yet, many don't have ears to hear it, and instead choose riches and power over what's truly good."

"Which does nothing for a person."

He patted her shoulder, his voice soft and low. "To be sure. They don't understand what is better."

When they were done eating, they thanked the monks and nuns for the meal and then went to their rooms to retire for the night.

Isabella couldn't sleep. She said a prayer for the men and women who lived there, listening to the quiet songs and shuffling of feet in the long hallways.

Amidst such splendor and richness, in such a grandeur setting, with so many opportunities for prayer and meditation and learning of the Holy Scripture, Isabella couldn't for the life of her understand how any of them could turn from the truth. When she finally lay her head on her pillow and closed her eyes, she drifted off to sleep to the sweet, gentle music all around her.

In the morning, she pulled her tunic over her head and slipped on her shoes, stepping out into the hallway to look around. Godhuwe had already left. He must have been on his way to get his new cart and bring it back to the monastery.

A nun in a long corridor motioned to her, and she quickly made her way down the hall.

"You could use my assistance?" Isabella wondered what it was the woman might want.

"I could, miss. There's a man dying in this room." She pointed to the closed door next to her. "He's not sick, merely very old. I've many things to attend to and wonder if you might stay with him, so he's not alone."

Isabella's heart swelled to be given such a task. She nodded enthusiastically. "Oh, I will, if you'll let my friends know where I am."

The nun spoke softly. "I'll tell them…and I thank you for this."

"Is he in here?'

The nun opened the doorway. "On the bed."

Isabella entered the dark, candlelit room. A slight rustling came from the corner, where she turned and saw an old, shriveled gray-haired man lying on a lumpy straw mattress, shivering, a wool covering half on him and half on the floor.

Isabella crossed the room and lifted the blanket up and over the man and then sat down on a wooden chair next to his bed.

His eyes were soft, but set in hallowed, sunken cheeks. They fluttered open. A smile curved his lips. "A pretty girl for the end of my days." He spoke in a quiet whisper, "You may call me Ailwin of Dudford."

Isabella smiled. Despite the fact that he was withered, thin and gaunt, with a gray pallor and little life left in him, there was an intelligent twinkle in his warm, brown eyes.

She looked around, and observed the cold, cracked walls of stone. It provided no place for a fire and left little to be desired in the small, dank room. It was a pitiful place to die. She determined to make his last hours bearable, and maybe even gratifying.

"I'm Isabella." She smiled, lifting the blanket back over him and moving closer to his bed.

His shivering lessoned. "Thank you for covering me. I couldn't reach the cloth."

Isabella sighed. "It's the least I could do. Are you feeling much pain? I hope not."

The man's eyes softened. "I have some pain, yet I'm old, and have learned it's the way with persons of my sort. But the Lord is my shield and my reward, so I can bear it."

She smiled.

He eyed her curiously. "Where are you from?"

Isabella hesitated, then thought it would be all right to tell this dying man the truth. "I came from London, traveling with a group of Christians."

A brief spark came to the man's tired eyes. "So you're visiting?"

"Yes."

He nodded. His eyes fluttered closed.

She could see he was close to the end, as he seemed to float in and out of consciousness and lose his speech for moments.

His breathing was labored, and he eventually fell into a deep sleep for a long period of time.

Isabella's eyes were riveted to him as he slept, watching his chest rising and falling unevenly. She studied his face, which was drawn into a smile. She was amazed by the joy radiating from him in his state so close to death.

Time passed as she sat there, and then she finally heard him stir again.

When he opened his eyes, she was still studying his face intently.

His expression was gentle. "I once knew a woman with the same extraordinary color of eyes."

Isabella was curious. She'd never heard of anyone having had the same color eyes as her own and was interested to know who this person might be.

But, before she could say more, he spoke again, barely above a whisper. "I lived in London for a time."

"You did?"

"I was a servant at Godfrey Hall, until I was put out, as was every servant at the place."

It was Isabella's turn to be shocked. Ailwin came from her home? "Godfrey Hall? You lived there? It was my home!"

Ailwin's eyes widened, surprised.

Isabella's mind was full of questions. They put all the servants out? She didn't remember such a thing, but he was old, and it was possible. Anything was possible at the manor in which she lived.

As if reading her thoughts, he asked the question. "Who were your mother and father?"

She sighed. Memories of her life with them and their death were not so pleasant. It was difficult telling others her parent's identity, without feeling it might bring judgment upon her own self. "Muriolda and Alward of London." She revealed their names to him hesitantly.

A line wrinkled his forehead. Yet, before he could speak, his eyes drew sleepily shut again, and his breathing became short and raspy.

Isabella took his withered hand in her own, giving it a gentle squeeze. She tipped her head forward and prayed for his time to be short, so he wouldn't suffer long.

His eyes remained shut, and yet he made a concerted effort to speak.

Isabella shook her head. "Rest easy, sir, and don't try to say anything on my account."

His hand closed around hers, and he struggled to sit up and say something to her again.

"Sir, lie down. I'll put my ear to your lips, so you can tell me what you wish for me to hear." She leaned over and positioned herself above him.

He drew an unsteady breath, the sounds weak in his throat. "The key. Find Hereward. He muttered it between gasps.

Isabella's eyes widened. "Find Hereward? Who's he?"

Ailwin's eyes began to roll back, his breathing suddenly becoming raspy again. He tried to speak, but the words came out in slight, vaporous gasps.

Isabella found it near impossible to understand what he was trying to tell her. She spoke in a gentle whisper. "What is the meaning of this? What is the importance of the key you speak of?" She leaned down again and heard nothing, and then sat back up.

He tried to speak one last time, but couldn't.

She scanned his soft features and ashen skin and sighed, suddenly realizing he would not speak again. She saw he was slowly fading away, and his life was clearly ending. It'd be moments, and he'd be gone. She was silent, watching closely as his eyes shut. She noticed the slightest rise and fall of his chest, as he drew in his last bit of life.

Her heart melted when she saw a gentle smile tug at his lips. The tired, worn lines in his face miraculously transformed into a most tranquil expression.

His eyes opened momentarily and she gasped, bending down to catch the glow emanating from them.

Such joy, as she'd never seen before!

She was astounded by the change in his expression, never having seen anything so beautiful in her whole lifetime. It was pure, unadulterated love she couldn't explain.

And then his eyelids closed peacefully.

She sat very still next to him for the longest time, reveling in the fact he'd passed from life to death before her in the most serene manner. She felt blessed to have been witness to his last moments and was glad she came to sit by his side. God was surely with him. There were no questions in her mind about the place where he now resided. The old man was at rest and in a better place.

She leaned back in her chair and took her hand from his, sighing. Then, she contemplated his last words to her. The key? She wondered. And who was Hereward? Most likely it was the ramblings of a confused, dying old man.

"Yes," she murmured to herself. "I must not meddle in such things. There's no reason to concern myself with this."

And yet she couldn't help speculating on the last two things Ailwin uttered. He seemed stable in thought and speech up until the very end, and so very persistent.

She sat in silence for a long time pondering the older gentleman's words, letting out a long breath. Maybe someday she'd look into the matter further and try to find out more for Ailwin's sake.

Isabella covered his shoulders with the blanket and then got up to find a nun to care for Ailwin's lifeless body.

Isabella turned before she left the room, taking one last look at the kindly, old man, wishing she could've had more time with him before he died. What a most worthy soul he was. It was a blessing to have had this opportunity to know him for the short time she did. When she entered his room, she believed God placed her in this particular room for the old man's benefit, and yet now, she knew she couldn't have been more wrong. His death was an assurance to her that there was a better place, one she'd be going to someday, and one in which she would be loved.

She was certain that Ailwin found a place with no more tears or pain. Someday she'd know him again and meet the Savior too, as Ailwin had.

\*\*\*\*\*

# Chapter 5

It was a relief to be riding on a cart the next day. The refreshed group was on their way to the town of Doncaster, a few days south of Cropton. They'd made it quickly to the Sherwood Forest and were traveling through at a good pace.

Isabella was spellbound at the beauty around her. The forest was lush with rich, green and brown foliage. A thick, mature oak with great twisting branches reached out to them. Over it a large falcon circled, lowering slowly and dropping out of sight.

"It's beautiful, isn't it?" Angnes leaned closer, her eyes wide.

Isabella nodded. Birds hopped from branch to branch, on thin, birch limbs and squirrels dashed to and fro beneath the golden-green canopy. Along the path were wild orchids lined in rows, which spread soft scents into the air around them.

The noise of the wagon wheels lurching forward along the hard-packed earth blended with the gentle forest sounds of melodious bird songs and soft rustling wind. Isabella leaned forward, enjoying the quiet sounds, along with the warm sunshine cutting through the trees.

Suddenly, Angnes poked Isabella a little too hard in the side.

Isabella turned quickly, eying her friend with a quizzical expression. Angnes didn't look at her, but seemed as if frozen in her seat.

"Do not turn round, Isabella." Her eyes were set ahead of them on the path.

Isabella felt alarms going off inside her. She drew in a breath. "What is it?"

Angnes spoke in almost a whisper. There was a calm, yet serious tone in her voice. "Godhuwe spotted Wolfhart riding a horse on the path in back of us."

An astonished sound came from Isabella. She suddenly felt as if it were difficult for her to breathe. Wolfhart was still looking for her. He'd been on the same path and didn't seem to be waning in his hunt for her. What might she do this time to escape him? She was glad for the hooded cloak Matheu of Thorneton Le Dale had given her.

A worried look came over Angnes. "Godhuwe told me you'll have to leap off the cart where the road ahead bends. You need to hide yourself in the forest, otherwise Wolfhart will catch you!"

"You are not coming with me?" Isabella's quiet voice came out in a squeak.

Angnes shook her head. "No, he'll see the two of us."

Isabella's was frozen with fear. She put her hand to her heart, trying to still the strong beat coming from within. "But, where will I find you again?"

"Stay in these woods, until we circle back." Angnes sounded confident and calm. Something in the way she said it, stilled Isabella's nerves.

Isabella swallowed hard. "All right." She felt the dark presence of Wolfhart behind them. She was fixed upon her seat next to Angnes, watching for the bend in the road, which was drawing nearer to them. Fear crept steadily into her heart. Her breath felt as if it'd been stolen away.

Yet, this was her chance to escape, as the horse and rider would be coming upon them very soon. She was Wolfhart's property, if she guessed what was most likely true, and there'd be no choice but to go willingly with him, if he demanded it. There'd be nothing Angnes or her friends could do to stop him.

Her chance came, and she took it, leaping from the cart and falling to the ground, rolling into a ravine that edged the path. She got up quickly, pulling up her tunic and running to the refuge of a large oak tree, ducking behind its massive trunk.

After the bend in the road straightened, she saw Wolfhart nearing the cart. She heard the wagon halt further down the road. She leaned up next to a tree near her, pressing her body against the rough bark and listened. Her heart was pounding in her chest. She thought if it were any louder, Wolfhart and the rest of them would hear it. She put her hand to her throat.

# Isabella's Shield

"Have any of you seen a flaxen-haired woman with the violet eyes of a witch? Her name is Isabella London, daughter of Alward. The young woman's missing, and I'm looking for her." Wolfhart was eying each of her friends suspiciously, holding tight to the reigns of his prancing horse.

Angnes looked down. Isabella hoped he didn't recognize her as a former servant at Godfrey Hall.

Wolfhart looked from her to Godhuwe, who stared at him boldly.

Godhuwe answered. "No, we have not, sir." He shrugged, nonchalantly, and then he turned to the others. "Have any of you seen this young woman?"

"No." Each of them said it, as if they hadn't a clue.

Wolfhart rubbed his heavy, full chin. "Where are you riding to?"

"North," Godhuwe replied. Then, he muttered something under his breath.

Leofwin piped in, "We've no real path, only the one that'll make us money in a town. We're troubadours and go where the wind takes us." He smiled.

A scowl formed on Wolfhart's face. He looked perturbed. "Might I ride with you for company? I'm heading in that direction, also."

Leofwin smiled graciously, yet spoke quieter than was natural for him. Isabella could see he was clearly disturbed by Wolfhart's question. "You could, but our cart would be a hindrance to you. It would surely slow you down."

Wolfhart eyed the forest around him, frowning. He rested his hand on his extended belly. "It'd be no trouble for me." His voice held a cantankerous tone, despite his trying to convince the others that he was responding with impeccable politeness.

Isabella could barely see the cart from where she stood, but stayed hidden behind the tree, only poking her head around when Wolfhart's back was turned to her. She watched the man closely, repulsed by his bad-tempered sulky behavior, not to mention his undesirable looks. He was definitely beyond the age Isabella considered appropriate for her station in life.

Godhuwe's lips tightened. He seemed to play along for Wolfhart's sake. "Well, we might stop to rest too often for your liking." He nodded to his horse. "This one here cost me a pretty coin, and I do not wish to push him in any way. If you've a pressing need to move quickly, our group might slow you down."

Wolfhart's eyes narrowed. "You're sure you know nothing of the young woman? It seems as if you're trying to rid yourselves of me." He eyed them closely, not able to disguise the mistrust he had for them.

All of them shook their heads. "No, you can ride with us to Doncaster. We'll get an inn there for the night. We've been traveling a long way and need the rest."

Godhuwe extended his hand, as if to beckon Wolfhart to join them. "We don't mind the company, if you're willing to ride at a slower pace. Come, let's be going."

Wolfhart smiled irritably, patting the side of his horse. "Yes, well. It'll be my pleasure to join your lively conversation." His sullen expression told a different story.

Godhuwe reluctantly clicked the reigns of his horse and made a clucking sound to start them on their way. The wagon rattled and shook as it came to life, making it's way down the forest path, as Wolfhart rode along beside them.

Isabella kept her eyes on Godhuwe's cart as it rounded the bend. She grasped the tree she was hiding behind, to keep her knees from buckling. The sound of the cart's wheels rolling down the road became steadily more distant and then disappeared altogether.

She felt faint, realizing she was left alone in this place. She'd never been in a forest without a guide and was unsure of how she'd find her way out safely. The dark woods seemed ripe with peril of more than one kind, and Doncaster was a great distance away. Along with the threat of wild animals roaming freely in the forest, there were also traveling bands of men and serfs who worked the open, sandy grassland areas of the forest leased to them by the king. Any of these might find a lone woman wandering in the countryside a likely target for abuse.

Isabella looked around her. The forest was quiet, other than the occasional skittering sound of small animals rooting beneath the woodland trees and the soft noises of twittering of birds above her. While it was still light out, there seemed to be little danger. Yet, Isabella knew that night would fall upon her very soon, and then the landscape would present a much different picture.

She came out from around the large oak tree she was hiding behind and began making her way through the dense brush as the sun was beginning to set in the sky. She tried to stay near the well-worn path, yet felt uncomfortable walking too close to it. If anyone should suddenly appear on it, she wanted to be able hide herself quickly.

She walked for a time through the dense foliage, until she noticed the shadows in the forest lengthening. She already spotted more than one traveler ambling along the road, unaware of the fact she was hidden from them, within less than ten horse lengths.

She'd have to find shelter soon as her friends wouldn't be able to find their way back to her with Wolfhart watching them so closely. She feared being alone amidst wild animals at night.

She listened carefully in attempts to escape the clomping sounds of horses, the chatter of men's voices and the soft padding of feet along the forest path, while looking for a safe place to lay her head for the night. There were no small cottages in sight or any signs of women present. The deeper she trod through the brush, the wilder the forest became.

Darkness was setting in quickly now. A disturbing feeling of trepidation welled up in Isabella's chest, while icy shudders ran through her, causing her to turn frequently and look over her shoulder. The outlines of the trees became shadows, their branches like fingers reaching out to take hold of her.

She suddenly stopped and turned when she heard hard, heavy thudding sounds like horses hooves trotting at breakneck speed toward her from deep in the forest.

She felt sick inside, because this time she wouldn't be able to hide, as she didn't know what direction the rider came from.

She held fast to a tree, breathing a sigh of relief when she realized it was only a deer bounding in quick leaps past her and then springing across the road in wild abandon. She never realized how loud a deer would sound as it ran through the forest. She'd always pictured them prancing and padding through the underbrush noiselessly. Yet, it made sense that they were louder than they appeared, as they were a wild animal and similar to a small horse in size and stature. She couldn't imagine a horse, running at breakneck speed and jumping over brush in the forest without a measure of discord.

Isabella let out a light laugh, but then the sound of her voice died, when she realized why the deer was in such a hurry.

She froze.

Her eyes lit on two lean, gray wolves that entered a clearing, a fair distance away from where she stood and then stopped when they spotted her. Their mouths hung open, large sharp teeth glinting against their salivating tongues.

"Go!" A shrill fear rose inside her, as she yelled at them.

She grabbed a stick and screamed again. "Go away!"

They both lowered their heads, their gray fur standing upright on their necks. They emitted low growls, moving in slow half circles toward her.

Her eyes stung with tears. She swallowed, but her throat was dry. Swinging the stick at them, she screamed, her voice shrilly. "No! Be gone, you! Go!"

As if on cue, both wolves took a running leap in her direction, ravening barks growing louder as they closed in on the distance from her.

A helpless groan stuck in her throat, while her whole body tensed, a shudder running through it. She was defenseless, unable to move.

She dropped to her knees, aimlessly lashing out at the wolves and then stopped, realizing any of her efforts would be in vain. Very soon she'd know what it felt like to be under the attack of these two, tremendous beasts.

She dropped the stick and covered her eyes with her hands. "Lord, help me," she prayed aloud, paralyzed with the chills running through her.

Almost instantly, Isabella heard a different sound, a sharp, whistling one that rang out. Next came a thud and a yelp, which sent one gray wolf tumbling to the ground, bleeding from its side and lying still.

The second beast stopped, suddenly apprehensive, yet continuing to growl and move toward Isabella. She remained frozen in her spot, unable to move, sick with fear.

She turned when she heard a crashing sound behind her, and before she knew what was happening, she was being lifted onto the back of a horse's saddle and found herself gripping tightly to a man riding on the seat in front of her.

The stranger quickly strung another arrow to his bow and let it fly, sticking it deep into the second wolf's heart and dropping the creature in its tracks. Then the man dug his heels into his horse's side, steering the animal back up the embankment and onto the path, racing wildly down the road that would eventually lead out of the forest.

Isabella shook. Her mind was flying with thoughts of what might have become of her if this stranger had not come along at the exact moment he did. Everything happened so quickly, and she'd not had the time or ability to react to any of it.

Her thoughts were jumbled, as she held tightly to the man in the saddle. She felt a calming presence invade her heart as they rode along.

God must have heard her prayer! Only seconds after she prayed, her requests were answered! Surely her Lord knew ahead of time what would happen and certainly provided her a means of escape at just the right moment.

Thank you, she breathed gratefully.

Just outside Sherwood Forest, Isabella spotted a town ahead. She leaned closer to the stranger. "Is this Doncaster?" She feared Wolfhart would be there.

The man's voice was vaguely familiar, but she couldn't see him in the dark. "It's Blythe. Doncaster is almost ten more miles, yet, I believe you'll be needing a rest for the night."

"Yes, it would be good to stop here."

As they neared an inn further down the road, Isabella looked around for any signs of Wolfhart. She didn't see Hastulf's chestnut stallion anywhere, so breathed a sigh of relief. She'd be all right in this place tonight. She wondered about the man she rode with. Surely, if he were a threat to her, he would've had plenty of opportunities to take advantage of her before this time. She felt safe in his company.

The man gently lifted her from the saddle, setting her firmly on her feet. She waited for him to get off the horse after her. Once down, he turned, his dark blue cloak opening to reveal a tunic underneath with the symbol of a stone gate on it, the same one Matheu of Thorneton Le Dale wore. His shield was one and the same.

She turned to him, her dark eyes inquisitive. "What? You?" She took a step back.

Matheu grasped her arms. "What were you doing in that dark forest? You took that path, alone?" He shook his head and scowled. "It was a foolish thing for any young woman to do!"

Isabella bit her lip, and her eyes began to fill with tears. She wiped them away with the back of her hand. His words were unfair, yet at the same time she was relieved to know she was safe with this man.

Her heart was only beginning to slow from the steady thumping she'd felt earlier, and her knees seemed at that moment as if they might buckle beneath her. She was more grateful than angry he'd come along when he did and was overwhelmed with a sense gratitude for his assistance. If it weren't for him, she wouldn't be alive at this very moment.

She feared she might drop to the ground, if she didn't steady herself. Without thinking, Isabella impulsively leaned closer and slipped her arms about his waist, gently enfolding herself in his embrace, letting tears fall with abandon.

Matheu took a deep breath, unaccustomed to displays of affection, having spent the better part of his life in the war. Immediately, his hands began to tenderly stroke her hair, and he drew her in to him, speaking in a quiet, calming voice. "There, you're all right now. Do not be pained."

He looked down at her, surprised by her reaction, her slender arms wrapped so tightly about him. He pulled his cloak around her and held her close until he felt her pulling away from him.

Isabella took a quick step back, meeting his dark blue eyes, suddenly embarrassed by the intimacy of their embrace and the strong emotions she displayed. She apologized. "I didn't mean to be forward with you, sir. I was merely overwhelmed by all that happened."

*****

Matheu stepped back reluctantly and bowed his eyes holding hers fast. His expression became slightly guarded. He shook his head. "You've been through much. I understand." He eyed her warily and then moved further from her, suddenly aware the young woman wielded a great power over him.

He could not forget his vows as a knight, as Isabella was already spoken for, and arrangements had been made between wealthy families. He'd been warned he had no right to be interfering with the whole affair.

Isabella smoothed out the folds in her wrinkled brown tunic and wrapped her cloak tighter about her, holding herself upright with quiet poise. "My friends are with Wolfhart, as he's following them. I had to leave them, so he wouldn't catch me. I was afraid to be in the forest alone, yet believe Wolfhart catching me, would be worse than the dark forest. I'd rather be eaten by the wolves."

Matheu tipped his head, eyeing her curiously. A smile stirred on his face, and he could not help letting out a laugh. After what had just happened, he seemed surprised she could say such a thing.

*****

Isabella stared at him. "You must not make light of my situation."

"But, m'lady, after what you've been through, I cannot believe you'd choose to be eaten by those wolves." His blue eyes sparkled.

She nodded, with more conviction than she felt. Neither Wolfhart nor the wolves would've been her choice, but maybe the wolves would've been better. "God's able to save me from both, and he's done it. When I'm afraid, I can trust him. He is my shield."

Matheu's heart melted with her words. "I agree that God is faithful and can be trusted." He pulled his horse to the stable and tied it to a post, as she watched.

She marveled at the way he maneuvered the great animal and was touched inside that he also believed in God as she did. The knights at Godfrey Hall were different than Matheu. She never met any man like him in her whole lifetime, aside from Angnes' friends. Before leaving her father's manor, she knew nothing but brutality and evil coming from men. She assumed all of them were like the men there, and she'd never known any who truly cared for and respected women. Now, she felt she might have been wrong.

Matheu took her arm and led her to the inn. "I'll get you a place to sleep, and then I'll take you to Doncaster in the morning to find your friends, without Wolfhart knowing."

She smiled. "I'm grateful to you, once again."

He bowed slightly. "It's my duty as a knight."

Isabella sighed. She forgot about the vows of the knights. For a brief second, she caught a glimmer of sadness in his eyes, but then it was gone.

She tipped her head to the side. "Where's your squire? Why's he not with you?"

"The king allowed me to hunt in his forest. Gawain is staying at the castle in Nottingham. He'll be looking for me in the morning and carrying my armor and lances. We can wait for him here."

She nodded then watched, as he went to the door and knocked. The wooden frame swung on its hinges, and the innkeeper appeared in the light of the room.

*****

Matheu bartered with an elderly man and then paid for rooms for both Isabella and him to sleep in. He saw to it she was safely inside her room, and then he went to his own and lay down for the night. He tossed and turned, as he lay on the straw mattress beneath him, thinking of Isabella.

As for her father's agreement with Wolfhart, he'd keep his vows as a knight and would honor positions of authority. And yet, he couldn't agree with the man that a woman as lovely as her should be given in marriage to such an evil man.

He struggled with his thoughts. He'd already had such strong feelings for this young woman, after only three brief encounters. He supposed he'd prayed for her so many times, he felt he knew her. She was like no other woman. Those lovely eyes of hers drew him in like a snare upon his very heart, and her silken hair felt like gold upon his hand. Maybe tomorrow, Gawain would help him see things more clearly.

One thing he did know for certain, was the fact that Isabella spelled trouble for him. The woman was entangled in too many of her own trials and unfortunate circumstances for him to find himself in the middle of. He let out an exasperated sigh.

Tomorrow he determined to find her friends quickly and safely deposit her back with them. Then he'd take a different path with Gawain that led to the manor at Thorneton Le Dale.

He pulled the woolen covering over his shoulders and sighed, closing his eyes and letting himself be carried off by sleep, reveling in the warmth of the blanket about him and the soft, inviting bed.

Morning would come early enough. There'd be much to think about then. Tonight, he'd sleep and wake up fresh at daybreak, hopefully able to see things in a much more clear and level headed manner.

*****

73

# Chapter 6

Isabella shook out her wet hair and then sat on a log next to a river to fasten the ties on her leather shoes. She felt better after having been able to wash in the clear, refreshing stream.

"Isabella!"

Upon hearing her name, she stopped what she was doing and looked up sharply, noticing Matheu standing above the rise next to the river.

Panic registered inside her. He'd called her by her name. He knew who she was? "How did you know my name, sir? Who told you?"

Matheu sighed and shook his head impatiently. "My lady, it was not difficult to know this, after hearing that Wolfhart was to be wed to the daughter of Alward of London. I was at the meal, when your parents made the announcement."

A slight look of discomfort crossed Isabella's face, and she quickly bent down to finish tying her shoes. "You were one of the knights at the end of the table?"

"Yes." He moved closer to her. "I attempted to discuss the matter with your father, yet he would not listen. I couldn't bear it that a young lady such as you, would be forced to endure that ungodly man in marriage. I prayed for you."

Isabella finished tying the leather laces, still not looking at Matheu. "I thank you for this. The Lord has surely listened."

He strode down to the edge of the river that wound past her and stood next to the large fallen tree she was sitting on. His eyes fixed on her. "You cannot leave without giving notice to others where you are off to. Do you understand that you've made a grave mistake in doing such a thing?"

Isabella turned and looked up at him with surprise. Her cheeks blushed crimson. "I was merely cleaning myself. I needed a bath, and the river was close." She sat up after finishing with her shoes, then straightened her wool tunic and stood next to him.

Matheu gave her an exasperated look, exhaling deeply. "Isabella, things are very different here, than at the manor where you were living. In the country, there are dangers you are not aware of, such as the wolves you dealt with, besides other wild animals and miscreants looking for trouble who might hurt a lady such as you."

She sighed deeply. She regretted the fact that he felt obligated to her and that she may have caused him distress. "I'm sorry. I've not been in the country. I know little of these things. I did not mean to trouble you, sir."

She shook out her hair and pulled her fingers through the silken strands. They were almost dry from the sunlight, creating soft waves of gold against the bodice of her tunic. She eyed the rolling green hills in the distance and the clear sparkling river and then turned, noticing Matheu was staring at her, his expression unreadable.

Her cheeks suddenly warmed again. "I won't leave again and cause you difficulty."

His expression softened, and his eyes met hers. "I'm glad, and hope you remember this."

Something lit inside her at the warmth in his eyes. She hoped he felt more for her than he let on, as she felt an incredible amount of affection for him, especially after all he'd done for her.

She reached down, itching the back of her arm. The wool was making ugly red marks on her skin. She wasn't accustomed to certain fabrics and spent more time in silks and soft weaves. Her body was definitely reacting in harsh ways to the rough, scratchy tunic.

Matheu lifted her arm and frowned, surveying the chafed skin underneath the brown wool of her garment. "You cannot have this cloth against your delicate skin. It is not fitting for you." He had a concerned look on his face.

Isabella pulled her sleeve back down over her arm. "Oh, but I must. I cannot let Wolfhart know who I am."

She gave him an uncertain smile. "I merely have days until I'll be at my sister's, and then I'll know what to do. It's not so bad."

The rise in his brow revealed to her that the answer she gave didn't satisfy him. He took her by the arm, lifting her to her feet. "Come, we must get back to the inn."

Isabella nodded. "Yes well, I will collect my things and be ready to go within the hour."

*****

"*She's* coming with us?" Gawain's expression was one of annoyance as he eyed Matheu lifting Isabella onto the saddle of his great horse behind him.

Matheu turned. "We cannot allow her to walk to Doncaster alone." He dug his heels gently into the side of his horse and began a slow gait down the path.

Gawain chucked to his own horse and edged up to the side of them. "She'll slow us down."

Matheu smiled. "There are many things that have slowed our time."

On top of the large steed, Isabella breathed a sigh of relief, knowing Matheu would be taking her to Doncaster. She was also grateful to him for freeing her from the scratchy, wool fabric against her skin. Before they left, he'd bartered with the innkeeper's wife for a linen tunic she could slip on beneath the rough material rubbing her raw. The itching had subsided, and she was glad of it.

Gawain snorted. "She can find her friends herself. We'll lose time with her along." He eyed Isabella with distaste.

Matheu smiled. "Gawain, you wish to be a knight, someday. Remember your vows."

Gawain grunted, then took his reins and made a clucking sound again to his horse. A look of contempt stole over his face, as he rode past Matheu. "A sting of the serpent, she is," he muttered under his breath.

Isabella turned her head, ignoring his comment. She looked out over the low, rolling fields, concentrating on the view. Gawain's familiar words stung, ones her relatives used often in reference to her. She chose to ignore his comment and not answer to it.

Matheu noticed her silence. "Do not allow him to offend you. He has a low opinion of women, because of his past. It will not be long before he sees you differently. He's a worthy lad and kinder than the impression he presents. His mother was not a fitting example, as she chose to wed the man who killed his father."

A breath caught in Isabella's chest. "Oh." Her heart softened. "I feel sorry for him. I cannot take offense after knowing his story. I'll treat him kindly."

Matheu nodded then leaned forward slightly, whispering in his horse's ear. "This is a worthy girl, Black. I'm thinking it's fitting we're helping her."

Isabella smiled and tugged at him to sit upright. "You're speaking to a horse, sir. And it will surely cause me to fall." Yet, something inside her lit at his favorable compliment.

Matheu laughed loudly. "You must hold closely to me, then."

Isabella's eyebrow lifted. "I'll merely hold you as close as is needed for me to keep myself on."

He laughed again. "Then be ready to go faster, as it's agreeable for me to have your arms around me."

Her mouth opened slightly, and she let out a light gasp.

Matheu dug his heels into the dark horse.

The animal lurched ahead and began to gallop, forcing Isabella to bounce forward, clutching him tightly in efforts to stay in her seat. As they sped along, she held him close, more so than she felt befitting for a lady, yet unable to loosen her grasp, as they raced down the path.

Her cheeks grew warm, and a smile formed on her lips as they rode. This dark knight, Matheu, was not what she expected him to be. On the surface, he appeared quiet and strong, sometimes even grim, a man one wouldn't want to come up against in a battle, similar to the knights she met at her father's manor. And yet, after spending time with him, she realized he also possessed other qualities, honor and respect, a high regard for women, and even humor, as she was seeing now.

In her childhood, Isabella was led to believe women deserved men's disrespect. And now, she was beginning to wonder.

It gave her great hope in the belief that Matheu was different. And maybe beyond the small world she came from, he showed her that life had more to offer than she ever thought possible.

*****

Further down the road, Isabella noticed poorly dressed children in ragged wool, dancing in a circle in front of a cement shack where a woman was drawing water from the river nearby. Their clear simple voices rang out over the rolling-meadows. "Ring-a-ring o' roses, a pocket full of Posies, A-tishoo! A-tishoo! We all fall down!"

Then, the tattered, unkempt group dropped to the ground screaming and sprawling in the grassy field, shrieking with laughter.

Isabella shuddered, upon hearing these gruesome words coming from innocent mouths of children. She recognized the chant as one that marked the Black Death, which was ravaging London when she left. They'd no understanding yet, of the effect it was having throughout the land.

Further down the road, she noticed the sky turning a bleak gray color, heavy with misty low-lying clouds, the valley losing its vivid colors in the fog. A screeching sound rained out overhead, and she looked up. A hungry-looking vulture circled the bloated remains of a lifeless carcass lying in the field. She sensed stillness settling over the land, an eerie silence and lifted her head, her eyes large. "It's the plague, making its way into the country." She said it in a hushed voice. Fear crept through her. These people had no idea as to the coming storm, seeming to go about their tasks, as if life would continue in the same unaffected pattern.

Matheu nodded. "It happens in a very short time and is not taking long to reach us." His eyes were dark and the lines of his mouth grim.

Gawain slowed his gray mare and edged up next to Matheu's larger, black horse, trotting beside them. He turned his head to them, but didn't speak. Words didn't seem to do justice to what they saw lying ahead of them.

Littered across the moors, there were at least twenty-five more dead animals lying motionless on the grassy knolls, mostly sheep, covered with dark gruesome swellings and distended bellies.

Isabella closed her eyes. "I cannot look. It's terrible." She rested her head on Matheu's shoulder, as she looked down. This is how the plague entered London. Not long afterward, people fell in heaps beside the blackened creatures.

The horse's gentle motion swayed beneath her to the rhythm of the great animal's steady gait. His considerable size and strength afforded her a certain amount of security, as they moved quietly past the latest fallen victims to the plague.

Further down the path, she heard the whimpering of a very young child reach her ears. She forced her eyes back open and looked around, searching for the owner of the small voice. It was a wounded sound, one she couldn't ignore. Where was it coming from?

To the right, she saw a small, cement hut with a thatched roof, the doors flung open and swinging in the breeze, slapping hollowly against the wall. More animals lay dead in a gated pen nearby, save one brown, speckled rooster sitting on a post making mournful crowing sounds.

She heard the faint cry of the tiny voice again and turned in the direction of it, spying a tiny child dressed in a disheveled, gray wool tunic, sitting alone in the dirt next to a shed, its blonde curls bobbing with each whimper. The small babe's clothing was torn and dusty, as if she'd had little care in the past few days.

Isabella eyed the child with a pained expression. Something inside her broke for the little one, and she felt as if she had to do something to help her. "Sir, you must let me off the horse. I must examine the child."

"Isabella, the Black Death is in this place. We can do nothing for anyone here." Matheu's voice was steady, and he didn't turn when Isabella pointed to the child. He kept his eyes trained on the road. "Someone will care for her."

Isabella was sure he refused to look, to keep up his resolve. He'd probably seen worse things in the wars he'd fought and had learned to put up defenses against them.

She tugged at his sleeve. "Yet, if those here are all dead, the babe will not survive on her own."

He turned, spotting the child, but said nothing.

Isabella struggled in her seat. Her voice became more insistent. "If you'll not help, I'll get down. She's crying and alone.

Please, sir." She took his arm and began to lift her leg over the horse.

Matheu put out his hand and held her there. "M'lady, it isn't safe for you to do such a thing."

Gawain slowed his horse. A ridge formed over his brows. "But, Matheu, we cannot leave the child. I believer Isabella is correct in her endeavor to help. It appears as if the babe has been abandoned."

Matheu's expression was grave, and he let out a slow breath. He eyed Isabella hesitantly. "I'll go to her, but you must both stay here."

A light shone from Isabella's eyes. She gave Matheu a quick hug and then let go. "Oh, thank you. I could not have left her, without knowing her situation."

He gave her a disconcerted look, and then swung his leg up over his horse and jumped down. He went into the weather-beaten house and looked around. When he came out, his expression was grim.

He strode over to the little child and picked her up, holding her close to him. "You will find yourself well with us, little one. We'll care for you." He patted the little girl on the back of the shoulder and carried her to where Isabella waited on the horse's back.

Isabella reached out her arms. "Give her to me. I was with my brother and sister when they were stricken with the plague, and I was spared from it. I spent two days in their company."

Matheu shook his head. "No, you must not touch her. I will walk beside you with her. At least, she does not appear to be sick at this time."

He reached into a pouch hanging from the horse and took out a thick piece of bread and began breaking off bits to feed the child with.

The little girl's blue eyes grew large, and she hungrily downed a fair portion. Then, she smiled at Matheu, reaching up a chubby hand and touching his nose.

He laughed. "It's time to find you a monastery little one, a good place." He took the reigns of the horse and began to lead them down the road.

Isabella gave him a disconcerted look. Even though the armor Matheu wore was light chain mail and Gawain was carrying his weapons, it still would be a long journey for him on foot.

She pleaded her case to him. "Sir, you cannot lead us with u child in your arms, I'll hold her. If it's God's will to keep me from the sickness, he will. But, you must trust him and not be afraid."

"Afraid?" His brow arched, and he smiled. "I only fear for your safety, m'lady."

Isabella let out a breath. "But, you are not trusting God when you won't allow me hold her. There's no need for you to fear anything." She looked down at him and put out her hand. They'd never make it to Doncaster in a reasonable time, if they kept this pace. Angnes and the others might think something happened to her and leave town.

Gawain rode up beside them, and a spark lit his eyes. He chuckled to himself. "Am I hearing you're afraid, Matheu?" A wide grin spread over his face, and he shook an errant piece of red hair out of his eyes.

Matheu looked up at Isabella, his eyes solemn. "I only..."

"Give her the child. Trust in God, as you tell me. If you refuse, it'll take us two days to make it to Doncaster, and then she'll never find her people."

Isabella held her arms out. "Please, the sickness will do nothing if God does not will it to."

Matheu shook his head and looked up at her with an annoyed expression. "For such a slight young woman, I believe you to be more hardy than some of the villains I've fought who would've run from the plague."

Gawain moved his horse forward and turned back grinning. "Maybe this gate of the devil is not so bad." He clucked to his horse again to move ahead in a slow gait, while Matheu reluctantly handed the child to Isabella.

Isabella held the child close, speaking sweetly to her, enjoying the feel of the soft tender babe against her shoulder. She was glad the little girl was safe with them, and they'd see to it that one of the monasteries in Doncaster would take over her care. She was also glad Gawain spoke kindly of her. She didn't wish for him to view women the way she had viewed men, which only led to sorrow.

\*\*\*\*\*

It wasn't long before a monastery came into view on the horizon. They were not far from Doncaster, which they could see further down the road from the monastery.

When they brought the child to the doorstep, the monks and nuns were receptive to taking the baby in, acquainted with the girl's family.

Isabella smiled. The people in this monastery lived simply, in quiet ways and would provide a good place for the child to be reared in.

\*\*\*\*\*

"Wake up, Isabella," Matheu whispered in her ear. "We're in Doncaster. Put your hood on. Wolfhart might be in the town."

Isabella opened her eyes and leaned forward, realizing she'd fallen asleep on the horse. She looked around, lifting her hood over her head. Her eyes widened, amazed at the splendor of the town. Doncaster was one of the richest looking villages she'd ever seen. Many substantial buildings lined the streets, along with great stone bridges scattered throughout the town. There were craftsmen and tradesmen on every corner, a large bakery, and even a bank and a hospital. Surrounding the town was a large wall with five enormous gates. Castles rose above the horizon.

Isabella spotted a familiar wagon just off the street. "Godhuwe! I know his cart. He has those markings on the side of it." She scanned the stables looking for Hastulf's horse, but it wasn't there. She let out a breath, relieved. Wolfhart wasn't with them.

The door to the inn opened, and Angnes stepped out onto the street. When she saw Isabella, she cried out, "M'lady! You're not harmed and are back with us!

Then, she quickly clamped her hand over her mouth. "I mean, my friend!"

Matheu lifted Isabella to the ground.

Isabella smiled. "Do not worry. They know the truth."

Angnes went to Isabella and took her hands in her own. She looked at Matheu, surprised. "Who are you? Weren't you the one who brought Isabella back the last time?"

"Yes, we seem to be meeting up by chance." Matheu tipped his head to Isabella, the lines in his face softening as he spoke. "I'm Matheu of Thorneton Le Dale, and this is my squire, Gawain Brooks."

Angnes had an interested look in her eye, as she studied Matheu. She smiled warmly at him and Gawain. "Thank you for caring for Isabella, again. I prayed to God that he'd protect her and keep her safe."

Isabella took her arm smiling. "Yes, I was cared for! In the forest, I was almost eaten by wolves, and Matheu, he slayed them! And then, he bought me these clothes when the wool scratched my arms. He found a place for me to stay last evening."

Angnes' eyes grew wide. She moved closer to the horse and reached out to grasp Matheu's hand, shaking it. "I thank the Lord and you, sir."

Isabella nodded. "I thank you, also and will miss your company. I'm beholden to you, once again."

Matheu smiled, his eyes gentle. "You're beholden to me for many things. Someday you'll pay me back, as I said before." He winked.

Isabella blushed and backed away from his horse. "Yes, well, maybe money."

"Well, this girl needs some rest, I see." Angnes' brows rose above her perceptive brown eyes. A smile lit her face.

Matheu let go of Isabella's hand. "Yes, my manor's awaiting Gawain and I. I regret to say we cannot be staying. We're late getting back."

"That's too bad. We would surely enjoy your company." Angnes smiled again. "And I thank you again for helping Isabella. I'm very glad to see her."

Matheu tipped his head. "Yes, well maybe I'll try and get to Cropton in the next few days, after I settle the matters of my estate. I would like to be assured that you arrived there safely."

Isabella clasped her hands in front of her, nodding. "I'd like that very much."

"If I weren't delayed in getting back to my manor and resolving matters there, I'd ride that way with you. But unfortunately, I cannot." His eyes were warm looking. "But, I am glad you're safe with your friends, now."

As his horse moved forward, he turned back one more time, and his dark eyes fixed on Isabella's large ones for a brief moment. He seemed almost hesitant to go and as if it conflicted him to leave, but then, after a nod and a smile, he took one last wave and then headed down the road.

Isabella fixed her eyes on Matheu and Gawain's horses as they slowly disappeared down the street and out of sight. She felt a dark pang within her chest, an empty feeling, as if she'd lost something valuable. In the brief time she spent with him, Matheu of Thorneton Le Dale had made a lasting impression on her, and his departure left a tender spot in her heart. Maybe if he came to Cropton, she'd see him again.

She turned to go inside the inn, looking forward to a much-needed rest. She was tired. So many things happened in a matter of a few days. It'd be good to be back safe with her friends.

*****

# Chapter 7

Blysse skipped over the cobblestone streets, her eyes shining and her dark hair flying wildly behind her. She couldn't wait to tell Alan the fair was on its way to Cropton. It would be there in two days.

Before she lived in Cropton with Alan, she'd never seen anything like it before. The last one was such fun and brought so many intriguing people. She couldn't wait to decorate the front of the home, picking massive bunches of flowers from the meadow to use for it.

She took quick steps forward and sniffed, noticing the old hag who called herself Mother Migg O' Cropton, hobble past her. The witch was hunched over, rubbing a crystal between her weathered, wrinkled hands. Ha! That old woman tricked others, but wasn't going to fool her.

Blysse frowned at the disheveled, gray-haired woman locking stares with her.

The old woman bared her teeth and hissed, milky blue eyes driving stakes into Blysse's dark ones. She looked down at her crystal and let out a throaty cackle, and then grinned at Blysse with her sharp jagged, yellowed teeth.

Blysse dusted off her jacket. Mother Migg O' Cropton, indeed! Calls herself a witch, when she can do no harm to a flea, much less me. She laughed. "Are you seeking to gain power again by pinching that piece of rock, Sabina Moss?" Blysse lifted her chin jauntily.

The old woman scowled, "Mind you, young woman. My powers are much stronger than anything you're brewing up. You should rein yourself in, as I see what's in your future. And my title is Mother Migg O' Cropton, and you should be calling me that, or I'll be telling the eyeless man who's breathing fire, to be coming around to the place where you reside."

Blysse laughed, as if the woman had told a bad joke. She waved her hand. "Be gone, Sabina! I'm not afraid of you. I do not believe in your silly superstitions, as others around here do."

She grinned, shaking her head, holding the edges of her woolen skirt and stepping saucily past the woman. Magic crystal, my eye. Blysse let out a sound.

She laughed again and fairly danced down the pathway to her house in town, leaving the old woman meandering along in an opposite direction, mumbling dark, poisonous chants, staring back at Blysse.

Blysse shook her head from side to side and let out an aggravated breath. Ever since she came to Cropton, she felt the old hag was provoking her, and going out of her way to try and scare her, most likely trying to bring her under her dominion, as she'd done with most all the other villagers.

Blysse figured Sabina Moss was bothered by the fact that she could see through the hag's foolishness and scoffed at it. The withered old woman wanted Blysse to be cowering in fear of her, as the other people in the town were. Her brown eyes rolled back. She'd no time for such rubbish. There were more important things that deserved her focus.

A smile lit her face, quickly replacing her drab thoughts of the ridiculous town witch. The fair! Now, that was something to hold one's interest.

Her mind was filled with things she'd seen last time she was at a fair, the troubadours, dancing bears and tournament knights. How fun! And now, Cropton would be host to one, and she would be able to enjoy it in her own hometown! The thought of it stole her breath away.

She eyed the shoemaker shop ahead and skipped toward it, bursting with news to tell Alan. She couldn't wait to find her husband.

Nearing the doorway that led into the shoemaker shop, she was about to reach out to grasp the handle and go in, when she heard a soft moan coming from the alleyway in between the buildings.

A hoarse low sound reached her ears. "Oh…"

She turned, tipping her head to the side, looking around. "Alan? Is that you?"

"Blysse, come into the alley. I must see you." His voice was barely a whisper. "My darling."

Blysse's eyes grew wide with alarm. She quickly stepped around the corner of the stone building, grasping the edge, when she saw her husband lying helpless in the shadow of the wall. He was hurt, bloodied and bruised, lying in a heap.

She ran down the narrow passageway, hastily kneeling beside him, her hand sliding underneath his head. In shock, she studied the purple bruises and swellings that covered his face and the dark blood seeping from his forehead.

"Oh, Alan! You're hurt! How bad is it? Here, here you'll be all right." Her eyes were ripe with fear, her large, thick lashes forming tears beneath. What happened here? Why would anyone do such a thing?

"Thieves. Blysse, they've taken all our money." His breathing was labored. "I tried to stop them."

Blysse's hands began to shake, and she clasped them together to still them. Her chest tightened, making it difficult for her to breathe. "How am I to help you, dearest? What can be done?" She leaned closer to him.

Her husband's eyes closed briefly, and then opened. He whispered in her ear, "I fear I'm hurt bad, Blysse." He took a breath. "I'm in such pain. "Please, if I do not live through this, I ask that you to go to Friar Dixon. Promise me. Ask him about truth."

A frown formed over Blysse's brown eyes. "Alan? Do not say this. You will be fine."

"Promise me, please. You'll see him? You must do this."

A dark look crossed her face. "All right, all right. I promise. But it will not be necessary. You'll rally. I'm sure of it."

He smiled, ignoring her. His voice was weak. "You're a strong young, woman and very pleasing to look at. It will not be long, and you'll find your way."

She shook her head, distraught. "Alan, no. Do not say such things. I will not hear of it."

She cupped his face in her hands gently and watched his eyes close again. Panic struck her inside, and she said his name again. "Alan?"

A slight, gargling sound came from within his throat, and Blysse felt his head loll back, heavy upon her hand. The silence of the dark alleyway overcame her, and she began to shake again, this time all over. "Alan?" She said it a third time.

She lifted him to her, staring blankly at his limp shoulders and his motionless chest. No breath came from his lips. "Alan? Speak to me."

She shook him gently and then more harshly when he didn't respond. "Speak to me. Please. Wake up!" Her eyes filled with tears, while watching his silent form for any sign of life, yet seeing none. "Alan! For my sake! You must wake up!"

The mute walls next to her echoed the silence of his still, lifeless body.

It couldn't be. It wasn't happening.

She let out a scream and then heard more strangled cries coming from her throat, which didn't feel like her own, while struggling to hold onto the dead weight beneath her. Sobs shook her body, and she was sick inside, deep breaths catching in her throat.

To her, it felt as if time had stopped, while she sat there weeping in the alley, holding her husband tightly, tears staining her swollen cheeks. She couldn't bear to leave him, and yet she wondered how long she'd be in the passageway beside him, before anyone found them there. She needed help, yet was frozen in her spot, unable to leave. How much longer before someone came?

*****

The day darkened and shadows were long before a kindly, older gentleman finally discovered Blysse. He stopped while knocking upon the shoemaker's door. "What's this? Who's there?"

He entered the alley Blysse was in, to investigate. "Young woman? What is the matter? Why are you crying?"

Blysse looked up, still in a state of shock, holding Alan, bloodied and lying in her arms.

88

The man went to her and pulled her from her husband, holding her close. "Tell me what's happened, dear one?"

Blysse gulped and spoke between soft whimpers. "The robbers, they've taken my husband. Alan's gone. They stole him from me, and I'm beside myself. I do not know what to do." She looked up at him, her eyes dark, and cheeks running with tears.

"He's dead?"

Blysse nodded, her face downcast.

The man bent down to check Alan, and then got up. "What you're saying's the truth."

Blysse put her hands to her cheeks and sobbed uncontrollably again, and when it seemed she could not cry any longer, she angrily wiped the tears away. Her expression was one of deep sorrow and bitterness, as she gestured to her husband.

The man's eyes were full of compassion. "I'm sorry for your loss. May God care for you in your trials."

Her eyes narrowed. "God? The one who is supposed to be faithful? What kind of a God allows such things to happen?"

The man gently took her hand in his. "Oh, child, do not question it, for he's against this dark thing. Do not blame him."

"What? Against?" Her eyes glittered. "He has never been there for me, when I needed help."

She tightened her fists and turned, eying her husband in the alley. "And do not even try to speak to me about a benevolent God. I want nothing to do with him, and refuse to discuss him after I've just lost Alan." Her cheeks flamed, and her eyes burned with anger at the thought of it. The man would never find her in agreement with him.

He seemed to know she'd had no intentions of listening to him, so quickly switched the subject. "I'll say no more. I'm sorry for distressing you." He looked down at Alan. "I understand this is sudden, yet your husband will need a proper burial. Something must be done, very soon."

She nodded, her dark eyes softening again. "But, I cannot leave him here. Will you help me?"

The man tipped his head. "Yes, child. Do not worry. I'll get an undertaker for you. But, I'm sorry to say, I must leave you here in order to accomplish this task for you."

Blysse nodded, then called after him. "Please what is your name, sir, so I'll remember you?"

The man smiled, tipping his gray head slightly forward. "It's Mauger of the Moors. I came for my shoes, but it is not important in this dark time."

Blysse bent her head.

Mauger turned to leave. "Another day, I'll be back for them. I'm sure you'll have need of my money in the future. My village is close."

Her solemn, brown eyes met his warm, gray ones, and she nodded, silent.

True to his word, the kindly old gentleman sent an undertaker to care for Alan's body and also a servant woman to sit with her and prepare her meals during the first grieving day.

Blysse did not see Mauger of the Moors again, but planned on thanking him when he came back for his shoes.

She'd much to think about with the sudden change in her situation. She felt as if a hole had opened in her heart, and her lungs were depleted of air. Despite the fact she married Alan to escape Wolfhart, she'd also grown to love him and depend on him. She couldn't fathom how she'd manage without him.

She paid the undertaker with most of the money she'd hid from Alan during his gambling stints. Her stash of coins was growing thin. She wondered how long she'd be able to buy food and pay her ten percent to the church, when she had little knowledge of her husband's craft and no skills of her own to earn wages.

The shoemaker's guild would care for her for a short time, while she sold the last of Alan's shoes, and yet, when they realized her insufficient understanding of the trade, and the money they were losing from her lack of participation, it would not be long before she'd be cast out onto the streets and her house occupied by a replacement for Alan.

She wasn't prepared for what she'd do then, and grappled with thought of a life without security and more than that, without Alan in Cropton.

*****

# Chapter 8

From the wooden cart where she sat, Isabella scanned the dark silent, cobblestone streets of York and then eyed an enormous tower set high upon a hill in the middle of town.

She shuddered, realizing this was probably Clifford's Tower, the tower where Jews took their lives to escape violent mobs awaiting them beyond the walls. Lighting the tower on fire and dying in the flames, seemed to them the best means to avoid the worst of persecutions.

She eyed a lone rider heading in their direction, dressed in a gray tunic with tall, leather boots. He was sitting on a chestnut horse, a green felt hat perched upon his head.

Isabella pulled her hood closer over her face, whispering to Angnes. "It's Hastulf's horse! But who is on it? I cannot be sure, but I do not believe it is Wolfhart."

Angnes touched Isabella's arm. She answered quietly. "I don't know, yet I can see you're right. It is not he."

Isabella let out a relieved sigh. She held her cloak tight about her, keeping her eyes averted. Whoever it was, he had her cousin's horse. He could be dangerous.

The rider approached, stopping a distance away.

Godhuwe shouted, "Whoa!" The wagon slowed to a halt.

The man put up a hand. "My name's Dauit of York. It would be prudent not to come closer."

Godhuwe eyed the man curiously. "Why, sir? We're merely traveling to the town fair for work."

The man shook his head. His voice was low and quiet. "Half the persons here are dying of the Black Death. It's stricken York very diligently, and no one's feeling hardy enough to have a fair. If you do not wish half your party dead with this sickness, it would be good to leave now."

Godhuwe nodded. "We'll need to travel through town on our way to Pickering, but because of you're advice, we will not stop. And we thank you for informing us of this travesty."

Kara S. McKenzie

The man tipped his head. "You're prudent to listen."

Godhuwe started to answer, but Leofwin spoke up first. He eyed Hastulf's animal, as if curious. "Was this horse a new purchase of yours?"

The man seemed surprised at first, and then a sheepish look crossed his face. "The person who owned it, was a man named Wolfhart Butler."

Theobald nodded.

The man tapped the side of his tunic in a nervous gesture. "Merely one day ago, he was at a monastery and died of the Black Death."

Isabella and Angnes both covered their mouths in shock. They looked at each other not saying anything.

Theobald stammered on his words, holding his chest. "Wolfhart Butler? Are you sure of this?"

A sudden relief coursed through Isabella. Wolfhart was dead. She sighed. The distressing burden she carried with her during her travels, lifted from her shoulders. She was free and would have no need now to fear for her life. She could travel the rest of the way to her sister's home in peace. She wouldn't have to worry about the hold he had over her life anymore.

The man nodded, "Yes. They told me I could have the horse. He was at the monastery, and his death was very quick. The disease came upon him very suddenly. Despite the fact he was such an ill-tempered man, I felt much pity for him. The Black Death is a gruesome way for anyone to spend their last days."

Isabella gulped. Her hand went to her heart, and a sick feeling welled up inside her. How could anyone feel secret joy at the thought of someone else's death, no matter how offensive they were? She personally witnessed the Black Death up close. Not even Wolfhart, as vile as he was, deserved such a thing. She crossed herself, conflicted by the incongruity of her feelings.

Angnes reached over and put a hand on her shoulder. "Don't be pained, Isabella. You're not wrong feeling lightened of your oppression. You did not wish this on him."

Isabella nodded solemnly.

92

The man on the horse, pulled back on the reigns to still his horse. "I assumed he was alone, and the horse would have no master, so I kept it. I never guessed it belonged to another."

The man was clearly distressed over having the horse in his possession. Isabella was glad he'd taken the animal under his care and obligation.

She took the cloak from her head and nodded. "It was my cousin's horse, and Wolfhart was using it. I'm glad it is being put to good use, as I cannot ride a stallion, and my cousin, obviously has no need of it. Do not worry about such things. It is of no consequence to me."

Dauit studied Isabella. His eyes traveled to her ragged clothing. You are not from this place?"

She pulled her cloak tighter about her. "No sir, I'm not. We're traveling to Cropton to my sister's home."

He smiled wide, his brown eyes twinkling. "I'm glad our paths have crossed. I felt pained I had the horse and had no permission to it. I thank you very much."

Isabella nodded. "I'm glad to have met you, sir." His news of Wolfhart's death was a welcome relief.

Dauit tipped his head, the smile widening again on his face. "Maybe we'll meet again, someday."

Isabella wondered whether she should encourage the man's attentions. Knowing she might never see Matheu again, she may have no other choice but to marry to survive. The man seemed a decent sort. She breathed deeply and then lifted her hood over her head again, nodding slightly, in a half acknowledgement.

Dauit grinned, sitting taller upon the horse.

Godhuwe turned to Dauit. "We should leave now. I thank you again for helping us." He clucked to the horses, and the cart began to move slowly ahead.

Isabella looked back at the rider, as they rattled over the cobblestone, noticing his eyes never left their cart. She wondered if she'd be seeing him again, hoping with all of her heart, she would not. She didn't wish to make any decisions at this time, which might end up sealing her fate. She knew the marriage would be one of convenience.

She turned back around in her seat and settled in for a long ride. She hoped they'd find an inn soon to sleep in, one untouched by the plague.

*****

"Here, I can help you, Angnes. You're in need of a hand." She reached for the container Angnes held in her hand.

Angnes frowned. "No, m'lady. It's beneath you to pull water from a well." She lifted the wooden bucked filled with water over the edge of the stone cistern. They were not far from Godhuwe's house, so had only a small distance to carry it.

Isabella took the bucket from Angnes. "But, I must earn my keep. I'm no longer the lady at the manor, and do not wish to take advantage of you any longer."

A soft wind tickled her shoulders, as she set the bucket down on the grass and waited while Angnes lowered a second pail into the well, shaking her head. "It makes me sad to see you brought to such low circumstances. You are not accustomed to such a lifestyle."

"I'm not grieved, Angnes." Isabella lifted her face to the gentle rays of light around her. "I did not have to marry a man I didn't love and have a place to stay with my sister in Cropton. I'm happy to help, as I feel I have much to be thankful for."

Angnes continued lowering the pail into the well, letting it sink under the water and then began pulling the rope hand over hand. "It will only be a couple days until you see your sister. Tomorrow you can ride with Godhuwe to Cropton."

Isabella put her hand on her friend's shoulder. She thought they would all be riding together. "Angnes, you won't be with us? What will you do?"

Angnes pulled the second bucket out of the well and set it on the ground, wiping her hands on the apron she wore. She took Isabella's hand. "I'm staying here at Godhuwe's place."

Isabella's mouth fell open. "Angnes, but why? I thought you would want to stay with Blysse and I?"

Light, brown freckles danced across the bridge of Agnes' upturned nose. She grinned widely, suddenly seeming much younger than when she lived at the manor. She giggled with delight. "Godhuwe's plan is to come back and marry me. He says we make a good pair, the two of us."

Isabella's eyes widened, and she grasped her friend's arm. "Oh my! Godhuwe? Angnes, this is good for you. You'll be a peddler's wife!" She laughed, her eyes merry. "I hadn't a clue! I'm sorry I didn't realize it, but am very happy for you! Godhuwe's a worthy man.

Angnes nodded, her eyes dancing. "Yes. We're sure it was God's plan. He spoke to each of us, and led us to this decision."

Isabella smoothed out the folds of her woolen dress. Angnes had said something as such before, yet Isabella had not understood it.

She cocked her head to the side. "But, Angnes? I'm not sure I understand. How do you know when God speaks to you? How does he do this?" If she were ever asked for her hand in marriage, she'd have not a clue as to what was right or wrong. How could they be so sure?

Angnes reached out and took Isabella's hand. There was a sparkle in her eye. "I can tell you from my own experience how I hear from him. And you must know it is only through much time spent in prayer and learning his Word that I find his answers. It is one of the ways he speaks to me. But, do not worry. He'll show you, and you'll know what is right. Listen for that still, small voice and follow it, if you know it to be right and true."

Isabella looked puzzled. "You hear him?"

"Sometimes, like a gentle whispering. Not so much a voice, but more like a feeling. When I feel hesitant, or not quite right about something, I wait and do nothing. But, when I feel peace in my heart about a decision I've an answer for, and I know it'd be something he'd honor, then I go in that way. But, I always pray and ask him for wisdom."

Isabella nodded. "I'll do this."

Angnes smiled. "Yes, it will lead you on good paths, ones where you'll find joy. I'm glad you're thinking of such things."

She leaned over to take one of the buckets, and Isabella did the same. They both walked up the path toward Godhuwe's two-story cement home between patches of purple and white heather that spewed sweet perfume in the air.

As they neared the place, Isabella's hands began to hurt from the bucket handle rubbing against her palm. The sun beat down on them, as they walked along. She set the container down in front of the door and wiped her forehead. "Angnes? Will Theobald or Leofwin be coming with Godhuwe and I to Cropton?"

Angnes shook her head, straining with the bucket in her hand, as they neared the door. "They'll stay here for the fair and then be moving south."

Isabella sighed. "Well, I'm happy I'll see them for a time, but, I'll surely miss them."

Angnes set down her bucket and straightened for a moment, giving Isabella a chance to rest. "Yes, but we'll not live far from each other. I can come with Godhuwe to Cropton and call on you when he's peddling his wares." Her expression lightened.

Isabella got up from where she sat. "Oh, I'd like that very much, Angnes. I'm glad I'll still be able to visit with you."

Angnes bent over and lifted the bucket. "Yes, it'll be good to be close." She smiled, opening the large, wooden door. "But for now, we must get this water into the house, or they'll all be coming out here, and wondering what's happened to us."

Isabella lifted the other bucket and laughed. "Oh my! You're right. There's little time for chatter. But, I am glad for your news, and so happy we've had this time together."

"Yes, m'lady. It's been a good thing."

\*\*\*\*\*

# Chapter 9

After the funeral, Blysse stomped across the road and down the street toward the broken-down old shack where the hag, Sabina Moss lived. She'd forego her grief to settle some things. She knocked loudly at the front door. The old woman would pay for the last piece of gossip she was spreading around Cropton.

"Sabina Moss! I know you're in there! You come out and speak to me! We need to talk!" Blysse shook her fist at the heavy, broken down door.

She heard a cackle through a crack in the entrance to the home. "Everyone else in this village calls me Mother Migg O' Cropton and are holding me in high honor. Me crystal's strong, and you should be heeding its magical powers."

Blysse yanked at the rusty latch on the door. "You don't scare me, old woman. And, if you don't come out, then maybe you're the one who's afraid? Are you afraid of me, Sabina? Come out and show yourself, if you're not!"

There was a moment of silence and then a stirring behind the wooden entrance. The old woman slowly lifted the latch and opened the door. Her blue eyes were slanted and glowing. She glared at Blysse. "What do you want, you wicked girl? You got what you deserved when you watched Alan die. I told you your future was bad, and you would not listen to me."

Blysse's eyes were black as night, thinking about the things that had gone on in town lately. She'd get to the bottom of it, if it were the last thing she'd do. She railed at the hag, "What did you tell my friends old woman? They're not speaking to me, and I suspect you're behind it."

Blysse's dark eyes bored into the hag's. She rested her hands on her hips, her brown leather shoes tapping rapidly against the weather-beaten doorframe.

She spoke again, the tone in her voice posing a harder edge to it. "Well? What've you to say for yourself? What've you been spreading around town about me?"

The old woman's sinister, slate eyes narrowed within the frame of shabby, gray hair around her wrinkled face. She snarled and lifted the crystal in her withered hands. "Only that it says it would be wise for others to stay away from you, as misdeeds will befall anyone who remains near a person of your disposition."

Blysse's expression was one of shock, her eyes wide. This woman had done more damage to her reputation than she'd done to herself. And most of it was undeserved. What was the woman thinking?

A strong, Moorish wind blew a gust against the door, shoving it aside wider.

Blysse held the swinging door frame open, and let out a breath. Looking inside the shack, she could see that it was in disarray, full of vials and potions, lit with one glowing candle that casted long shadows on the walls.

A dank smell of bitter herbs made its way to the open doorway. Blysse wrinkled her nose in distaste. "So this is why there had been no one to comfort me in my distress. You've been scaring them all from me, because of that silly crystal."

She stared at the woman who rubbed the rock in her gnarled hands with a self-satisfied expression, the corners of her mouth lifting. Blysse wanted to throttle the old hag, squeezing the life out of this woman who seemed to hold the power of the town in her withered hands.

"I told others you'd lose your husband. Were you aware of this?"

Blysse looked skeptical. "No, you never said a word. I heard nothing of the sort."

Sabina cackled, "Yet, I told those friends of yours, that my power was proven true by his death."

"Whom did you tell this to? I don't believe it."

"Belle Walker. She was one of them, and Heloise. You're aware of the girl?"

Blysse stomped her foot. Her words came out in a cynical tone. "It's a rock, Sabina."

"Yes, but a very powerful one you do not believe in. The others in town see things more clearly than you."

Blysse eyed the crystal again, this time warily, a sudden sickness striking deep inside her. Her father's own words haunted her. You bring trouble on yourself by your impulsive actions.

She shuddered at the thought and of the timing between Alan's death and the old woman's predictions. The anger in her suddenly was replaced with fear. Her hand went to her chest, and a doubtful look crossed her face. It could not be true? No? Was it possible to draw power from a rock?

Sabina's wrinkled fingers rubbed it more fervently beneath Blysse's gaze.

Blysse shuddered. Was she wrong about the power of the crystal? A hollow chord of fear sickened her, and she pushed it down deep inside her. She used anger again instead, to mask her dark feelings. The foul smell from the room unsettled her stomach. "I'll be watching you, Sabina Moss! Maybe it was you who was arranging my husband's death? You'd best be watching yourself, or I'll find out things about you, to get you in trouble with the town."

The old woman's icy eyes met Blysse's, and she cackled. "You're not so sure about the crystal, I am guessing? Be leaving me alone now, and stay far from me."

Blysse wiped her sweaty palms on her woolen skirt. She lifted her chin. "Believe me, I'll leave. Yet, I warn you, Sabina Moss, stay far from my friends, or you'll regret it."

She took one more wary glance at the crystal, twisting between the hag's fingers, and she turned to go.

There was a light hiss from behind, as she left the old woman, but she kept walking. She let out a long, slow breath and pulled up her skirt, tromping down the dirt path that lead to the main road into town. She'd have some convincing to do, to unravel this old hag's meddling in her life.

The wind was beginning to howl, and darkness was setting in. She had to get back to the shop. She looked back over her shoulder, jumping at the sound of a hoot owl and then letting out a nervous laugh.

She shivered, as the fog rolled in around her.

Tomorrow, she'd attempt to alleviate the town people's fears, this woman had instilled in them. It was wrong for Sabina Moss to rule a whole town. It would be a task to persuade the others who lived here that they were wrong to listen to the old woman, but if she were to survive in this town, it was something she necessary for her to do.

But first, Blysse needed rest. She was tired and ached to lie down and sleep.

The toll of her husband's death weighed upon her like the pails of water she carried daily from the well. She felt a dark oppression holding her down and wished for release from it. She held back the tears that threatened to destroy her.

Her fist tightened, as she walked, her thoughts on the old woman and her rock. Why couldn't the wizened hag leave the townspeople alone?

Eying the shop ahead, Blysse suddenly broke into a run in efforts to free herself from the unsettling feelings running through her. Her shoulders went back, her chin up, and she snorted, "Baaah!!" Crystals, power and superstitions could hold no power over her!

She ran faster, shivering until she reached the doorstep of her home and quickly lifted the latch and went in, locking the door behind her. She clenched her fist and crossed the room, taking a seat by the hearth, staring at the dying embers. That witch would never succeed in her heartless ways! She wouldn't stand for it.

Tomorrow she'd set it all to rights. Sabina Moss would surely lose her position, and people would know her for the fraud she was. Blysse assured herself it'd take little to convince them, and then all would be the way it should. She took a quick drink and sighed. She hoped sleep would come quickly this night.

\*\*\*\*\*

Chills struck Blysse in the middle of the night. She wrapped the woolen covering on the feather mattress tighter around her, tossing and turning in her sleep.

She couldn't erase the images of the crystal out of her mind. Flashes of Alan dying in the alleyway, and of Sabina Moss, cackling and rubbing the stone beneath bony fingers, kept her from drifting into a deeper slumber, of which she would've been grateful.

Alone in the dark, she felt less sure of herself. The crystal was a rock dug out of the ground. How could anything such as a translucent stone contain powers Sabina claimed it to have?

She shook her head. Surely, Sabina picked it up out of the dirt. Anyone could find one on the road similar to it, in less than a day.

Silent echoes filled the room. Her heart thumped unsteadily. Ridiculous as this so-called magic rock was, Blysse couldn't rid herself of the idea that there might be a connection between Sabina's words and the sudden death of her husband, after witnessing both incidents in the same day.

She shivered again and pulled the covers up to her chin, a sudden draft chilling her bones. The wind was causing eerie creaking sounds in the room and a groaning in the walls.

Blysse guessed a storm was moving through.

It was spring. Surely, that's what it was.

Then, suddenly she felt another ungodly rush of cold air. Immediately, images of Sabina flooded Blysse's mind. The woman's disorderly, gray hair poked out around her evil, smirking face as she rubbed her glowing crystal beneath her withered fingertips.

Blysse couldn't contain the inner fears she constantly pressed down deep inside her. Her breath became short, and the panic she felt so often as a child, swelled up within her pounding chest. It gave rise to a paralytic state she'd grown accustomed to. Would it never end? Would she ever be free from the demons that constantly haunted her?

She took long drawn breaths and held her hand to her heart, trying to dispel the strong beat beneath. The thought of God pervaded her mind, and yet she pushed it out.

Her eyes narrowed. Nothing could bring her close this one who had deserted her as a child. He listened to prayers at dinner tables of those chanting sweet, yet fake incantations in attempts to hide their own black hearts, but had no time for the likes of her. This God did nothing for her, and she wanted no part of him.

Her heart continued to pound. She turned over and beat her fists against the mattress beneath her. "You'll not prevail against me, Sabina Moss. You will see, tomorrow."

She pulled the wool covering completely over her head and lay there in the stillness of the night, listening to the groaning walls. She remained like this for hours, until she finally fell into a fitful slumber.

When morning came, she was exhausted, having had minimal sleep. Despite the distress she felt when she thought of it, she lifted herself wearily from the bed and got up to ready herself for the day.

There was one task she promised her dying husband she'd do. She'd make good on her promise, despite the distress the thought of it brought her, especially after such an unsettling, sleepless night. Out of respect for Alan's last wish, she'd go see Friar Dixon.

She sighed deeply with regret, lifting a comb to her tangled hair. She wouldn't stay long. She promised she'd see the man, and nothing more. It'd be one visit she'd make sure to bring to a close quickly.

*****

Blysse rapped impatiently on the front door of the simple, whitewashed wattle and daub hut. She let out a quick breath and looked down the street, hesitating for a second and then turned to leave.

Alan's last wish just might have to wait. Friar Dixon apparently wasn't there.

She took a quick step away from his home, and then heard the sound of the door behind her creak open.

The monk's low, gentle voice beckoned. "Blysse. You're looking for me?"

She crinkled her skirt tightly in her fist and turned back, suspiciously eying the tall, elderly man standing in the doorframe. "It was Alan's dying wish, that I speak with you."

Friar Dixon's eyes crinkled at the corners. He reached up and smoothed back his thinning, gray hair with his hand. "Come in. I'll get you something to eat."

Isabella's Shield

Blysse smoothed out the sides of her tunic. "Oh, I've no time to stay and eat. I must get back, as I've work to do. But, I must ask you something, and then will be leaving." She began to twist the fabric of her apron.

He smiled. "The others are out in the fields working, Yet, you are welcome to come in and visit." The wooden cross around his neck jingled, as he ushered her into the room.

She sighed. "It will not hurt to stay for a short time." She lifted her skirt, stepping over the doorframe and followed him into the room. An uneasy feeling swept over her, as she made her way across the room.

Friar Dixon sat down on a wooden stool and pulled another up next to him, motioning for her to sit. He leaned forward and patted her arm. "Tell me what Alan's last wish was, and I will listen. He was a worthy man."

He took her hand in his, which caused tears to form in the corner of her eyes. She looked down at the dirt floor, pulling her hand back. "He said you must explain truth to me." She looked chagrinned. "But, if you do not understand what he meant by it, I will leave, and you can go about your tasks."

She began to get up, but Friar Dixon motioned for her to sit back down. His brown eyes twinkled. "No, stay, dear. I understand this very well and am able to explain it to you."

Blysse sat back on the stool. "Oh." Her foot danced lightly up and down. "I'll listen then." The eerie feeling that always crept into her, when she sat in a church pew, suddenly coursed through her. Her stomach felt as if someone took a spoon to the contents of it. Men of God surely made her nervous.

Friar Dixon fingered the wooden cross dangling about his neck. "It was Alan's desire that you understand the way to eternity through the truth I am to impart to you."

The toe tapping continued. "I'm at the church Sunday." Blysse could not rid herself of the impatient feeling drumming in her. Her desire to leave Friar Dixon's home and be on her way grew with every moment she was in the house. She figured she knew what was coming and did not wish to hear it, another lecture on the woes of her life. She hoped he'd spared her the tragedy of it all.

Friar Dixon sighed, and his eyes softened, as he looked at her.

Blysse crossed her arms in front of her. She almost gagged at the way he portrayed himself, innocent as a baby fawn. Auch! These priests understood what they were doing. The fact that he could appear so guileless and kindhearted only served to bolster her suspicions of him.

"Going to church is not enough, Blysse."

Blysse let out a breath, her expression wary. "Nothing is ever enough for you men of God. You seem to derive satisfaction making others suffer?"

Her eyes lit with fire. "I suppose you will tell me next that you believe me to be the gate of the devil? Or better yet, the sting of the serpent, or a perilous object. Oh, I know them all." Her eyes narrowed, as she studied his face. "And I must pay for my waywardness? Is this correct?"

Friar Dixon fingered the cross hanging around his neck. He laughed, his eyes merry. "No, I have no time for such sentiments." He touched his cross again. "Alan hoped you might find tranquility in praying to God for forgiveness."

Blysse's dark eyes rolled back, and she snorted. "Tranquility? Did God give Alan tranquility when the robbers stole his last breath from him?"

She got up from the bench. "I do not believe I'll be needing this tranquility! Alan was surely not seeing things clearly when he asked me to speak with you."

Friar Dixon took her hand in his. "He did understand, Blysse. He wanted you to know that God would listen to you, even after you've turned from him, if you take the time to talk to him. Can I pray for you?"

Blysse pulled her hand away as if burned. "Do not waste your time. You seem a good man, yet I cannot believe in any of it, when God has done nothing for me."

Friar Dixon's eyes were a somber brown. "So, I will not vex you with it, but surely will pray."

Blysse nodded. Something about this man disconcerted her. Even though she didn't wish to hear what he had to say, she could not help liking him. "Well, I best go. There are things I must do."

She crossed her arms and shivered, despite the warmth from the fire and the cozy snug atmosphere emanating from the room.

"Come back again dear, if you have need of anything." He watched her go through the doorway, a concerned look on his face.

"All will be well. Do not worry on account of me." She stepped out into the street and walked away, leaving him standing in the doorway, holding his cross with his eyes closed, murmuring a silent prayer.

*****

On the way back to the shoe shop, Blysse met Heloise, a young girl from one of the serf's homes.

Heloise ran across the road and stopped short of Blysse. Her red hair was swept back from her face and her cheeks were flushed, as if she'd been running for a time. The girl grabbed Blysse's arm and leaned forward choking on her breath.

Blysse took her hand, wondering what might have caused such a scene. Her friend could barely speak. "Slow down, Heloise. What is the matter?" She waited, while the girl struggled to catch her breath.

Heloise put a hand to her forehead. "Oh, Blysse! I should not be speaking with you, but I must! Mother Migg O' Cropton told me it is apparent you hear this!" She made the sign of the cross and then practically choked while gasping for air.

Blysse's eyes narrowed. She squeezed Heloise's hand. "What did the old hag tell you now? What story did she give you, the wicked bat?" She could not imagine what that wizened snake of a woman was spreading around town now. The pit of her stomach felt as if a fire had been lit in it.

Heloise's eyes widened, and she loosened her grasp. "Oh, Blysse! You must not say such things! I fear for you!" She took a step back, a distressed look in her eyes.

Blysse let out a breath. "Do not be afraid. I will say no more. Merely tell me what she said." This ought to be interesting, another of the old woman's lies. She could not imagine what Heloise was commissioned to tell her.

Heloise sucked in some air, her eyes wide as pools. She stammered as she spoke. Her voice sounded strained and high-pitched. "Mother Migg O' Cropton told me the crystals did not lie and that death has taken another of your friends. Because you were not listening to her, Alan's dead. And now, your friend, Belle Walker is too, because of the sickness! The old woman said that you're cursed at this time, and that others will be dying, also."

Blysse sucked in a breath. She began to shake and felt the blood draining from her face. Belle Walker? Her sweet friend?

"No." She eyed her friend cautiously. "This is not so. Tell me it is only a tale being spread round."

Heloise choked out her next words. "I would not lie. I saw them take Belle from the street. She was cold as the river in January and pale as ice. She lay there as a dead person, her breath gone."

Blysse was frozen in her spot. She didn't move or speak.

"Blysse? Did you hear me?" Heloise began to back away from her.

Blysse wrapped her arms around her waist and doubled over, falling to her knees. A cloud suddenly blocked out the sun, sending a dark shadow over her. She felt the rough stone of the road up against her knees. It was as if a wine press had squeezed all the contents out of her stomach and left her empty inside.

She looked up to see Heloise running down the street toward her home. A shadow raced across the path, as if following the young woman.

Belle? Oh, by the blessed monks! It could not be.

Was this the work of the crystal again? Sickness gripped her heart. She couldn't comprehend what was happening. Was she responsible now, for her good friend's death?

She was nauseous. She got up and lifted her skirt and ran. She had not a clue as to where she was going, but raced out of town along the road, fleeing from the fear raging inside her beating chest.

Was the old woman truly a threat to the others in town? Blysse was dumbfounded.

She took a smaller path and ran for what seemed miles, until she slowed to a walk. The road was empty, without even a small animal to be seen. It was eerily quiet, save for a creaking of trees in the wind and the occasional flutter of leaves. Her eyes fixed on the Old Wives Well up ahead, a large, dark hole cut out of the ground, surrounded by a rocky wall.

She stopped walking and stood there, memories of her friend flooding her mind in raging torrents.

Her cherished friend. There could not have been a more light-hearted soul with a genuine golden-hewn heart than Belle. Belle reminded Blysse of her sister, Isabella with that sweet smile, and honey-colored hair that shone like the sun. There was never a time Blysse could remember when Belle did not have a kind word for her, or a smile on her face.

Belle surely didn't deserve to die. It was the second death that had come about since Sabina Moss' prophesy.

When Alan died, she believed it was only a coincidence. But, now? She was beginning to wonder if she might be cursed.

What if another person died because of her denying what had been proven true twice? Could she ever risk being with friends and company, knowing what she knew now?

She looked over the edge of the well. She heard the screech of a raven overhead, and turned to watch it swoop and land on a rickety branch of a dead fallen tree. A dark mist was forming over the moors.

Could she live a life set apart from her friends, saving them from death this way? She sighed, knowing she'd never survive without the company of others.

She loved people. Her friends were the ones who helped her forget the dark child of the devil who reigned deep inside her. How could she ever cope without human company? She was sure she could not.

She grasped the edge of the Old Wife's well and peered deeper inside. The dim, murky waters below were as still as death. There was a damp, moldy odor welling up from the bottom. She wrinkled her nose in distaste. Not knowing how to swim, she wondered what it would feel like to drop down inside the well and plunge into the dark liquid beneath. Maybe it would be best if she were dead? It might prevent any more tragedies caused by her willfulness and derision.

Tears sprouted to her eyes, and she found herself weeping, at first in quiet sobs, and then in great heaves. She edged closer to the well and leaned over it, droplets falling from her cheeks into the cold, hollow hole. They made plinking sounds when they hit, far below her. Surely, it would be over quickly. She'd not remember a thing; by the time she fell to the bottom and plunged below the depths.

As she crawled onto the top of the cistern, she gripped the edge. The sounds of her tears dropping, seemed louder and closer together and then stopped altogether. Was it her tears she heard?

Then, she heard a loud shout and the clomp of horse's hooves behind her. "Wait, miss! Stop!"

Blysse's eyes were blurred, making it impossible to see the intruder. An ache struck her heart with such intensity; it felt as if she could not breathe. She clutched the wall, unsure of what to do.

And then her eyes narrowed. She let her legs slip over the edge and started to fall, but not before her wrists were clamped onto in a vice-like grip.

"No!" She screamed at the top of her lungs. "Let go!"

The sure, firm hands that gripped hers tightened. "But, I cannot. You do not understand what you're doing."

Blysse gritted her teeth together. "You're wrong! I do! You must let go!" It infuriated her that the man wouldn't loosen his hold. He'd no business making these decisions, having no clue what he was getting involved with. He was interfering in matters he knew nothing about. It was better for everyone this way. He was ruining her plan. "Stop, I said! Leave me be!"

Her lips pressed into a firm line, and her eyes sparkled dangerously, as she fought to escape the stranger's hold on her. And it seemed, the tighter he held, the more enraged she became. One thing she hated more than anything, was the feeling that she was trapped, and she'd lost control of herself. The man had unleashed a flame within the pit of her, and she suddenly wanted to direct it all at him, blackening him to ashes.

She began kicking and pushing against the man, as she dangled against the inside wall of the dark well. Great sobs choked her, as he lifted her out of the opening and dragged her onto the ground, despite her protests.

Outside the hole, she attempted to squeeze out of the man's grasp, but was unable to break his hold. "Let go, you imbecile! By the holy moat, you'd better or I'll..." She tried to twist away from him, but found it near impossible. The longer he held her, the more she wanted to pummel him so that he hurt.

"No, m'lady. You do not understand. You'll hurt yourself." His voice was insistent.

She struggled violently, as the anger within her burned against him. When she finally felt she was making a little headway, she leaned down and bit the man on his hand.

"Ow!" He pulled it away, but wrapped his fingers around her waist, holding her back with his free hand, as she continued to kick and scream. "Stop it, you little fool! I told you to settle down."

Blysse tried anything she could to wriggle out of his tight hold, and tear herself from him, but soon realized she was getting nowhere in the struggle. There was no weakening this tyrant. It maddened her that his grip was as strong as when he'd first took hold of her.

She let out a long breath, suddenly ending the struggle, putting her hand up to her face to quell the tears beginning to flow. She ached, and even though she wished she could shove the loathsome man's hands off her, and maybe even pull him in the well with her, she found herself giving up.

She was tired. After losing Alan, her friend Belle, and now this, she felt as if all her energy was spent and draining from her. She wanted so much to fight to the bitter end, but the strain of the last couple days overtook her and weakened her to the point of exhaustion.

She let out a weak cry. Why couldn't this man have allowed her to jump? What reason did she have to live? Now, she'd neither the strength, nor the resolve, to even crawl to the well.

Her cries turned to sobs. She felt the stranger rest his hand on her back and pull her to him. She turned, pressing her face into his chest, allowing him to hold her there.

"There, m'lady. You'll be well, soon. You'll not hurt yourself, again." His voice was comforting and full of compassion.

Her mind raced with questions. How could one who wielded such strength, be so tender and so quick to forgive at the same time?

She began to cry.

All the while the stranger patted her arm and tenderly held her to him, whispering in her ear. "Things will be better. You'll see."

Blysse couldn't seem to stop rivers of tears flowing down her cheeks. It was as if every injury she'd ever forced down inside her, was making its way out, each and every one unlocking a secret to a past grievance. Strangely, it felt good, and she let the tears flow freely, for longer than she thought possible.

It wasn't until the sun rose into the sky, and the warmth of the midday sun washed over her, before her shaking and tears finally began to diminish. She wiped her face dry on her apron and made a soft sound, slipping back comfortably into the stranger's arms.

He said nothing, but held her there for a long while, occasionally smoothing back the damp tresses from her forehead.

Eventually, she felt the puffiness and ache in her eyes lesson. Her rage disappeared, and she became curious. What kind of man would spend such time to care for her? He'd taken pains to save her from her own impetuous decision, placing her wellbeing ahead of his own agenda.

She wrenched herself from him, but he gathered her back.

"You will not return to the well?"

She shook her head. "No, sir. Much has happened, and my thoughts were a jumble. But, I am better for it now."

She turned to face him, and her eyes widened. She was struck at how handsome the man was. There was no doubt in her mind of his Viking ancestry, with his tremendous build, keen blue eyes and white-blonde hair. Blysse eyed the fine weave of his clothing and the markings on it. A knight to be sure. His eyes were bright, and his grin somewhat roguish, his mouth curving up on one side.

She pushed herself from his embrace, suddenly uncomfortable to be in the arms of another, so soon after her husband's death. "You must leave me, sir. It is not fitting, and I'll bring you misfortune as Mother Migg O' Cropton has told everyone. You could die, the same as the others."

He let out a snort and laughed. "And you're believing such absurdity. You do not strike me that you would care so much what a witch as her would say to you."

Her dark eyes began to glitter. "I didn't at first. But it's why all this happened."

His mouth turned up at the corner again, and he gave her a look that said he was clearly not convinced.

She pushed on his shoulder. "It is true. My husband Alan's dead, and now my close friend Belle, too. And it's what Sabina predicted would happen." Then, she wrinkled her nose at him. "But, you would not know my beliefs, sir, as we have never met."

The stranger laughed. "After that battle, I believe one old witch wouldn't be scaring you away."

Blysse let out a short breath, her hair wild about her shoulders, thick lashes against her tear-stained cheeks.

He lifted her chin.

Her eyes met his. They were somber. "It's taken my husband being beaten by robbers to death, and my friend dying of a sickness, to make me believe. I do not wish to see anyone else losing their life because of me."

The man's slate, blue eyes never wavered from hers. There was a serious expression in his face. "I'm sorry you've lost those who were close to you. It must be very difficult for so much to have happened so suddenly."

He turned and looked across the moors. "But, she has no control over you, if you do not allow it, and there's a greater power above a witch's magic."

Blysse eyed him skeptically.

He reached out and pushed a dark stray piece of hair from her eyes.

She pulled back reflexively.

He sighed. "You've a suspicious nature? But, I'm not surprised, with the day of age not holding much promise for women."

Blysse turned to him. "You're right in saying I do not trust easily."

He smiled. "Then, I've helped you, now. So, there is a reason to trust me."

She eyed him with uncertainty.

He smiled. "You understand you can be assured that God's power is stronger than any witch's. I lived for too long, far from him, and you should not allow this to happen."

Blysse crossed her arms. "Auk! I'm tired of hearing talk of this today. It seems everyone must go on about it."

The stranger's voice grew soft, despite his rugged appearance. "I suppose you're running from him as I was, and he does not wish for you to escape. He loves you too much to let you go your way."

Blysse sat quietly, not saying a word. She bent her ear to the sounds around her and listened, waiting in silence for something, anything that might save her from the turmoil churning within her. She pondered what the man had told her.

The Moor winds called to her with a beckoning wail, and the trees above her began to rustle, as if whispering their consent. She could smell the delicate scent of heather that enveloped her. She began to weaken at the beauty that seemed to be reaching out to her.

Tears formed again in Blysse's eyes. She was exhausted from all that passed and felt powerless against the witch, Sabina Moss. She closed her eyes.

Her balled fists loosened, and she let out a long breath. She put her hands on her cheeks and held them there. "This is the second person who's spoken to me this way in one day." She closed her eyes.

The man's voice was quiet. "It may be that God wants you to pray, so that he might help you and work in your life. But, you must believe him."

Blysse knew she was in deep waters far above her head, and there was no way out, save help from God. She pictured the cold dark walls of the well imprisoning her and the water rising above her head, offering her no escape. She suddenly wished for deliverance from this present darkness.

She nodded and bowed, as the stranger took her hand in his. She prayed for forgiveness and asked for God's guidance and for her own salvation.

For a long while afterward, she was motionless, afraid of breaking the spell of the peace pervading her heart. She heard clear sounds of birds and the crackle of nature around her. She felt the mist, cool on her skin, refreshing and replenishing in the stillness and silence of God.

Blysse felt freedom for the first time in her life and was in awe knowing it. The misery of her former life was like teardrops in the well, disappearing into the depths.

When she lifted her head, her dark eyes were brimming with tears. "I have done as you've said and prayed. I only wish I would have done it sooner."

The stranger grinned, his mouth turning up at the corner and blue eyes sparkling. "I'm glad to hear this, miss." He reached out and took her hand. "And now you will see his certain grace."

Her dark eyes were shining. "I already have."

The man smiled and then pulled her to her feet. "I cannot stay long, but will take you back to town for your security. I believe you'll have no need to take your life now. God will watch over you at this time, and Sabina can do you no more harm."

Blysse nodded, suddenly feeling as if a massive weight had been lifted from her shoulders. Sabina would never have power over her, ever again. The power of God was unquestionably stronger.

The man turned to her. His blue eyes danced. "I do not know your name. If I come by this way again, I could find you."

Blysse pressed her small, pouty lips together. "But, I might not want you to."

He laughed. "Let me guess. Something pretty, like Marigold or Lilly or maybe, Rosalie?"

"Ha!" She let out a playful sound, lifting her chin. "My name is Blysse. And I believe, sir, you're teasing me. I might be walking alone to my place."

His lopsided grin worked its way into a full smile. "You are right in saying, that I'm teasing you. But, I mean to take you back, whether you wish for me to or not."

Blysse's eyes narrowed and then softened after recognizing the man's playful nature.

He reached out and tugged her skirt. "Blysse. Who might have bestowed on you, such a lovely title?"

Blysse stiffened and pulled away. "It is not important."

The man eyed her curiously. "You're difficult to understand. What did I say to displease you this time?"

Her expression was one of regret. "I'm sorry. It has not been a good day. I did not mean to wrong you."

"Pardon me, m'lady. I wouldn't want to hurt you. I know you've been through enough at this time."

She lifted her head and looked across the moors. "Don't worry. You meant no harm."

The man smiled. "Your name, Blysse, suites you. You're as pretty as heaven."

Her dark eyes widened slightly, and she laughed, her voice a ringing sound. "You must tell me who you are? Maybe I'll write a letter, to let you know how I'm faring."

The man seemed puzzled. "You write? I thought you were a peasant's wife? Is not Alan, the shoemaker in town? I believe you told me your former husband's name was Alan?"

Blysse fidgeted with her hands. "He was, but it's as much as I care to discuss."

The man smiled. "Well, I'm Dante and live in a little town southwest of this place." He turned to his horse, nibbling grass along the edge of the road. "Might I take you back now? Here, let me get my animal."

He got up and took the horse's reins, tugging on them, and the horse followed.

Blysse stood next to him, reaching up to pet the side of the horse's face. "She's beautiful."

Dante didn't take his eyes from Blysse. He seemed almost spellbound. "Yes, she is."

She cocked her head to the side, taking the horse's reins from him. "We best be leaving, if we're to make it back before dark. I do not need to give that town one more thing to gossip about."

He smiled, lifting her onto his horse's back and walked beside it, holding the reins.

Blysse yawned, tired from the exhausting day. She allowed Dante to lead the horse back to the shop, while she rode along, as the sun lowered in the sky.

Safely on her doorstep, Dante watched as she opened the door and turned to him.

"Thank you for your help." Her dark eyes sparkled. "This is a day I will not forget."

He eyed her curiously. "Yes, well. I wish I could stay to see you settled, but I must get back to my own residence. I've matters to attend to."

She smiled, as she reached up to wipe a smudge from his cheek. "There. I must have caused you some trouble."

He grinned. "More than a little. But, I know where you live. So, I may be coming to see you again, to make sure you're staying out of it."

She straightened, tipping her head to the side. There was a sparkle in her eyes. "In time, I might see you."

"Yes, I'll come calling, when I'm able."

And he turned and got up on his horse, waving to her.

She watched him ride out of sight.

*****

# Chapter 10

Godhuwe was silent while they rode down the wide lane leading to Cropton.

Isabella scanned the horizon as the cart ambled along. The moors stole her breath away, as she eyed the sweeping hillsides sprinkled with glowing purple and white heather interspersed among stony crags. The smell of lavender and sweet scents was strong all around them, while the cool, daylight air produced a rosy glow upon Isabella's pale cheeks.

She spied Cropton ahead. The town was set upon a hill surrounded by a deep vale of green fields. Finally, Blysse's home. A motte and bailey castle rose to greet them at the very center of the town. They took the path that meandered up the slope toward the great building at the entrance to the city.

It was the last day of the journey to her sister's home. She couldn't wait to see Blysse again. It wouldn't be long now. Soon she'd be at the shoemaker's shop.

"Oh, look Godhuwe." She pointed to a small goat meandering down the path in front of them. "I think she's lost. Let me give it some of our feed. Maybe she'll follow us into town."

Godhuwe chuckled and handed her a container full of oats, as she got down.

Isabella went into the field and called to the small, chestnut-colored animal. She took a path through the tall grass in the midst of flowers spraying the hillside. "Come, little one," she cooed. She held out the oats.

Godhuwe laughed as the goat turned and headed for Isabella.

Isabella smiled. "See how she comes?"

Godhuwe chuckled, "It's true. I think you have a way with her." He looked impressed.

The goat ate out of her hand. After it had it's fill, Isabella got back onto the cart.

The goat followed them to the next bend, then wandered off the path and down the trail leading to a small cottage.

"It looks as if she found her way." Isabella smiled, as the small animal disappeared from their sight and their cart ambled down the road toward the town ahead.

As they rolled to as stop in front of the doorway to her sister's home, Godhuwe pulled back on the reins, and the horse slowed to a halt. He tied the animal to a post and lifted Isabella from the cart. The anticipation of seeing Blysse welled up inside her Blysse had no idea she was there.

"I'll finally see her, Godhuwe! I cannot wait! She'll be so surprised!"

Godhuwe smiled, revealing a missing tooth. "I'll see that you're safe with her, before I leave." He reached down and gave her a pat on the shoulder.

She smiled. "I understand you cannot stay. But, tell Angnes I made it to my sister's, and wish you both a happy marriage."

"I hope you find life with your sister here a blessing as well. Let us know if you ever are in need of anything, and we will surely help."

"I will." She watched him climb back onto the cart, as she knocked on the door to the shoemaker shop.

She waved to him, when her sister opened the door.

Godhuwe nodded and smiled, clucking to his horse. The wagon began rolling down the wide street.

Isabella turned to her sister. "Blysse! Finally!"

Blysse's hands flew to her face. "Isabella! Ach! My sister! What brought you here?"

Before Isabella could speak, Blysse pulled her into her home. "Come, I cannot believe what I'm seeing! Come inside. There have been many changes here in the last few weeks!" Blysse's eyes were a deep somber brown. There were dark circles beneath them.

Isabella couldn't help noticing that something about her sister was different. Most likely, life here had been tougher than they were accustomed to in London. "You would not believe what a trial it was to get to Cropton."

"Here, take a seat. I'm sure you're weary." Blysse pulled out a stool for Isabella to sit on. "Tell me. What brought you here?"

Isabella sat down, smoothing out her skirt. "There is much I have to tell you. I am not quite sure where to begin."

Blysse took Isabella's hand in hers and sat beside her. "Please, it will be good to talk again. We must tell each other what has happened since we've seen each other last. But, I must warn you. Things have not been good of late."

Isabella sighed. "For our family, either. I'm sorry I must bear such bad news, but I cannot help it."

"What has happened, Isabella? Why the graven face?"

Isabella's voice quavered as she spoke. "Our family, Blysse. They're dead from the plague, and Hastulf, our cousin has taken control of the manor." She gulped back tears threatening to spill upon her cheeks.

"Mother, Father? And Henry and Anabel, our dear babies? Dead?" Blysse reached out and took hold of the wooden table, steadying herself.

"All of them. Hastulf was with our parents, and I stayed with the other two."

Blysse dropped her hand in her lap, and choked back a sob. "Oh, my! I was not expecting such tragic news. We've had little experience here with this terrible sickness, but from what I'm hearing, it is heartbreaking."

Isabella nodded, wiping back tears. "Yes, I believe God spared them pain, as it happened very quickly. I prayed diligently for all of them."

Blysse's face was one of shock. "You're a believer?"

Isabella nodded.

"And Henry and Anabel, too?"

"They made a commitment to him, before they died."

The room was quiet, other than the snapping and crackling sounds coming from the fire.

Isabella looked at the floor. She spoke softly. "Everyone is gone, but us." She took Blysse's hand in her own. "I was left alone, when Hastulf took charge of the place. He wished to see me married to Wolfhart, as it was Father's plan before he contracted the Black Death."

"Wolfhart? Oh, no! You lost everyone, and to think." Blysse wiped the tears from her face.

She got up and began to pace the floor, her long pointed, leather shoes making tapping sounds against the floor.

Then, she put her hands on her hips, and made a face. "That pig of a man. Isabella, you pitiable thing! I know why you're here!"

Isabella choked out, "It does not matter. He's dead, now He contracted the plague, also, on the road."

Blysse looked shocked for a moment, then she pursed her lips. "It's serves him right, to come to such a horrible end. He deserved such a thing."

Isabella chided, "Blysse, you cannot think this way, not after our own family has perished from that dreadful disease. It was horrible."

Blysse frowned, her lips in a pout. "It's difficult for me to think any other way, when I remember that filthy dog who cared a naught for others. I've enough to grieve over and think about. Too much has happened here."

"What do you mean?"

Blysse sighed. "I've had my fill of tragedy, and the ache I feel inside is so deep, it's difficult to go on about it."

Isabella looked concerned. "Blysse?"

"So much has changed here, and I'm very grieved because of it."

Blysse lowered her head in her hands and spoke quietly. "My husband..." But, she couldn't say more, as tears dropped from her eyes.

"Are you well?"

Blysse looked up. "Alan, was beaten by robbers and died merely days ago. And my best friend, Belle Walker, fell sick and died shortly thereafter."

Isabella reached out and put a slender hand on her sister's arm. "Oh, Blysse, I didn't know."

Blysse swallowed and lifted her chin, sopping up tears beginning to drop again. "My husband is gone."

Isabella nodded. "I'll pray. Yet, I fear it must be difficult for you."

Blysse took another drink of ale. "I must put it behind me. I cannot think of it. Our money will be gone very shortly, and I must find a way for us to make a living."

"How long will we have money to live on?"

"Merely a week or two."

Isabella's hands went to her cheeks. "Oh, Blysse! What will we do?"

Blysse laid a hand on Isabella's shoulder. "There, do not fret. We'll find a way. There's hope even in the worst of circumstances."

Isabella nodded. "Yes, I believe this, too."

Blysse sighed. "But, there is more, and some of it is very difficult to believe."

Isabella drew back. "Must I fear the days ahead?" Trouble seemed to follow her sister everywhere she went. What might Blysse have gotten herself into this time?

Blysse reached out and patted Isabella on the arm. "Ah, I am sure you'll not be pained, when you hear this."

Isabella looked wary.

"There are other things that happened before you came, one of them being, the commitment I made to walk in faith in God."

Isabella's eyes grew wide. "Blysse?"

Blysse nodded. "It is true."

Isabella's cheeks glowed. "Oh! This is good news! I was afraid there would be trouble, instead."

Blysse's expression sobered. "Well, I regret to tell you that things here will not be easy. There is much that has happened."

Isabella smoothed out the folds of her ragged brown tunic. "It cannot be as bad as it seems, can it?"

Blysse paced the room again. "Well, it seems I've found myself in a bit of a disagreement with the town witch, and she's none too pleased with me."

"Town witch?"

Blysse laughed, seeing the look on Isabella's face. "The woman's name is Sabina Moss. The town people call her Mother Migg O' Cropton. She's an ugly, drooping thing, always carrying this crystal with her and threatening the people here. Everyone fears the old bat, except myself, of course."

Isabella shuddered, her dark eyes growing by the moment.

Blysse stood up and filled two wooden mugs with wine and set them on the table, drawing one to her lips to take a sip, and then setting it back down. "She's a malicious old hag, and at this time is very upset with me. I've not exactly made friends with her, and no one in this town is speaking to me, because they believe I'm cursed, or at least most of them. Friar Dixon is one exception."

"We'll pray and trust, and things will work out." Isabella rubbed her eyes and yawned.

"You must be very tired. I realize the road you took was long."

Isabella nodded. Flames in the hearth crackled and danced, the heat from it, enveloping her. Her eyes closed and she yawned again. "You must be tired, also, as you've been through many difficult things. I suppose we should get rest and speak of more of it in the morning."

Blysse sighed. "Yes, I believe you are right in saying so."

They dressed in their nightclothes and lay down on the cozy, straw bed in a room attached to the shop.

Both quickly fell into a deep slumber until the next morning.

*****

After the girls finished a meager breakfast, and Blysse counted the last coins in their purse, a knock sounded on the heavy wooden door.

Blysse hurried to open it. "Might I assist you, sir?"

"I'm looking for a young woman, I passed on the road. Someone told me she might be in your home."

"Who is it, Blysse?" Isabella's heart skipped. Was it Matheu of Thorneton Le Dale? Did he come, like he said he might?

The door creaked open.

Isabella was dismayed to see the man she'd given her cousin's horse to, Dauit of York. He stepped out from behind the heavy, oak-framed entrance. A Moorish wind blew in, carrying with it some dust.

Dauit tipped his green felt hat to her, a wide grin spreading across his face when he saw her and he brushed his jacket off.

"What've you come for, sir?" Isabella eyed him with uncertainty.

His thick, dark brows rose slightly. "To make sure you made it safely."

She nodded, not sure what to say.

Blysse held out a glass of ale. "Stay and have a drink with us. I'm Isabella's sister." She turned and winked slyly at Isabella.

Isabella reluctantly turned to Dauit. "I appreciate you taking the time to come here, sir, but it was not necessary. Our travels were uneventful, and my friends saw to it that I was quite safe. There was no reason to oblige yourself to me."

He moved to the table and sat on a stool. "I would appreciate a mug of ale and a rest. It is good to know your name. It was difficult to find you."

He leaned closer to her. "Now, what's your merry sister's name? You must introduce us."

"Her name is Blysse, but we're not feeling so merry at this present time. We've lost family and friends." Isabella moved away from him and gave him a look of angst. She put her hand on the table in front of her, her fingernails tapping on the rough wood beneath. "There is much we've endured in the past days."

"I'm sorry. Was it the Black Death?"

"For our family, but Blysse lost her husband to thieves."

"It is not a good time, then."

Blysse handed him a wooden cup with dark liquid in it. "It'll be good to take our minds from our sorrow. You're a welcome relief to sitting here thinking about it. And I see you have taken an interest in my sister. I'm glad you took the time to see that she made it here safely."

Isabella lifted her chin. "Blysse, I'm sure he was merely passing through, and it was a second thought." She clenched the coarse surface of the table tighter.

Dauit looked down his slightly thick nose, his eyes resting gently on her. "On the contrary. I didn't come for any other reason than to see to your security. I was quite taken by your sweet face on the road."

Isabella's cheeks colored. She got up from the stool from where she sat, putting another log on the fire and poked the charred wood with a long stick. "Well, it was of naught. You can see that I arrived intact."

Blysse put her mug on the table. "Tell us, what is your name, sir? I would enjoy it very much to know my sister's suitor."

Isabella let out a sound, swinging her head around, still holding the hot poker in her hand. "Blysse! You must not be so forward! We merely met once!"

The man ignored Isabella's discomfort. "Dauit of York. And I hope to visit frequently. I believe you're in need of a good man here."

Isabella stared into the flames in front of her, watching the embers die out. "My sister and I will find our way in time."

Blysse patted her arm. "But, we will be happy to see you again, Dauit."

Dauit got up and stood next to Isabella. "Pardon me. I didn't wish to distress you with my forward behavior. I will remain friends with you, if this is what you wish, but will certainly hope for you to see me differently over the course of time."

Isabella sighed. "I see nothing untoward in this, yet, I do not wish to encourage more than a friendship at this time."

Dauit took his hat off his head and held it in his hand. "Then, I will ask for nothing more." He extended his hand to shake hers.

Isabella could not deny the man company, as he seemed genuine. She took his hand and shook it half-heartedly.

Blysse poured more ale into Dauit's mug and beckoned him to eat a slice of bread.

Dauit sat back down, eying Isabella curiously as he ate, while she tended to the fire.

When he finished, Blysse took the trencher from him. "I hope the meal was to your liking. I suppose we must get back to our work, but we're very glad you came. Since my husband died, I must learn his trade. We've very little money and will need to find a way to keep fed."

Isabella touched her sister's arm. "It is not so bad, Blysse. I'll help. We'll make it in time."

Dauit put his hat back on his head. He tipped it forward. "Do not hesitate to ask for help. I would be happy to oblige."

Isabella straightened her skirt. She eyed a wooden cross hanging on the wall. "God will surely provide for our needs, yet I thank you for the offer."

He got up from his seat and winked at Blysse. "I'll stay in town, until I know you have both found your way. I look forward to our next time together."

Blysse got up and went to the door, letting him out. "Yes, come to visit again, sir. We'd enjoy your company very much."

He tipped his hat to them, the brown curls on his head falling forward. "I'll be back to check on you."

Another gust of wind blew some dried leaves onto the floor. Isabella bent over and picked them up, tossing them onto the fire, watching them burn.

When the door shut behind him, Blysse turned, her eyes solemn. "Dauit is surely our way out of this disaster, Isabella. He is a good man, and seems very enamored with you. And I can see by the weave of his clothing, he is not a poor man. In answer to our prayers, God has provided for us."

Isabella got up from the stool she was sitting on. "Dauit? How can you say such a thing? I cannot comprehend it. It seems no better than one of father's schemes. At this time, I've no desire to marry this man. You might consider him yourself, if you think so highly of him."

Blysse gave Isabella a disconcerted look. "Isabella, he's not as Wolfhart was. He would treat you very well. I meant no harm. Yet, we're in such a time of poverty, I was merely thinking of our next meal. He came when we were praying."

Isabella eyed the table, scant with food. She knew their supplies were drawing thin, and her sister was only searching for a way to feed them both. It was true. They had prayed for God's provision.

She eyed the empty shelves and the last couple of coins sitting in full view on the table.

Blysse was right about the timing of Dauit's entrance into their home. Was it a coincidence that he should come so soon after they prayed? Did God send Dauit to provide for them? Or was it a test of her faith and of her ability to follow Him, against her own heart?

A hollow emptiness tore through her. She hoped with all her heart, God had not intended for her to marry this man.

Deep down inside her, a quiet yearning stirred in her soul. She recalled the security she felt in the strong arms of Matheu of Thorneton Le Dale and envisioned his clear, blue eyes resting upon her gently. She could not forget the handsome dark knight who came to her aid twice along the path to Cropton. She longed to see him again.

Was this the still, small voice Angnes spoke of? Was she hearing correctly?

And yet, had it been merely a chance meeting with Matheu, no more than it had been with Dauit. She knew little about either of them. Matheu might have been carrying out his chivalric duty toward her when he'd found her in distress. Knights followed orders to care for and protect those weaker than themselves. He'd made no commitments to her and no professions of courtly love. He merely suggested he might call on her in Cropton, to find out if she arrived at Blysse's home safely.

Blysse's situation at the shop was disparaging, and neither of them would be able to wait much longer without an arrangement of some sort. Isabella could not allow herself to be swept away by her own heart and desires, but by the path God would make known to her.

It was right to pray and ask for his guidance and seek to follow him.

She sighed. "I see the merit of your thoughts, Blysse. I realize our situation is desperate. And it is true, that Dauit is showing interest in me."

A thread of guilt stole through her when her eyes swept the bare room. They had little left to live on and little prospect for the future. "Dauit does seem to be a kind man. I will be more considerate from now on."

"Isabella, you mustn't marry the man out of guilt. I'm only asking that you give him a chance. You might see things differently after a time. God may have chosen him for you."

Isabella nodded. "I'll give him a chance, as this may be true." She eyed the dusty floor and then looked about the room. "Enough. We must do our chores. I will think on it."

Blysse's eyes sparkled. "Good. I'm glad for this."

They spent the rest of the day carrying water from the well, tending the garden out behind the house, making bread with their scant resources and studying the leather and tools Alan used for repairing the shoes in the small, two room shop.

*****

Over the next few days, Isabella followed her sister's suggestion and allowed Dauit to escort her for walks and take meals with them. She was beginning to give up on ever seeing Matheu again, so made efforts to try and develop feelings for this other man.

Dauit brought them food for the table and other much needed supplies and even paid the ten percent to the church they lagged behind on. In this way, they were able to keep the place they were staying at and live comfortably.

Isabella found Dauit to be kindhearted and caring toward her and Blysse. He proved to be a generous man. She guessed he was in a position of advantage over the serfs, with some money to spare. The plague was devastating the town of York, so he'd made the decision to stay in Cropton, until it ran its course.

"Come walk with me this evening, Isabella." Dauit poked his head in the doorway.

Isabella hesitated.

"Go on. I'll finish the chores." Blysse waved her hand at them.

Isabella sighed. "All right. I will not be long."

They walked down the wide lane, leading out of town to the south and stopped when they encountered a bend in the road alongside a craggy cliff. There was a cool mist settling over her shoulders and face. A light wind bent the tops of the tall grasses in the fields on the other side of the road. The moors presented a lonely, almost dreary picture this day, with clouds hanging low and heather weeping and smelling of dampness.

Dauit stopped and took her by the shoulders. There was a serious expression on his face.

Isabella drew back. She didn't appreciate the way he stared at her, or the way he nervously wiped the sweat that formed on his brow. "Blysse will be waiting. I told her I would not be long."

"But, there is something I must say, first. Your sister will understand."

Isabella was anxious to be getting back. "We should be leaving soon."

Dauit reached out and took her hand in his, his thick, dark brows furrowed. His fingers were trembling. "But, M'lady, I planned to ask you something first, which is very important."

Isabella let out a long breath. It was not difficult for her to guess what he was going to say. And she did not wish to hear it. "You might ask this another time. Look, it's going to storm soon. Blysse will wonder what we're doing out in this."

Dauit shook his head, perturbed. "You can most likely guess what I'm going to say. Please, Isabella, you must hear me out."

She had a good idea of what he planned to ask her, yet, she was not ready to hear it. Despite the kindness Dauit shared with her and Blysse, something inside her railed against the thought of ever becoming his wife.

"The rain is almost here." She pulled her hand away and smoothed out the folds in her skirt. "Dauit, let's keep this for another time."

She felt a tiny droplet of rain on her cheek and brushed it away. Visions of Matheu of Thorneton Le Dale invaded her thoughts. She'd wished he'd have come back for her by now.

Dauit wiped his brow with his hand again, and then took her by the shoulders. "I've a shop in York and am a mason. I can provide for both you and your sister. You will do well to consider the offer."

Isabella sighed. A mason? Blysse would tell her to grasp this chance, while she still had it and marry the man, regardless of her feelings for him. It's what her sister had done with Alan, and it'd all worked out for the best in the end. At least it's what Blysse kept repeating to her.

And, if she said no, what would happen to her and Blysse? Dauit had been their sole provider and support for weeks. And without him, they'd have barely a coin to spare.

An uneasy expression crossed Dauit's face. "I cannot wait any longer, Isabella. I ache for you to consider my proposal. I cannot bear another day without you. You must tell me what your feelings are in regards to me. For to prolong the agony, will only serve to make it more difficult for me in the end, if you'll not have me."

A light misty rain began to fall around them. Isabella felt her breath in her throat, as she watched the light grow in Dauit's eyes. She attempted to take a step back from him, but he held her there firmly in place, his hands clasped around hers.

Her eyes grew large, when he leaned down and kissed her on the lips, first gently, then more insistent. His desire for her seemed to grow with each attempt he made to sway her.

Isabella shook her head. She put her hands out and pushed against him. "No." She whispered it softly at first, and then more insistently.

His lips against hers felt foreign and as icy cold as the Moor rain. She couldn't imagine ever feeling anything in his arms.

He backed away, his expression solemn.

It pained her to tell him what she knew to be true, that she didn't love him and could not go through with this charade. Blysse would not understand. But, she knew what had to be done.

She spoke softly. "Dauit, I do not wish to hurt you. You're a good man. Yet, I feel we're not right for each other, and I cannot lead you to think there will ever be more between us."

She shrunk further into herself, her eyes a dark violet. She knew it was devastating to him for her to speak in this way, yet it was necessary. He had a right to know the truth.

Dark clouds in the distance threatened a downpour. Isabella looked up at the sky, realizing it would soon be upon them, if they did not hurry back. She shivered, lifting the shawl that slipped over her shoulders. "I believe you should take me home. It's going to rain, and we'll be wet."

Desperation flooded Dauit's eyes. She turned away from him, realizing she'd hurt him. She couldn't bear causing him any more pain.

He took her hand and swung her around to face him again. "You and your sister will be broken without my assistance, as I'm unable to remain here in Cropton to support you. I must return to my business in York as supplies there are wearing thin. If you leave with me, I believe you'd be very happy in time."

Isabella shook her head and pushed him away. His desperation was more than she could bear. He was a caring, kind man and did not deserve less than he'd given. She felt responsible for his distress.

Then, she heard the light clomp of a horse's footsteps behind them, and realized Dauit and her were blocking the road. A traveler needed enough room to pass. "Come, we must not block the path."

He took her hand, and they moved a couple steps back.

Isabella was uncomfortable with the thought of someone having come upon her and Dauit, at such a time. Her emotions were in such a frenzy, that whoever it was might misconstrue what was happening, by the passion displayed in both their faces. She did not wish to be the subject of the next day's town gossip.

But, when she looked up at the rider, her eyes registered surprise. Matheu of Thorneton Le Dale was sitting straight in his saddle on his great, black horse. His hand was upon his sword. "Isabella? Are you in need of assistance?"

Her violet eyes widened, and a blush set upon her cheeks. The words tangled in her throat. "No, sir. This is a friend, Dauit of York." She wondered how much Matheu saw and what he might have determined as a result of it.

Matheu eyed her warily, his expression suddenly solemn. "A friend?"

She pulled her hand away from Dauit's and clasped her shawl. "Yes."

Dauit smiled. "Come now, Isabella, you must be truthful. Our times together have extended beyond mere friendship." He gave Matheu a wide smile.

Isabella wished to explain, but didn't know where to begin. She stood there dumbfounded.

Matheu tipped his head. "From what I gathered, it was obvious as to the intensity of your relationship with this man, which I cannot deny. It appears your future is clearly fixed, and you will be headed to the church in time."

Isabella swallowed, her eyes huge. A gust of wind tossed strands of hair across her face, and she pushed it behind her. She wanted to say something, but found herself at a loss for words once again. How could she explain the passionate embrace he must have seen between her and Dauit and the kisses that were not her own?

Dauit nodded. "We are currently working on that aspect of our situation at this time."

Isabella felt the heat spread in her pale cheeks and took a quick breath of air.

Before she could reply, Matheu pulled back on the reigns he held tautly and circled his horse around, facing the oncoming storm. He looked back, a frown drawing over his brow. "I came to make sure you made it to Cropton safely, and can see that you have. It appears you are in good hands. A storm is coming, and it might be prudent that you find your way back to your homes."

He looked down the road. "I must make the next town by nightfall, so will need to be on my way."

Isabella stared at him, speechless. She ached to tell him she didn't want him to leave and that Dauit meant nothing to her, but she fell silent. The lengthy training in decorum she received as a young woman, and her lack of knowledge of Matheu's own intentions toward her, kept her from calling out to him. In this moment, with all her heart, she wished she were more like Blysse.

Matheu's dark horse impatiently pawed at the dirt. He held the reigns tighter to keep the large animal on the path and spoke quietly over his shoulder. "I wish you both many good days in the future." And then he turned away.

A hollow pit formed inside Isabella, as she noted how he dug his heels into the animal's side and caused the horse to charge ahead.

Matheu looked back only once and then turned in his saddle, as his horse tore down the path, kicking up dirt along the road.

Isabella didn't take her eyes from him, until he rounded the bend and disappeared from her sight. She lifted her hands to her face, her eyes brimming with tears, knowing she'd probably not see him again in the town of Cropton. From their conversation, he'd be of the understanding that she was to be married to Dauit.

A mournful sound escaped her lips, and a deep sadness filled her heart.

"Isabella, who was he? Did you know him well?" Dauit frowned.

She shook her head from side to side. "No, he helped me along the way."

Dauit eyed her curiously. "He was following his knight's orders and wished to see you safe? Is that it?" He lifted her chin.

She shook her head, hesitating slightly. She wondered if it were true. Was Matheu merely helping her out of duty, or did he hold deeper affections for her?

Her eyes trailed the empty road, a thin cloud of dust disappearing in the dense meadow air. A great emptiness grew inside her, and the hollow ache formed in her heart.

She felt Dauit's arms encircle her, and this time she didn't push him away, but solemnly laid her head on his shoulder and sobbed, tears dropping freely down her cheeks. Matheu of Thorneton Le Dale was gone. He would not be back.

Isabella had been hoping he'd return and might call on her as Dauit had, with the chance of a match between the two of them. But now, all hopes of that were gone.

And in regard to her and Blysse's situation, if things didn't change soon, they'd both be living on the streets, with the choice of either selling themselves or starving. She could not even begin to imagine her sister or her living such a life.

As long as she held hopes of a union between her and Matheu, she'd put Dauit off. Yet, now with Matheu having left, Isabella knew there was nothing she could do to save her and her sister from the poverty they'd surely be subject to, unless she accepted Dauit's offer.

He was proposing marriage to her and promising her the life of a tradesman's wife. He was an honorable man, kind toward her and her sister. Marrying him would bring her and Blysse the security they lacked. Without him, they'd be begging for food in a fortnight, with no protection.

She pulled back from his embrace and straightened, a grave expression in her eyes.

Light drops began to fall, obscuring her tears. She took a deep breath. "I believe you might think me silly as to what I have to tell you, Dauit, but I'll be honest with you."

He took her hand. "Yes, my dear? What have you to say to me?"

Isabella wiped the tears from her cheek. "I do not love you as a sweetheart at this time, and I wish I could say I did."

Dauit nodded. "I see what you're saying is true."

She stopped, unable to go on.

"Please, Isabella. You must tell me what is on your mind. I will not judge you."

She stammered out the words she didn't want to say. "Blysse and I, well, we cannot make it on our own with no trade or possibilities, unless of course we were to make the streets our profession, or we took some other lowly position. But, as you know this type of life would be very difficult for us, and we'd rather starve to death, than resort to do such a thing."

"Yes, go on." He seemed to guess what she was going to say, by the solemn shine growing in his eyes, and how he looked at her with great interest.

She looked down at her feet. This was one of the most difficult things she'd ever had to do, and it made her feel as if she were a common beggar on the streets. "Well, my sister and I are in great need of your support as to our distressing situation, and I know the good man that you are. Anyone could see what kind of a husband you would make."

Dauit nodded. He looked eager, as a cat might if he were going after a ball of wool.

A faint blush stirred on Isabella's face. "How do I say this delicately?" She turned away, pained.

He took her hands in his own and whispered in her ear. "That it might be best for us to marry, so that I might sustain you and your sister?"

Isabella cringed at the thought of making such a deal. It seemed no better to her than selling herself to the highest bidder, as her cousin had planned to do with Wolfhart. Yet, the prospect she yearned for, would not happen. Matheu was gone. Dauit was surely a more promising figure than Wolfhart.

"I'll make it my aim to develop deeper feelings over time."

"Yes, your sister said it herself, that it was possible for her."

Isabella let out a slow breath. "It is true."

His eyes widened, the thick brows above them rising. "So, you are sure of it?" He scratched the top of his head, anticipatory of her answer. "Could you accept my offer in this way?"

Isabella nodded, resigned to her decision. "I know you're a good man, and Blysse thinks it, too. I believe it'll merely take time, and I'll find in the end, it was the right thing to do."

Dauit nodded, with the full realization that she was merely agreeing to his proposal, as a means to support her and her sister. Regardless, she saw that he was glad she changed her mind, and it would give him the chance to prove he was a worthy husband. "You'll see, Isabella. I'll make you happy."

He took her arm, as if to ignore his own misgivings. "Your sister will be very happy." His eyes glowed. "And maybe in days, we will be husband and wife! I would like that very much!"

Isabella sighed deeply and nodded. "Maybe." Her eyes followed the trail back to the village. "Can we speak of this another time, Dauit?"

He nodded. "Yes, m'lady. If it's what you wish."

"I'm tired and would like to rest. I wish to go back to the shop."

Thunder rumbled in the distance, and the sky was turning increasingly dark. A wind began to shudder across the moors.

He nodded again and smiled. "Yes, the storm will hit us soon. I must get you back there before it's here. It is a big decision we've made. You'll need your rest for the days ahead."

He gestured for her to leave with him, taking her by the arm and guiding her down the path, a slight bounce in his step.

Neither spoke on the way back. A dark mist landed over the moors and shadows deepened as they walked, the rumbling closing in on them, and the rain beginning to fall.

Relief washed over Isabella, when they finally reached the door of the shop and Dauit left to go his own way for the night. She closed the heavy, wooden behind her, securing the latch. The wind pelted the cold rain hard against the shop.

Inside, Blysse was sewing the leather on the seam of a shoe. She was curled up on a rug by the fire. Her sharp eyes met Isabella's dark violet ones. "What is it, Isabella? Are you not well?"

Isabella stared at the floor as she took off her wet shoes. "I'm to be wed to Dauit. He asked, and I told him I would."

Blysse sat upright. She grinned, surprised. "You said you would?"

Isabella nodded again. She strode across the room and placed her woolen shawl on the table. "We'll have money again and a place to stay."

Blysse put her needle down and stopped what she was doing. "And you're happy with this arrangement?"

Isabella forced a smile and sat on the wooden stool next to the table. "I'm sure I will be. I merely need time to adjust to it."

Blysse tipped her head to the side, eyeing Isabella curiously. "This was the answer to our prayers, was it not, sister? It must be God's will for our lives."

Isabella gave her sister a forlorn look. She remembered the chance meeting with Matheu of Thorneton Le Dale on the road. Maybe, it was God's way of telling her, this was the way it was to be. "I suppose so."

"I think you'll see, in time Dauit will be a fitting husband for you and that it was in your best interest to marry him." Blysse's eyes danced. "He's a fine man, Isabella, and will make a pleasing partner." She seemed to want to assure her sister of the worthy decision she'd made.

Isabella nodded. "Maybe it will be that way."

Blysse lifted the shoe in front of her for inspection and then set it back down. She was uncomfortable with her sister's silence, but didn't say anything.

Isabella stared at the hard packed, dirt floor. Matheu was gone, and she was to be married. She could not help thinking of him, even now. She cupped her hand over her mouth, pretending to yawn.

"You seem tired, Isabella. I put warm stones in the other room. You will find it ready for you."

Isabella nodded. Even though she'd no desire for sleep, she wanted nothing better than to wrap up in a blanket and drown herself in her sorrows. "Yes, I believe I'll retire early this night."

"And it'll be a good thing, too. You'll need your rest for the days ahead. The fair will be upon us soon, and we must plan for the wedding. We've much to do."

Isabella got up from the stool to retire for the night.

\*\*\*\*\*

In a short time, Blysse heard her sister quietly sinking onto the straw mattress in the adjacent room. She hoped she hadn't been too insistent on her own wishes being fulfilled. She knew Isabella was swayed by guilt and obligatory duty. For Isabella to comply with her wishes, it'd merely take a little push and a few persuasive words. And it was exactly what she had done.

Maybe she had pushed too hard this time to get her way? Would she herself have married Dauit to pull them out of this situation? Alan was persuasive, holding a certain charm, she could not deny. But, what if there was none of that for her sister?

She lifted the shoe she was working on to her and drew a needle through the leather and out again. Was what she'd done an attempt to follow God's will, or had she done it out of fear and lack of trust in his provisions? She could not be sure.

Blysse laid the needle in her lap and laid a hand on her heart, disturbed by the dark feeling residing there. She turned eyed the pelting rain against the window, and she sighed.

It was nighttime. Everything seemed grim in the absence of the light, especially in the midst of a storm. Maybe things would seem brighter when the sun lit the sky in the morning. Maybe Isabella would see things differently too, in the light of the day. Tomorrow would stand the test of time. Tonight was a time for prayer. She'd pray for God's way to be clear and for Isabella's decision to be made in His steps.

\*\*\*\*\*

135

# Chapter 11

Matheu eyed the heather-covered hillsides surrounding the small village of Thorneton Le Dale. The road leading into town was lined with shacks made of cement, wood and straw, while peasants worked the fields.

He spotted Gawain on his gray mare trotting toward him at a good pace, past merchants, who rode on heavily laden, wooden carts along the stony trail.

Matheu's jaw clenched. He pulled on the reigns of his horse, coming to a stop and patted the side of the dark animal. "This is a difficult thing to tell my squire, Black. He'll think poorly of Isabella again."

He sat straight in his saddle.

Dust kicked up a cloud on the path behind Gawain, while he closed the distance between them.

Matheu sighed. Nothing was as he thought it was. Nothing in Cropton turned out the way he guessed it would.

Gawain stopped when he reached Matheu's black horse and drew up beside him. He rested the reins in his lap and grinned. "You must tell me what happened? Where is Isabella?"

Matheu didn't respond, but looked at him solemnly. What could he tell his friend, so that the young woman's reputation would still be intact? He knew what Gawain would have to say about it.

Gawain stared at Matheu. "What is the matter, sir? Why the look of concern? What do you learn of Isabella?"

Matheu patted the side of his horse. "Only that she's safe in Cropton and is with her sister."

Gawain's horse began to dance. He tightened the reigns. "I believe it'd make you glad to have seen her, yet you do not seem happy."

Matheu nodded. "I'm glad she's safe."

"Was she happy to see you again?" Gawain tipped his head to the side.

Matheu raked a hand through his dark hair. His eyes were guarded. "She's marrying, Dauit of York."

The pallor of Gawain's skin reddened, and his mouth tightened. "To be wed! And to think she acted as if she were sweet on you?" He shook his head. "I told you she would spell trouble."

Matheu reached out and laid a hand on Gawain's shoulder. "No, Isabella was merely taking our help. You cannot blame her."

Gawain snorted, shrugging off Matheu's hand. "It's not true. She did more than that. I know it. I tell you, you cannot trust women. They *are,* a path of wickedness, in my opinion."

Matheu sighed. "Gawain, you mustn't believe Isabella led me astray. It is her decision whom she'll be happy with."

"And you have accepted this?" Gawain did not look convinced.

Matheu shrugged. "There's no choice. She didn't wait for me and is with another. It is God's will." He tugged on the reigns of his horse and turned in his seat, his blue eyes pensive. "I feel tired and need rest. Let's get back to the manor. Tomorrow, I must to go back to Cropton, as I have one more tournament there."

He patted the side of his horse and looked down the road. "Also, I do not wish to speak of it again. Can you honor this? We'll finish the last tournament and be done with it."

Gawain nodded. "Yes, sir. If it's what you wish. I'll do as you say."

Matheu sighed. "I thank you for this."

They each gave a quick snap of the reigns, gently digging their heels into their horses' sides. Both animals simultaneously began to trot, picking up speed until they were racing swiftly across the moors toward a large manor on the other side of the town.

Matheu's horse flew beneath him, carrying him further from Isabella and further from the hope lit inside him in the recent days.

He aimed to forget the softness of Isabella's sunlit hair, her gentle laughter and the feel of her small hands encircling his waist. He prayed God would help him forget her and let go of the ache he felt inside.

He'd prove himself faithful in following God's path, which might or might not include her. Someday, he'd look back and understand God's faithfulness in fulfilling the best plan for his life.

*****

Blysse tugged Isabella's hand, her dark eyes lit. "Come, sister! Let's speak of the wedding tomorrow. The fair's here, and I'll not miss it."

Isabella's heart beat rapidly in her chest. She smoothed out her brown woolen tunic and stepped beside her sister as they moved between people on the crowded road. Street vendors met them on the path, calling prices and gesturing them to look at the goods they brought with them to sell.

Lilting tunes hung in the air. Her spirit was lifted somewhat by the scents of the many flowers set out on the streets. Wine was flowing, people seemed happy, and famine and disease were all but forgotten. An electric excitement rang through the air in the town streets.

She realized there was reason to hope, that the emptiness within her, would someday fade. Maybe, with Dauit, she'd find peace in the end.

Blysse was nearly dancing and skipping next to Isabella, when they reached the jousting tournament. "I haven't seen anything like this, Isabella! It's beautiful!"

Isabella could not help smiling at the frenzied emotions whipped up in her sister. Blysse never found occasion to mope.

A roar arose above a great crowd when two of the contestants stepped into the ring for the last joust, to determine the winner of the day.

An uneasiness surged through Isabella, as she sat down on a makeshift wooden bench in front of the area set aside for the competition. The knights cantered into the open field, while the crowd burst into applause.

Her heart skipped a beat, when she saw a familiar stone gate emblazoned on the front of one of the men's tunics. Her eyes rested on Matheu of Thorneton. There was no mistaking his dark, wavy hair and clear, blue eyes.

Blysse stood next to her. Her hands were clasped and one of her leather shoes was tapping the ground. "I wonder if Dante is in attendance, the one who helped me at the well. I might see him!"

Isabella let out a breath. "But Blysse! You're in mourning for Alan!"

Blysse whipped her head around and sniffed. "It's been at least a month, Isabella, and I'm tired of the pain and talk of the dead. I loved Alan, yet cannot ponder on these things that were done to him over and over,. I cannot bear the pain. It will slowly kill me to keep remembering it."

Isabella sighed. She knew Alan's death was more difficult for Blysse than she let on. Maybe, it was best for her sister not to dwell on it.

Isabella smiled. "I know you loved him and merely wish to forget what you've been through. Some might think it wrong, but I understand it breaks your heart to think of it."

Blysse fought back tears. "And why I distract myself." She looked back at the field, and then wiped the wetness from her face. "I'm glad you understand."

Isabella turned, spotting the black horse carrying Matheu. She took hold of the edge of the bench, while he lined up his horse to battle the last competitor. The gruff looking man on a white horse was heavily armored. He held a large, red shield and a jousting pole. Isabella's heart sunk at the size of him. A panicky feeling, rose in her chest.

Matheu turned in her direction, hesitating when he spotted her in the crowd. His stone blue eyes gentled when they regarded her unsettled ones.

Blysse laid a hand on her shoulder and shook it. "Oh, I hope the knight on the black horse wins, the handsome one!"

Isabella ignored her sister's remark, a sudden fear coursing through her.

Matheu backed his horse into position, taking a pole from Gawain. He lifted it up and waited for the call to fight.

Both horses faced each other, motionless.

Blysse shouted over the roar of the frenzied crowd.

Isabella clasped her hands tightly in her lap, wishing she were anywhere but in this place and that she hadn't come. Memories of duels at the manor left her panicky inside. Even though there were stringent rules that encouraged the safety of the participants, knights could still be badly injured. It pained her to think that anything might happen to Matheu.

Despite the fear brewing inside her, she was transfixed, unable to move. The signal sounded, and both horses charged forward, lances held high above thundering hooves.

Isabella hid her face in her hands.

Blysse tugged on her arm, laughing. "Look! You'll miss it!"

A great resounding clang and shattering noise rang out. Isabella lifted her head, and breathed a sigh of relief, realizing Matheu wasn't injured.

He circled the animal around, guiding it back to the starting position.

The other knight laughed, the tip of his lance broken. "It's shattered! I've earned three points over you!"

Matheu's lips curved upward slightly, and then he laughed. "I'm merely starting. Do not get too high in spirits, until we finish."

When the men made their second charge, Isabella held her breath, covering her eyes again. A soft cry escaped her lips.

"Isabella? Blysse leaned against the wooden fence that enclosed the area the men were fighting in. Her eyes gleamed. "There's no need to worry. Do not fret."

Isabella twisted the folds of her tunic. "But, it is difficult not to." She heard a thud and armor clanking, then realized one of the knights fell from his horse. She quickly looked up to see what had happened.

The older man was lying on the ground unhurt. His squire ran onto the field to help him up.

The tightness in Isabella's chest loosened. Matheu was still on his horse.

A self-satisfied grin spread across his face. He looked over at Isabella and smiled.

Isabella's cheeks grew warm.

Matheu circled his horse and trotted back to where the man lay. "Do you need a hand, so we might resume the fight from the ground?"

The other man sat up with the help of his squire. He chuckled, and then groaned. "I felt the strength of that blow and do no believe I stand a chance. No, I understand when it's a good time to quit. I saw what happened to the others before me."

Matheu nodded and then waited for Gawain to help him with his lance and shield.

The announcer strode onto the field and held Matheu's arm up. "We've a winner…Sir Matheu of Thorneton Le Dale!"

Matheu turned, bending his head slightly.

The crowd roared their approval.

Isabella breathed a sigh of relief and got up, standing next to her sister.

Gawain helped Matheu from his horse, tied the animal to a post, and then both men ducked into a small tent on the other side of the stands.

Blysse laughed. She clapped her hands, eyes sparkling. "I knew he'd win!" She looked around. "I wished I could've seen Dante, though. He isn't anywhere."

Isabella gave a look of annoyance. "I do not understand what you see in these matches. The joust is a silly sport, and a poor excuse for entertainment. It's the last time, I want to see it." She stood, lifting her woolen shawl over her shoulders.

Blysse pointed to the tent. "He's coming back out, the knight who won."

Isabella turned.

Matheu immediately sought her out, and took a step in her direction. Then he suddenly stopped, when Gawain grabbed his arm and pulled him back.

"Isabella."

She heard a voice and turned.

Dauit was behind her. "I was looking for you. Friar Dixon said he is able to marry us tomorrow."

She ignored his remarks, suddenly uninterested in the talk of marriage, or Friar Dixon, for that matter.

She looked back across the field and searched the area near the tent. Matheu was gone. He left without a word. She put her hand to her mouth and let out a soft cry.

What had she done? Why had she agreed to marry Dauit? If she hadn't have said yes to his proposal, and he had not been at the tournaments, Matheu might've approached her. Things might've been different.

A sudden emptiness struck her inside.

Isabella realized she still harbored feelings for him and they hadn't lessened with time. With Dauit, she'd only been confused and unsure. She suddenly knew that, if she were to marry him, she would be making one of the biggest mistakes of her life,. Her motives for choosing him didn't seem right or pure.

Maybe this was the still, soft voice Angnes told her about.

She lowered her head in prayer and wondered why hadn't she done this before. How was she to know truth, if she never asked for it?

She whispered a prayer, not pleading for an answer or for help, but asking in faith that God would reveal to her the path he wanted her to follow.

She did not expect to know the answer immediately, but maybe because it had been in her heart all along, she already knew what it was. Immediately, she was filled with a sense of peace inside her, and she understood what she needed to do.

She turned to Dauit, her eyes solemn. "Sir, there's something I must say to you."

Dauit took a step toward her, a wary look in his eye. He took her hand. "Whatever it is, it can wait. We are to be married soon, and you can tell me then. You see, everything is going according to plan."

Blysse nodded. "Do not be anxious, Isabella. Dauit is making sure the preparations for the wedding are in place."

"But, it does not concern them." Isabella lowered her head. She took a deep breath and sighed, smoothing out her tunic.

Dauit shifted uneasily. "My dear, do not say it. I fear you may be overthinking the matter."

She let go of his hand. "I do not wish to hurt you, but I must be truthful. I feel God is leading me on a different path than I have been taking."

Dauit nervously raked his hand through his hair. "Please, if you're going to tell me what I think you are, then you best consider carefully what the consequences will be."

"Isabella?" Blysse stared at her sister guardedly.

Isabella scuffed the ground with her shoe. "If I do not say it, I will be living a lie. Would you want this?"

Dauit shook his head. "But, it would not be a lie. I know what you told me, and you said it'd only take time for you to adjust."

"Dauit, I accepted you for the sake of my security and my sister's, and have no desire for marriage at this time. It'll never be the way you imagine it. I'd despise you for talking me into it. You'll want a bride who loves you the way you deserve, and one whose heart will never stray."

Dauit paced back and forth, then stopped and took her by the shoulders. "But, we will make it work. God will help us."

Isabella sighed. She didn't say anything.

Blysse's eyes grew wide. She tugged on Isabella's sleeve. "Have you lost your mind? This is necessary for us to survive."

"I know it, but, I cannot go through with it." There was full conviction in her eyes.

Dauit was silent.

Blysse tipped her head back in frustration. "You would not do this if you were thinking straight."

Isabella's eyes filled with tears. "But I am, and I have to. What would you do, if God spoke plainly to you? Would you listen?"

Blysse ignored her sister's question. "But, Dauit has a place for us, a home."

"Yet, I must not let this determine the path I take."

Blysse tapped her fingers on her side. Her expression was incredulous. "But, I thought…"

Dauit put out his hand and touched Blysse's sleeve. He suddenly looked as if he was beaten down, but was resigned to it. "It is as it should be. She is determined."

"Dauit?" Blysse turned to him.

He shook his head. "It is apparent she'll not marry me."

Isabella's head lowered, and she fidgeted with her hands in her lap. "I tried to go through with it, but the longer I thought on it, the more convicted I felt it wasn't the right thing to do. And I'm truly sorry for the trouble I've caused."

Dauit sighed. "I can see you've done nothing rash. Do not be grieved."

"I do care for you, and telling you this has certainly pained me." Isabella brushed a wayward strand of hair out of her eyes.

Dauit smiled tenderly. "All is well." His expression was solemn. "I'll talk to Friar Dixon." He took his cloak from the bench.

Isabella nodded. She wished she would not have hurt Dauit. She could tell by his expression that he took the matter to heart. "You're a fitting man, and I will not forget what you've done for us."

Blysse didn't say anything. Despite the forlorn look in her eyes, she smiled at him and shook his hand.

Both girls turned, as they watched him walk away, following the cobblestone path back to the shop.

When he was gone, Isabella shakily took her sister's hand. She felt a rush of uncertainty run through her. "I've felt so sure, but now, am suddenly afraid. Did I make a good decision?"

Blysse cocked her head to the side, eying her sister skeptically. "After this? Now you waiver?" Then, she laughed. She shook her head, a twinkle in her eye. "You never wanted to marry him, and I knew it. I suppose I should have married him, yet I suspect he would not have wished it."

Isabella straightened, the conviction returning to her eyes. "It's true, I did not want it from the beginning, and I feel a weight has been lifted, even though the situation we're left with is dire."

Blysse tugged her woolen shawl tighter about her. "Come what may, God will surely carry us through the days ahead."

Isabella smiled. "I believe this, too. Now, let's take time tonight in prayer and meditation. He will surely provide for us, whether in poverty or wealth."

Blysse smiled, agreeing with a nod of the head.

*****

Blysse pulled one coin from the leather pouch sitting on the table. A kettle of watery stew bubbled over the flame in the fireplace.

Isabella lifted it off the spit and carried it to the table, laying it down in front of them. A faint scent of onions and potatoes made Blysse's stomach rumble. She spooned meager helpings into each of the wooden bowls and set the pottage next to their cups of wine.

Pushing the coin aside, Blysse sipped the broth and put the bowl back down on the table. "It's the last of it, and needs to go to the church for our ten percent."

Isabella sat on a wooden stool, eying the stew. "I thought it was God's plan to take this path, yet it makes me wonder. We've nothing left, with no possibilities."

A log fell from the fire, sending a couple sparks flying onto the dirt floor. Isabella crushed them with a stick.

Blysse smiled and patted her sister on the arm. "He surely does not promise money and the good life to everyone. Look at Friar Dixon, and that poor woman in the Holy Scriptures Angnes told you about, how much her last coin meant to God? I suppose what's truly important, is whether we're following him, and to remember the assurance we have, that he'll be with us, even in the face of death."

She got up and crossed the room, when a knock sounded at the door. She lifted the latch and pulled on the handle.

Three men from the craftsmen's guild entered through the opening, taking felt hats from their heads. The tallest of the three bowed slightly to both the woman and then dropped his hand to his side. Sweat gathered in beads on his forehead.

Blysse sighed. A look of annoyance crossed her face. She rested her hand on her hips, tapping her foot on the dirt floor. "Well, are you going to tell us why you're standing in our doorway?"

The shortest of the men, well dressed in a blue tunic, tied with a wide, brown leather belt, clasped his thick hands together behind him and let out a breath. "We're grieving for you, as to Alan's passing. We hope you understand how much we regret this senseless thing that happened to him."

Blysse's eyes narrowed. "And yet you're here anyway, ready to take over his shop. Am I right in saying so?"

The shorter man sniffed, raising a finger to scratch his bearded chin. "We wished to help you as his widow, and yet, this is a time of hunger. We can't carry you along at the expense of our own families."

Blysse stomped her foot. "But, you see we're trying, even with little to add to our pottage."

All eyes went to the empty bowls and the pot of thin, watery stew sitting on the table.

The tallest man stepped forward. "We see this, and yet you are not paying the guild your money, and it's necessary for our very lives."

He looked around again, surveying the room's contents. "If another shoemaker moves in, we'll have money in our own pockets. You do not understand the trade, and we must have someone here who does."

Blysse glared at the men. "So are you saying I must leave my home?"

Isabella fidgeted with her hands. "Blysse, please, you must listen to them."

A log fell on the fire, snapping angrily. The flames flickered and then died.

The taller man sighed, as if pained by what he had to say. "It is true. We've come to tell you that you must take your things and leave, as we have need of it. You can't pay the rent, and you're not familiar with what needs to be done."

Blysse didn't move.

The man leaned against the wall, a hard glint stewing in his eye. "You do not have to make this difficult. You can leave quietly, or we will be forced to usher you out."

Isabella gripped her sister's arm. "If we don't go, they'll put us out, Blysse. There's nothing we can do. We surely must do as they say."

A gust of wind blew the door against the wall, making a loud, banging sound before one of the men reached out and caught it. He held it firmly, righting himself, while awaiting her response.

Blysse lifted her chin. Her eyes flashed. "I knew what you were going to do before the door opened. I merely asked for more time."

The man in the middle of the group spoke for the first time. He fidgeted with his hands. "We cannot give it to you. We need the place, for we've found a shoemaker who wishes to possess it."

Isabella pulled her shawl about her and shivered, the cold Moorish air from outside settling over her.

Blysse jutted her chin higher and she glowered at them. "We don't need it anyway. We can manage without this place." She sniffed. "We will collect our things."

The men nodded, eyeing the little provisions left in the room. They held the door open, waiting for the girls to leave.

Blysse and Isabella gathered their meager stock of food, coin, a change of clothes, two wool blankets and the last pair of shoes that were sitting against the wall.

On their way out the door, Blysse turned back to the men. She tossed her thick mane behind her. "I hope you're happy, putting women out on the streets. Hmph!"

The taller man looked chagrinned. "Look across the road. They may be in need of a laundress. You might find a place to stay there. You can't make much, but enough to survive."

Blysse stared at him coldly. "If the man Mauger comes for his shoes, you might send him there."

He fidgeted with the hat in his hand. "We will let him know, miss."

Isabella followed Blysse outside.

When the door closed behind the men, Blysse turned to her sister. "Auk! Putting us out with little but the clothes on our back. Worthless, they are! The whole lot of them!" Her foot made tapping noises against the cobblestone beneath her feet.

Isabella put her hand on her sister's arm. "Yet, they were only thinking of their own families. We cannot provide the money necessary to keep their children fed. You understand this." She turned to the shabby inn standing between two of the buildings on the other side of the road. "But, you see! God has provided for us already. There is the job across the street. We can go there, until we find something more suitable."

Blysse quit tapping her toe and took a breath. "They can have that old place. It's bad memories for me, anyway."

"Blysse?" Isabella tugged on her sister's arm. "You know we are called to forgive them?"

"And you must remind me?" Blysse let out an annoyed sound. And then she smiled. "Hmph! I know what I have to do. It'll happen soon enough."

Isabella's eyes warmed at the thought, and she shook her head. "I'm sure you'll do right by them."

Blysse eyed the structure across the street. The lines in her face eased. "I suppose we've no choice. We'll bring our things with us." She lifted her chin, dusting off the edges of her skirt and motioned for Isabella to follow.

They carried their meager belongings across the cobblestone street to the run-down building. They might secure a job there and a place to stay.

The air was cool, sending chills running through Isabella. She wrapped the wool shawl tightly around her, shuddering upon hearing the gruff voices inside.

Blysse lifted her fist to the wooden door, rapping on it softly.

Both girls held their breath, waiting for the door to open, wondering what their fate would be.

*****

Isabella found her way down the cobblestone street past wattle and daub huts to shops along the main street.

She poked her head into the doorway of their small, one-room apartment spotting Blysse lying on a cot against the wall; her laundress apron still tied about her waist.

"Did Friar Dixon have any food for us?"

Isabella shook her head.

She sat on the bed next to her sister. "All he had to spare was this little scrap of barley bread and a small bottle of milk from their cow. Hunger's spreading all over the land, and they can't afford to help us more than this."

# Isabella's Shield

The cement walls of the building seemed to close in on them, as Blysse's dark eyes rested on her sister uneasily. "Isabella, what are we to do? We cannot live this way for long. We'll die very soon. We barely have money to pay for this place."

The damp cool smell of the room made Blysse turn up her nose.

Isabella's stomach rumbled. She broke a small portion of bread into two pieces and handed the larger to her sister. "I don't know. In this time of poverty, there are not any villagers who are willing to help. I'm aware Friar Dixon was giving us food from his very own stock. He told me his path was not always easy, either."

Blysse hungrily shoved the small piece of the bread into her mouth and chewed quickly. She took a small sip of milk from the bottle. "We must come up with a plan. We need more money. We've been here for more than a month with very little to eat. I'm feeling weak."

Isabella nodded, her eyes large. She chewed on the edge of the slice of bread, trying to savor each small bite. "When we were living at the manor, I did not understand how terrible it was for the serfs who were begging."

Blysse sighed. "I didn't either, and I wish I'd been more sympathetic."

"Yes, I gave so little to others at the time, and we had so much."

Isabella and Blysse finished eating their meal in silence, while they listened to the dying sounds of the street, an occasional door locking and animals being shut up in their pens or brought into their homes for the night.

Both girls suddenly turned, when a knock sounded at the door.

Blysse touched Isabella's ragged, woolen sleeve. "Maybe it's the man, Mauger of the Moors, from out of town, coming for his shoes?"

A slight stirring of hope lit in Isabella's eyes.

Blysse got up and brushed off her skirt.

Isabella did the same, and they both made their way across the room.

Isabella tapped her sister. "Is it the man?"

Blysse nodded. She opened the door a crack. "You're looking for me, sir?"

Mauger's brows rose. The naturally rosy cheeks of the girl he met weeks ago, were now sunken and hollow, and her clothes weathered and wrinkled. "I came for my shoes."

Blysse curtsied. "Oh, I kept them for you. I knew you'd be back."

"You're not with the shop anymore?"

A blush stole over Blysse's cheeks. "The craftsmen's guild could not allow us to stay there."

His eyes lit on a thinner girl with large, luminous eyes standing next to her. "And this is?"

"My sister, Isabella, from Godfrey Hall in London. She came to live with me after I fell into this sad circumstance. At this time, I cannot be caring for her as I should. We're trying to pay for this place with the money from our laundress jobs, but are not doing well."

The man's eyes narrowed. "You said, Godfrey Hall?"

Isabella nodded. "My family's home." She wondered why the man was staring at her in an unusual way.

Mauger's usually upbeat manner changed to one of reserve. He lifted a hand to his brow. "Last time I was in this place, I told you my name was Mauger of the Moors. Did you look into my family's history after I left?"

"I did not. I had not the time or energy. Why?" Blysse gave him a questioning look. She pointed to the hearth behind them. "I have the shoes my husband made. I can get them for you."

Mauger nodded. He watched her cross the room and take the pair of large, leather shoes in her hands, bringing them back with her. Both girls stepped out onto the porch to speak with him.

Blysse's smile was wide. "I don't know the price, but am thinking you're a fair man. We can use the money, until we know what we're doing. We've been keeping them in this safe place for you."

Mauger's brow softened. He pulled a pouch from his green woolen jacket and counted out coins to match the cost of the shoes.

Isabella smiled. "Darkness is closing in. You should get a decent room at an inn soon, but that's on the other side of town."

He nodded. "Here, this should be the right amount." And then he slid a couple extra of his coins into their hands.

Isabella's eyes sparkled. "Thank you, sir. We have not eaten for so long. You do not understand what this means to us."

Mauger suddenly looked puzzled. He leaned closer to Isabella, scrutinizing her face more closely.

Isabella took a step back. "Why do you look at me so? What do you see, sir?"

Mauger seemed curious. "Who were your mother and father? Your violet eyes are much like someone I knew, and your voice, I feel as if I've heard it before."

Blysse rolled her eyes. "She's nothing like mother and father. And we've no desire to speak of them."

Isabella sighed, reluctant to answer. "Our father was Alward of London, and our mother, Muriolda, daughter of William. There is no one in my family with my color eyes."

"Muriolda? She's your mother?" Mauger took his felt hat from his head and held it in his hand.

Isabella swallowed. "You knew her?" She blushed and turned away. She hoped he wasn't judging her from what he knew of her parents.

Mauger took her arm. "I did, but do not think poorly of you. She was my sister."

Blysse gulped, realizing this man was her uncle. She quickly backed away. "I suddenly do not feel so well," she said. "Sister?"

Isabella went to her side and took her hand. "Blysse?"

Blysse put her hand to her chest and crouched down. "My heart. I find it difficult to breathe." Her words came in gulps. "Please, pray for me. It is that dark feeling that haunts me."

Isabella bent down and took Blysse's arm. She closed her eyes. "Father in heaven, take this from her. In Jesus precious name, let her remember that you're with her."

Blysse took a breath, still struggling to breathe, yet her expression grew less anxious. She got back up, steadying herself against the table, lifting the pouch and handing it to Isabella. "I can

151

breathe again, and my heart is slowing." She stood to full height, collecting herself and lifting her chin. "It is better."

Then she turned to Mauger. She spoke calmly, yet there was an edge to her voice. "We do not want your money, sir. I'd die before I'd take money from you. Give it to him, Isabella."

Isabella frowned. "But, Blysse, we're in need of it very badly." They had used their last coin. They'd be out on the streets without this money. Tears formed in Isabella's eyes, and she rubbed them away.

Blysse pursed her lips. Her cheeks were flaming. "But, he's our mother's brother. We cannot keep it." She grabbed the pouch from her sister and thrust it at Mauger.

He didn't take it from her, but shook his head. "But miss, your mother didn't speak to me for many years. I regret that she treated you poorly." His brown eyes softened.

Blysse studied him warily. "It matters not." She waved her hand nonchalantly. "Anyway, they hold no power over anyone, and can do no more harm, dead of the plague, getting what they deserved." She watched for his reaction.

"I didn't know this." He looked solemn. His eyes became moist.

Blysse took a step back, contrite. She cupped a hand over her mouth. "I'm sorry. I should not have brought this news to you in such a way. She was your sister."

Mauger sighed. "You've done nothing untoward. It pains me to hear this, but my sister and I were never close."

"Well, I am truly sorry." Then, her lips drew into a pout. "But, do not think poorly of me. They've wronged my sister and I sorely, and I cannot forgive as easily as Isabella can."

She lifted her chin, her eyes flashing. "I know I must, but am not ready for it, yet. Forgiveness must be done with a sincere heart."

Mauger's mood seemed to lighten. He smiled. "You're right in saying this."

Isabella eyed the small cross, embroidered on the him of his robe, and pointed to it. "You have made a commitment as a believer?"

Mauger nodded. He eyed her curiously. "One of the monks living near my home is my good friend. He helped me understand what walking with God meant." His gentle crinkling eyes sparkled when he said it. "I have learned we rarely take the popular route, but one that leads down the path he sets out for us."

Isabella regarded him curiously. "It's good to know. I hope my mother and father found the same peace in the end."

He sobered. "If they'd asked for it, even in their last hour, they surely would have been forgiven."

"I believe this too, sir, with all my heart and have spent my lifetime in prayer for them." Isabella smiled, and then turned to her sister. "Our uncle is a good man, Blysse. I hope that you can see it."

"He may be, but is also a relation of the worst kind." She put her hands on her hips and tapped her toe on the hard ground beneath her.

"And yet, he helped you when Alan died." Isabella smiled again.

Blysse flinched. "Oh, Isabella, you're too trusting. You always believe everything people say." And then she sighed. "But, you are right in saying that he offered help to me when I most needed it. I cannot forget his kindness to me the day I lost Alan. This is true."

"It was. You told me about what he did." Isabella moved to the window and looked out. She watched Friar Dixon bending down to take a small child's hand and help him up from the street. "He took care of all the arrangements for you concerning Alan, and came back for the shoes." Her eyes lightened at the thought of it.

Mauger smiled, and then he extended his hand to Blysse. "I suppose you've earned the right to be suspicious. Yet, I will not treat you in an unkind way. I did not return to inflict more pain on you or your sister, but to offer my support."

Blysse tipped her head in a show of consent. She put out her hand for Mauger to take. "I'll give you a chance, because it's true that you have proved yourself on more than one occasion."

Mauger grinned. "I hope so, because after having spent time in your company, I'm sure that we are blood relations, now. There is no denying it. It was no coincidence, but surely an act of God that brought us together."

And then he tipped his hat to them. "My full name is Mauger Godfrey of the Moors. But, you both may call me Uncle Mauger."

The sun came out from behind a cloud and lit the walls around them.

Isabella smiled. My sister's name is Blysse, and I'm Isabella. We're twins, if you can believe it, fraternal."

He seemed surprised. "I would not have guessed it."

Mauger was suddenly curious. "So you must tell me. How are your Uncle Stewart and Aunt Bela faring in London?"

"Uncle Stewart? Aunt Bela?" Isabella tipped her head to the side, a puzzled look drawing over her face. "I did not know them. Did you, Blysse?" This was certainly an interesting piece of information. Maybe her Uncle Mauger would reveal to them other family members they were unaware of.

Blysse let out a breath. "We do not know these relations." She looked perturbed.

"It was your Aunt Bela who had your eyes, Isabella. She looked much like you. I have a portrait of her at my home I would like to show you."

Isabella lifted her hands to her cheeks. "Oh, I wish I could've met her." She could not imagine. Neither, her father or mother resembled her. Blysse at least had some of their mother's traits. She hoped she'd get to see the portrait at least once.

"You would've liked her. She was sweet." Mauger could not seem to take his eyes from Isabella, as if he were seeing a ghost. "Forgive me. But, the resemblance is uncanny. I definitely can see my older sister in you."

Isabella suddenly swayed, grabbing Blysse's arm. "Oh my." She caught herself and quickly sat down on a chair at her side. "I feel faint."

Blysse look was one of concern. "Are you well, Isabella?"

"I believe I am tired. I must rest a while."

"And eat, after I find you some food." Blysse let out a pained breath.

Mauger Godfrey went to Isabella and knelt beside her. "My dearest girl, I regret taking so much of your time. You need both a meal and rest. Please allow me to provide food for you, and then we will see about a coach to carry you to my home. I've a large manor with many rooms. You are welcome there."

"To stay?" Blysse looked confused. "You mean for the night?"

Mauger laughed. "No, my girl. It is not what I meant. I'm your uncle, your close relation. I could never leave my own flesh and blood suffering in a place such as this."

Isabella took his hand and kissed the top of it. "Oh, sir! We've no more coins left, other than what you brought. You have no understanding of what this means to us."

"Remember, you must call me uncle. I will take you to the inn where I'm staying this very hour and get you something to eat, but, we best be going."

Isabella beamed. "God surely brought you to us, the answer to our very prayers." A tear slid down her cheek, and she wiped it away.

Blysse smoothed out her skirt, the rosy glow in her cheeks returning. "I'm sorry, uncle, for doubting you. The fact that God placed you here at this moment is surely a sign. I must give concession to that."

Mauger laughed heartily, his brown eyes twinkling. "It is true. None of it was of our making. It never is."

He looked at them both, concerned, as if suddenly noticing the gauntness of their expressions and the paleness in their cheeks. "Now, I must get you fed and give you some proper attire, suiting your station as my nieces. And I must learn in time, how you found your way to Cropton."

Isabella nodded. "We thank you, uncle, and will tell you both our stories along the way."

Mauger paid the owners the money due them, and they left the place, without turning back for a last glance, with the promise that they'd leave Cropton for good. He made it understood that in the morning he planned to take them to his town in the Moors, a few miles south. Tomorrow, they'd be on a different path to another home, one with food to sustain them and a roof over their heads providing shelter, more than they ever dreamed.

God had surely answered their prayers, and they were grateful.

*****

# Chapter 12

Isabella twirled in her light blue, damask gown in the solar room and dropped onto the bed on her back. Her hair fanned out on the mattress around her. She studied the dark beams above her that created stripes across white ceiling and the two massive, central ones that arched overhead dropping to the floor.

"Blysse, it's lovely here! It is so beautiful in this place, and Uncle Mauger even has a bower room to eat in, away from the great hall." She felt as if she'd been taken to heaven, after coming from the dirty, broken down room they were living in.

Blysse stood in front of a long, oval mirror set in a stand, while combing out her hair. She eyed her new outfit, a red silk gown with a flared skirt and jacket to match. She patted rose water on her neck, smelling the sweet scent upon her skin.

She laughed. "I cannot believe that merely days ago, we were almost starving. I will not forget how it was for the peasants. I hope to help them, after knowing what I do. We merely suffered a short time, while some suffer over the course of their lives."

Isabella sat upright, a grave look on her face. "I hope we can make Uncle Mauger understand this. We can't give away what's not ours."

Blysse set her comb on a dresser next to the mirror, walked over to the bed and sat down next to Isabella. "We can ask him."

"Yes, and we will. You were saying before, you were going to walk around the grounds? After I speak to Uncle Mauger, maybe we can go together?"

Blysse nodded. "Yes, let's go see him now. I'm interested to see the bower room."

Isabella got up and picked up her matching blue jacket from the bed, slipping it on. She attached a dark blue veil to her head, letting it flow down her back. Never before had she appreciated the comforts of living in a manor, as much as she did now. They were blessed in so many ways, and she'd never forget what her uncle had done for them.

They walked down the hall, past whispering servants, and into the bower room where they found their uncle sitting on a low bench before a great fireplace.

He looked up when they entered the room, the edges of his eyes crinkling at the corners when he saw them. "Isabella! Blysse! It is good so to see you! Come in!"

Both of them stepped across the grey, stone floor and took a seat on a carved wooden bench next to him.

Isabella smoothed out the delicate fabric of her gown,. It was so much softer than the homespun cloth they'd been wearing, which had been rough on her skin. She was still unable to get over the fact that this was their home, and they'd never have to go hungry or be forced to beg ever again, as long as their uncle was the owner.

Isabella admired the surroundings. The dark wooden doors, carved with a cross design on each, opened from the inside, near an intricately designed, rectangular wooden table.

Despite the space in the room, the massive, red circular rugs and crackling fire gave it a feeling of warmth and hominess.

She spoke up. "Uncle, I'm reticent to ask, but, do you have any books around your home?" She hadn't seen a library, but surmised there was one here. She'd never been able to read from the ones in her father's library, as he kept the door locked when he wasn't in the room. She guessed her uncle might be more lenient towards them, and allow her the privilege.

Mauger was curious. "What for? You could not possibly read them?"

Isabella looked at the floor, worried what he would think. "My little brother, Henry; he taught me without my father knowing." She blinked, a rose color setting in her cheeks.

Mauger laughed, shaking his head. "Is your sister able to read, also?"

Blysse's expression was one of mirth. "I'd prefer to experience living, rather than sitting with a book. Henry taught me also, and I can read, yet I've little time."

Isabella nodded. "She reads quite well, yet loves horses, and I'm sure would enjoy a brisk ride across the moors. She is an excellent rider."

Mauger smiled. "Then you will take Spook, our black mare. You will enjoy her."

Blysse's eyes began to well up with tears, but she wiped them away quickly. "I would like that."

"Good." Mauger turned to Isabella. "And, I must say, I do have some of the Holy Scripture for you to read. For Blysse too, if she so desires."

"The Scriptures! Oh, yes. So rare to possess, but necessary. I'll treasure reading them." Isabella's face lit.

Blysse turned. "I'll do this, also, for it is as Isabella said, necessary."

All three looked up when a young servant girl came into the room. "Pardon me, sir. You've a visitor." She waited to see what Mauger would say.

He gestured to the door. "Guests! Don't let them wait, by all means."

The servant girl smiled and left, appearing a few seconds afterward. "Sir Matheu of Thorneton Le Dale, sir."

Isabella's eyes widened when Matheu came through the door with a young girl at his side. He quickly surveyed the room, his eyes moving from Mauger to Blysse, and finally resting on her. Although his brow lifted slightly, years of training kept him constrained, disclosing little emotion. "Isabella? What are you doing here?"

Isabella's cheeks warmed, and she smiled, her heart racing at the thought of him addressing her with such familiarity. "'Tis a story, sir, and when time warrants, I would be glad to share with you." She was both surprised and pleased to see him, and yet after the brief encounter with Dauit on the road, she could not be sure how he felt about her.

Blysse stared at them both, suddenly curious. She nudged Isabella on the shoulder, none to gentle. "You knew him? The one at the fair? And you kept this information to yourself?"

Isabella brushed a stray strand of hair aside. An anxiousness welled up inside her. She'd no clue what Matheu's true feelings for her were, even though she cared for him deeply. She feared what her sister would say. "I was in need of assistance. He helped me on the way to Cropton."

Blysse studied her sister closely, a wicked sparkle in her eye. "You knew him, yet kept it to yourself, and would not look up during the competition." She suddenly smiled saucily, a twinkle in her eye.

Isabella's voice was constrained. She shook her head. "I did not watch, because I do not relish the joust. I never did." She smoothed out the folds of her skirt, fidgeting with her hands, a faintness overcoming her.

Blysse laughed. "Oh, my dear girl. So, this is why things happened as they did." She tilted her head to the side. Her eyes began to dance. "And you're blushing."

A curious expression crossed Matheu's face, and his eyes softened as they met Isabella's large violet ones, which stirred with discomfort.

Blysse laughed again. "You should have told me the reason you did not wish to marry Dauit."

Isabella drew in a short, quick breath. "Blysse!" She cringed inwardly, hoping her sister would stop, while she was ahead. "I told you, Matheu assisted me when I needed help. You must not be so forward, sister."

A slight smile twitched at the corner of Matheu's mouth.

Blysse nudged Isabella on the shoulder, taking a turn about the room. "What was father's name for me...gate of the devil? You do not remember?" She grinned wickedly.

The young girl standing next to Matheu pursed her lips, as if she didn't like the direction the conversation was taking. She didn't say anything. Her eyes were stony and cool.

Isabella shook her head. "Oh, Blysse..." A smile found it's way onto her face.

Mauger chuckled. He turned to Matheu. "So you *do* know, Isabella?"

"I do," Matheu nodded. "She found herself in more than one distressing situation in her travels, and I was obliged to help her. It was my pleasure to spend time in her company."

Blysse put her hand to her mouth, holding back a smile.

Mauger scratched the top of his head. "So, you were not aware of the connection she had to my family?"

"I knew she was Alward of London's daughter, yet had no idea you had family connections with them."

"I see." He went to the fireplace and added another log to it, stirring the coals beneath with a poker. "Well, I only found out yesterday that they are my nieces. Alward's wife was my sister."

"So, they'll stay here?" Matheu eyed Mauger with interest.

"For as long as they choose."

"I'm glad you found them. It seems to be an act of God himself."

"Yes, and they're both safe. Wolfhart was after them, but died of the plague along the trail, so both sisters are hindered by him, no longer."

"I see." Matheu looked pleased with this new piece of information.

A warm feeling settled over Isabella. For a brief second, she caught a soft look in his eyes, before she turned away.

Mauger shook his head. "I do believe this wasn't a coincidence to have met up with them. When I found out both young women were from Godfrey Hall in London, and I saw Isabella's eyes the same color as my sister's, I knew at once what they were telling me was the truth. No one else I knew had the same eyes and sweet voice."

He got up from his chair and went to a painting on the sidewall. "It's here, Isabella, the painting I spoke of."

Isabella got up and went to stand next to her uncle. She let out a sound when she saw the woman's likeness. It could've been her. "I see what you mean."

Matheu agreed. "The resemblance is uncanny. I've never noticed the painting before."

"It is true," Mauger answered.

Then, Mauger motioned to one of the seats in the room nearest Matheu. "Could you stay? For a visit? We would enjoy it very much."

Matheu sighed, as if deeply chagrinned. He had an apologetic look on his face. "I cannot. The reason I came, was to bring the girl here."

Isabella eyed the young woman, who was staring at Matheu with rapt attention, a smile playing on face. She wondered if the girl was relation of Matheu.

"What do you need?" Mauger looked concerned. "Maybe I can be of assistance."

"This is Hawise Ellis. She was being beaten at the place where she was living. I bought her from the lord of the manor, to get her out of there. She is in need of assistance."

"So, how might I help?"

Matheu sighed. "The plague's hitting the town of Thorneton Le Dale, and there are some in my manor who were recently stricken with it, my mother included. I was warned to stay clear, so have not been there, yet. Luckily, when I got back from the tournaments, I found Hawise had not been exposed. I thought I'd bring her here, for her safety."

Mauger nodded. "So, what will you do?"

"I must return to care for my mother. One of the villains is caring for her, until I return."

Isabella's eyes grew wide, but she refrained from speaking.

Mauger got up from his chair and paced the floor. "We can keep Hawise here. I understand that you must tend to your mother."

Matheu nodded solemnly. He took the Hawise by the shoulders. "You wait, and when the plague's over, I'll check on you."

She pleaded with him. "But, you must not go, Sir Matheu. You might contract that plague, and then who will care for me?"

Matheu patted her cheek and smiled. "My mother's sick, Hawise. Mauger will tend to you, and I will return when this is over."

Hawise fell into his arms, holding him tightly. "But, if you fall sick to this horrible disease, sir?"

Matheu pulled her arms from him and wiped the tears spilling out over her cheeks. "When the Lord wills it, it will happen, but not before then. Mauger will care for you, and you'll have his nieces here to keep you company."

The young girl sniffed. Her lips tightened, as she gave Isabella a sullen look.

162

Isabella's Shield

Isabella eyed the girl curiously, wondering at her relationship with Matheu.

Matheu handed Hawise to Mauger, who held her hand tightly. "I will watch over her for you, and Isabella and Blysse will spend time with her."

Matheu stared out the window. He seemed reluctant to resume his task. "You must keep the main gate closed. And do not allow anyone in or out until you have word that plague has run its course in town. If I find myself ill, I will send Gawain or a friend to inform you of it."

Mauger nodded solemnly. "We'll be waiting for you to come back."

Matheu dropped his hand to his side, then turned to Isabella, whose complexion was pale. "Say prayers, as I'll need them."

Isabella nodded. Words were caught in her throat, and she was unable to speak. She remembered how Matheu carried the young baby who had been exposed to the plague, so it might be that he was resistant to it. It killed so many people, yet not every person was affected.

She wished she could go to him, as Hawise had, but it wouldn't be proper. She was forced to wait and see if he came back for her.

Matheu sent her an encouraging smile. "I'll come back, m'lady, and see you, again."

Isabella smiled back. "I'd like that very much."

Hawise's eyes narrowed and she fixed them on the object of her consternation. While Matheu's back was turned, she shot Isabella a glance that could snap a drawbridge, then pursed her lips and went to the window to look out.

Isabella turned; fixing her eyes on the man she'd formed an attachment to. An ache settled deep inside her at the thought of him leaving. She reached up to wipe the moisture forming in her eyes. It pained her to think of him being near those with the Black Death all around.

Matheu's expression mirrored Isabella's. He eyed her tenderly, and hesitated, but then turned away.

They all watched, as the door closed behind him.

Isabella took the Holy Scripture from Mauger and excused herself to the solar room to lie down on the bed and read. Her prayers that night were longer than she'd ever had prayed before, and it was late into the night before she was able to fall to sleep in faith that God would protect Matheu, his mother and Gawain.

Isabella drew her strength from verses she read from her Uncle Mauger's book, speaking of God's peace in the midst of trials, and his love for his followers.

*****

# Chapter 13

It had been weeks since Matheu had visited the manor. Isabella looked out a tall rectangular window in the great hall and checked the gate again. No rider.

She said a silent prayer.

She reached across the table and took a playing piece from a checkered game board and jumped over Hawise's piece with it. She clutched the black chess piece she'd jumped and set it to the side of the board. "You're still winning, but maybe this time I've a chance."

"None, from what I can see, with the wit you lack." Hawise tipped her head back, her eyes narrowing slightly. She looked as if the game they played was an annoyance to her.

Isabella sighed. She tucked her legs up underneath her on the chair. "Tis unkind to say such a thing."

The room echoed with an edgy silence. The dark wood in carved designs on the stark white ceiling and massive beams were the only measure of warmth in the large, empty room. There was no fire lit upon the grate.

Hawise's brown eyes widened with feigned innocence. She reached out and took a piece off the board and smiled. "I meant no harm. Do you want the truth, or should I hide my true thoughts?"

Isabella let out a short breath. "I merely wish for us to be friends."

"I'm playing this." Hawise pointed to the game they were playing. "You could be grateful."

Isabella got up and went back to the window. She looked out again, her eyes fixed on the gate.

Hawise followed suit and stood next to her. Her brown eyes slanted upward. "Matheu has plans for him and I, when he returns. Marriage to him should not be far off."

Isabella didn't reply, tired of this girl's antics.

Hawise smiled, her brown eyes glinting. "When he rescued me, he made it clear to me. I'm near fifteen now."

Isabella turned quickly. "I don't believe he would give you that impression."

"His mother showed me the dress she wore when she married his father." Hawise lifted her silky tresses behind her again and leaned against the sill of the window, stretching confidently.

Isabella tilted her head sideways. "Have you prayed to know God's will?"

Hawise frowned. "I'm sure Matheu has, because he believes in it, but I haven't."

Isabella wondered. It was not uncommon for a girl to be married at the age of sixteen. Hawise *was* unusually pretty.

Isabella's heart skipped a beat. Weeks ago, when Matheu learned she was going to marry Dauit, would he have made a proposal to this girl?

"Did he ask?"

Hawise let go of the windowsill, not answering immediately. Her lips tightened. She turned to Isabella, a dark look quickly replaced with narrowed eyes and a smile. "Of course he did. Were you aware of the pains he took when he brought me here?"

Isabella remembered the last moments at the door before he left. She recalled him taking special care with the girl. She shook her head. She couldn't imagine such a thing. "When was it?"

Another pause. "Merely weeks ago. After the last fair in Cropton."

Isabella took hold of the window ledge. She looked out over the valley, and her eyes rested on a bronze cross on the top of a church that glinted in the sunlight. Surely, Hawise's faith in God would matter to Matheu. "Do you share his beliefs?"

"I would go to the church with him, but have none of it. Not the way the hypocrites in that place carry on."

Isabella turned back to Hawise. "Those who struggle, go there, because they are not perfect. And surely none are good, but God."

"Ha! Tell that to them." Hawise sneered. "I've seen the way they profess to be holier than thou, and then turn around and do the opposite." She took quick steps across the room, reaching for the

Isabella's Shield

chessboard and pushed the rest of the game pieces off and onto the table.

Isabella watched her, sighing. "You judge them harshly."

"Not true! Tis them that do it, not I!"

Isabella's expression softened. "I did not mean to offend."

"Yet, you have a way of it."

"Well, it was unintended, and I'm sorry for it."

Hawise let out a snort. "I'm tired of all this useless chatter." She threw up her hands and crossed the room, stalking out the doorway.

Hawise's gown swished down the hallway. Her quick footsteps eventually faded out of hearing.

Isabella went back to the window for the third time and looked out over the moors. A mist covered the purple clad meadows, obscuring her view. She was tired of waiting for news from the outside world about the Black Plague and afraid of what she might find out when it was all over. Her prayers at this moment seemed to fall on deaf ears.

Her mind drifted back to what God had done for her each time she felt herself in an impossible situation. She suddenly remembered his constant care and presence.

She decided, that whether Matheu came back to her or not, she'd trust that God's will was being done.

Her eyes fastened on a beautiful swatch of purple heather next to the house. A bright ray of sunshine suddenly broke through the clouds, lighting the patch of flowers, intensifying the color to a brilliant hue. Radiant, was the only word she could use to describe it. It was surely a sign that God was all around her and around Mathieu, too. She'd keep praying.

Isabella twirled a piece of her hair around her finger and then let go. Godhuwe had been insistent Isabella utter prayers about everything, listening for the right direction to go and following the path God set for her, the narrow one, that few followed. Could she continue on it? Could she draw upon God's strength?

She lifted her silken skirt in her hands and made her way across the stone floor through the arched wooden doorway to her room.

She'd pray for Hawise.

Isabella made her way down the hallway toward the bower room and shook her head. His path was definitely was not easy. And yet, it always seemed to be about love.

*****

A few days later, Isabella sat in the Bower room at a desk, lifting a quill pen from a bowl of ink, resting it against a thin piece of tree bark. She began to write.

14 July 1349

Dear Angnes,

I am sending this to find out how you're faring in the midst of these dark times. When you hear what's in this letter, I hope to find you and Godhuwe well and happy, even amidst this ghastly plague. It appears to be dying out, yet we're waiting for word of its end.

I want you to know that both Blysse and I are doing well, despite the many hardships faced. Alan died before I got to Blysse's place, and that's when we met my Uncle Mauger. We're living with him at his manor. He's a very good man, and we're both very happy with him. I feel this place has become more of a home to us than any other.

God's been good to us, as the Black Death came to this town, yet it has passed us by, and we have not been harmed. It's difficult to be cut off from the world for so long, yet, I'm glad we are safe for now.

I've seen Sir Matheu of Thorneton Le Dale. He's a friend of my Uncle Mauger. He's caring for his sick mother who contracted the Black Death, and said he would let us know when the sickness in town was over. It's been months, and we're still awaiting his return.

My feelings for him are strong, yet I'm praying for God's will in regards to him. A young girl, Hawise Ellis, has informed me that he asked her for her hand in holy matrimony. She's very pretty, yet possesses a sullen and moody personality. I am not sure if she has told me the truth.

A servant disclosed to me that he would transport this letter for a great price. He seems to be immune from the Black Death, as he's not contracted it, despite being around those with it. He'll bring a letter here, if you're able to find someone to write it for you.

I hope all of you are well. I'm also hoping to hear from you in time. I think of you kindly and will wait for your reply.

Yours faithfully,
Isabella of the Moors

Weeks later, a return letter was slipped into her hand. Isabella quickly carried it with her to the solar room and lay down on the bed. Carefully opening it up, she smoothed out the edges of the note and began to read.

29 July 1349

My Dearest Isabella,

I hope this letter reaches your ears in good time. I was so very happy to hear from you. Theobald Gray read your letter to me. I'm glad to know that both Blysse and you are in good hands and are being treated well.

The Black Death was hitting our town hard, but the sickness is over. I'm sad to tell you that Leofwin was sick of the plague and died merely a month ago. Osbert was also stricken with the Black Death, yet God spared him. I've seen none other than him surviving this horrible death, after they've contracted it. It's been like no other tragedy.

Godhuwe and I didn't catch it, so we helped others in their distress. We're beholden to God for keeping us from it.

I came upon a man named Hereward Walker, and we talked. When he knew I was from Godfrey Hall, he told me he was searching diligently for you and your sister. I was glad to get your letter, so I could tell him where you were. You might see him. He's a good man.

I believe it is not a coincidence that you've seen Matheu again. I am sure God has a plan for you in regards to him. I cannot believe Matheu would show interest in Hawise Ellis, other than to offer her support. It seems as if she is young. I'll keep you in my prayers regarding the matter. Do not forget that God has a path set for your life, and his way is always best. Ask him to show you it.

I must end this letter and am hoping you'll get it in a timely manner. Maybe someday, we'll meet up again.

Yours Truly,
Angnes of Malton


Isabella read the letter a couple of times before she folded it and slid it back into the envelope. Tears spilled onto her cheeks. Leofwin! He was dead, having endured the horrible symptoms of the Black Death. She wiped her cheeks and lay down on her bed, a intense pain striking her chest. She put her hand on her heart, holding it there, a sadness enveloping her.

That night, while the others slept, she lay looking up at the ceiling thinking of Matheu. He hadn't returned or sent a message. She wondered what could be delaying him, and whether he'd survived the sickness ravaging the land and their town.

She closed her eyes and lifted her hands clasping them together and began to pray. Maybe another day and they would see him back at the manor safely.

\*\*\*\*\*

# Chapter 14

Blysse lifted her red satin skirt and skipped down the flowered path leading to the main gate of the manor, anxious for word from town. From the great stone hall, she spotted a rider in the distance and was curious to know who it was and what he could possibly want.

Her Uncle Mauger had very few servants who chose to stay within the confines of the walls for the long months of quarantine, so there was no gatekeeper.

She called out, "Uncle! A visitor. He's at the gate!" But, she was loath to wait for him to come open it, as they'd had so few guests.

As she neared the heavy, thick wooden door, she heard horse hooves on the other side slow to a stop.

Her uncle yelled back from the arched doorway of their home. "Go ahead! Open it! It's a good friend!"

Isabella and Hawise both peered through the windows of the manor house.

Blysse pulled on the great iron latch, but quickly found it difficult for her to budge. She yanked harder. "Awk! It's stuck!" She tried again and found it fastened tightly. After a couple more futile attempts, the strength in her arms was beginning to wane, so when she wasn't getting the results she wanted, she resorted to kicking the door with her foot.

"Ouch!" She whimpered, enough for the sound to carry over the wall.

She heard horse hooves prancing in their spot, and then, a hearty laugh resound on the other side. She rolled her eyes. The nerve of the black-hearted cur. "Sir? If I'm not able to open this, you do understand, you will not be coming through."

The man let out another amused sound, and she could hear him getting down from his horse.

Mauger called to her again. "Do you need help, dear girl?"

"No! I can get it, uncle!" She grabbed the latch, again and yanked, struggling. The bolt was still strongly in place and wouldn't move. She beat upon it with her fist. "By the blessed monk! It won't open!"

The man's laughter on the other side deepened, and Blysse's dark eyes narrowed. "Sir, if I do get it, whoever you are, you will surely regret your poor manners, when we finally meet!"

The man's mirth was curtailed for the moment, as if he'd covered his mouth with his hand. "I'm sorry, miss. I suppose I must be minding you then, so that I do not face grave consequences."

Blysse's mouth curved up into a smile. "Which might be very grave, indeed."

He spoke again, this time in a low tone. "I might divulge a small secret concerning this particular gate to you. Might I share it, to lessen your struggle?"

His voice held a certain charm, and Blysse could imagine a slightly roguish gentleman on the other side. She lamented, letting out a short breath. "You might've told me this a time ago."

He chuckled quietly to himself. "Push the metal ring to the side, and then lift the latch. It'll work this way."

Blysse reached out and slid the ring to the side, and when she pushed the bar this time, it slipped open with ease. Her lips drew into a pout, as the wooden door swung free.

Her eyes widened, when she saw the tall, blonde-haired, blue-eyed man on the other side of the gate. "Dante?"

He whistled. "The pretty lady at the well? What're you doing here? I heard Mauger call you his niece?"

She bent down and brushed off her silken skirt and then put her hands on her hips, eyeing him curiously. "He did, because I am. He found my sister and I and took us in to live with him. It's a long story."

He grinned, his lip curving up on one side, revealing straight, white teeth. "So, you're the brute I feared when I was on the other side. I do remember you to be quite strong."

Blysse rolled her eyes. "You should watch yourself, sir. My uncle might not like it that you're using the term, brute, to describe his niece."

He took the felt hat from his head and swept it below his waist bowing low, a rascally grin on his face. "Pardon, m'lady. I regret calling you this. I'll not do it again, since I know now, who I'm dealing with."

She lifted her chin. "And it would be good to remember."

He laughed at that. "I suppose this is true."

Mauger Godfrey called from the house. "Dante! Blysse, show him in."

Mauger went inside, closing the door, and Isabella and Hawise disappeared from the window.

As they walked up the path toward the house, Dante reached out and touched a ribbon tied about Blysse's waist. "I rode back to Cropton to check on you, but couldn't find you anywhere."

Blysse nodded. "It wasn't long after, when my sister and I came here. I looked for you at the fair."

His eyebrow rose slightly. "I'm glad to see you well."

She stepped quickly along the path to keep up with his long stride. "Did you bring news of Sir Matheu? Is he well?"

He studied her face and then frowned. "You're interested in him?"

A grin stole over her face, and her eyes began to sparkle. "Very much so! He's a good man."

Dante scowled. "I brought news of him. But, you'll hear of it in the manor."

"So, he is well?" Her eyes slanted.

He reached for the door, holding it open. He had a perturbed expression on his face. "He didn't get the Black Death, if that's what you mean."

Blysse smiled, an impish look in her eye.

When they entered the house, Mauger was waiting in the great hall with Isabella and Hawise. They all looked up, when Blysse and Dante met them in the room.

Mauger spoke first. "I see you met my niece, Blysse."

Dante nodded. He didn't go into any explanation of their former relationship.

Mauger turned to the other two girls. "This is Blysse's sister, Isabella. And you know Hawise Ellis, Matheu's ward?"

Dante took each of their hands and bowed. "It's an honor to meet you Isabella, and I'm glad to see you again, Hawise."

"Did Matheu send news?" Mauger looked concerned.

Dante nodded. "He'll be here, shortly. He has matters of his estate to attend, before he could come, but is doing well."

Isabella looked relieved.

Dante sat on a chair across from Mauger.

All three girls took a seat on an opposite bench facing him.

"He said it is safe to go into town at this time. He knew your stocks were most likely running low." He looked around the room, as if noticing the scant amounts of supplies on the shelves.

Blysse let out a relieved sigh. She lifted her hands to her cheeks, her dark eyes sparkling. "Finally…we're free again!"

Mauger chuckled to himself. "Blysse is finding the limitations on her life exceedingly bothersome, and we are feeling her frustration."

"It is not difficult to see your niece is probably weighing on you." His blue eyes twinkled.

Blysse's lips drew into a pout, and she stood, walking to the window to look out. "I care little what others think." She lifted her chin. "I look forward to town and the shops again."

Dante drew his hand through his thick, sun-streaked hair, his eyes following Blysse's movements.

Isabella watched them curiously. Dante turned and smiled at her, winking and then looked back at Blysse again.

Mauger turned to them. "I'm merely happy we were able to live off the gardens and drink from the spring water on my land. Yet, there are things that are much needed we could get from town."

Dante shifted in his seat. "Yes, it's a relief it's over now, and we can go safely, yet many are dead. The Black Death killed off scores of people."

Mauger's look was one of concern. "How did Matheu's mother fare with the sickness?"

Dante's expression was sober. "She didn't. She died." He was turning and twisting the felt hat in his hands. "It's been difficult for Matheu."

174

Isabella closed her eyes. A hollow ache welled up inside her. She held back from replying.

Mauger expression was grim. "This is bad for him."

Dante nodded and quickly changed the subject, clearly not wishing to speak of the shocking details of this death and the plague itself.

He cleared his throat. "There is another thing I must mention, a man who told me he wished to speak to Isabella and Blysse about an important matter."

Blysse moved to the table, standing next to Dante. "Was it Hereward Walker?"

Dante nodded.

Dante eyed her curiously. "He wishes to disclose some very important details about your family, but could not share it with me. He had business in London to attend and hoped to meet the young women there."

"London?" Isabella's violet eyes grew large. "There? How will we know whether he is working for our cousin, Hastulf or not?"

Blysse shook her head. "Isabella, remember the dying man at the convent. You trusted him, and he told you to find Hereward. The man was never acquainted with our cousin. And Angnes said the same in the letter, that Hereward was a good man."

"Oh. I suppose you are correct in saying so. The man at the convent was dying, and I trust Angnes." She looked at Dante. "Did he say where he wanted us to meet?"

"At a tailor's shop on Threadneedle Street. He's taken a position as an apprentice and lives in the back of the shop. After the Black Death, there was a need for workers."

Blysse turned to Isabella. "We must go. It sounds very important."

Isabella eyed her uncle, as if uncertain as to the path they should take. "What should we do?"

Mauger leaned over the table and touched Isabella's hand. "I'd go if I were you, but not without help. I can ride along with you. I'm curious to know about this business that calls for you both to ride such a distance. I could carry you to London on my best horses, and put you up in good inns along the way. We'll take some servants and speak with this man."

A gray, striped cat jumped off the windowsill and onto the floor.  Isabella started slightly, watching it wander into the hallway.  The thoughts about going back home made her jumpy.  "That would be a help, uncle."

Dante shook his head.  "I'm not able go with you at this time, and Matheu will not, either.  We must finish business at our estates, first."

Blysse straightened, smoothing out her tunic and sniffed.  "It is not necessary that you come."

Isabella put her hand on Blysse's arm.  "And yet, we might wait for them."

Blysse shook her head.  "We'll be with Uncle Mauger and the servants.  We have both journeyed on this path before.  This time we'll have horses and good places to stay.  There is no need for anyone else to go with us."

Mauger smiled.  "We will do well enough, if we stay together."

Dante looked unsure.  "But, if you wait for Matheu and me, we'd assure your safety."

Blysse tapped the floor with her foot.  "I'm sure you would, but there is no need for it."

Dante shook his head, his cool, blue eyes meeting her fiery, dark ones. And then he smiled, eying her raised chin and crossed arms.  "Then you are certain, two knights for your protection, will serve you no purpose?"

Blysse's eyes sparked.  "I'm sure your service would be greatly appreciated, yet is not a necessity for what we plan to do."

Dante shook his head, and let out a breath as if defeated.  And then he laughed.  "Ha!  I'm sure you will fare well enough, regardless of the situation."

Mauger chuckled, his brown eyes twinkling.  "With the help of her Godfrey blood."

Blysse rolled her eyes, choosing not to answer.

Dante stood up.  "Well, I'll tell Matheu.  I hope you'll reconsider and wait; yet I can do nothing to stop you."  He tipped his head to them, his eyes resting on Blysse a few seconds longer.

They watched as Dante took his leave.

After he was gone, Hawise got up from her seat. A smile lit her face. "I've things to do as Matheu is free, now. I suppose I'll pack my things to get ready to go back to Matheu's manor."

Mauger took her by the elbow, his expression grave. "You must not, just yet." He looked pained. "I'm sure he'll need time to grieve for his mother. You stay here, until he's ready to make a decision. The house servants will see to your needs while we're gone."

Isabella nodded. "I believe you must listen to Mauger. I'm sure it will not be long before we're back."

Hawise's eyes narrowed. She pulled away from Mauger, giving him an annoyed look. "I suppose he will need time alone. But, it's no matter. I'm sure he'll visit before then, anyway."

"As I said before, you must wait until he is ready, and do not venture out to see him, until he is." Mauger was not usually impatient, yet with Hawise, he seemed to have difficulty hiding the fact that she was a strain on his sensibilities.

Hawise looked squarely at Isabella. "I'm sure it will be sooner, rather than later." Her brown eyes glowed.

It took all Isabella had, not to roll her eyes, but instead smile.

Hawise got up from her chair. "Now, I am feeling low in spirits. I must take to the solar room for a much needed rest. It'll surely offer the needed comfort."

"Rest easy." Isabella smiled kindly at her.

Hawise glowered, not responding. She took quick steps across the stone floor through the arched doorway, not looking back, disappearing down the long corridor, leaving Isabella, Mauger and Blysse to discuss their preparations for their upcoming trip.

They decided they'd leave on the morrow, so there'd be little time to change their minds. It would be a lengthy ride, but each of them knew it had to be done. They all were curious as to whom Hereward Walker was and what mystifying secret he held to the family's past.

*****

# Chapter 15

"You what?" Matheu took hold of the front of Dante's overcoat. "You told them it'd be all right to go without us?"

"It was impossible to keep them from going. They insisted on leaving suddenly." He pushed Matheu's hands off of him and dusted off his jacket.

"Isabella, also?"

"Well, she was not quick to agree to the plan at first, but accepted it well enough, after her sister convinced her it would not spell trouble for them. Mauger is sure to watch over them."

Matheu's face drained of color. He sat down on a bench and put his head in his hands. "I cannot believe you allowed them to leave with little protection."

Dante sighed. "They're with their uncle, and Hereward had no connection with anyone in London before he made his trip."

Matheu got up and began to pace. "But, Isabella's cousin is there, having inherited the manor. It might very well be a trap they are walking into."

Dante let out a breath. "I do not believe so."

Matheu shook his head. "Yet, if it is, you'll be sorry you sent them. And my plan was to propose to Isabella."

Dante turned. "Isabella?"

"Yes. She is the one I spent time with on the trail and the one at the dinner party."

Dante looked surprised. "I thought it was Blysse you admired greatly? She is not the one, you've been speaking of?"

Mathew turned, his eyebrows rising. "Isabella's sister?"

Dante nodded.

Matheu smiled. "Ha! I've no Viking in my blood. That woman would be too much of a trial for me."

Dante laughed. "It is true. And she is most definitely the one I've set my intentions on, the young lady I'll take to my manor, when she accepts my offer."

Matheu's eyes sparkled, and then quickly grew serious. "We must go to them. When did they leave town?"

"About four days ago. I could not come here directly to tell you." Dante looked chagrinned.

Matheu lifted his sword and chain mail off the chair next to him. "I cannot remain in this place, as the matter might not end well. I am leaving as soon as the horse is ready. Are you coming?"

Dante turned, taking his cloak in his hand. "I will, and I'm sure if we leave immediately, we'll get there about the same time they do."

Matheu looked out the window and then down the hallway. "I will send Gawain to placate Hawise. We'll travel light."

Dante nodded. " So we leave within the hour?"

"Maybe less than that. Pack your provisions and meet me at the stables. It would be best to catch them before they reach London."

\*\*\*\*\*

Gawain stood at the door of the manor sighing, not appreciative of the job of playing nursemaid to a young girl. He waited until the massive, wooden structure was opened by one of the servants.

"I'm here to check on the Lady Hawise." He shook the dust out of his red hair.

"This way, sir." The servant led him down a hall and into a spacious room.

Gawain limped on his bad foot, keeping up to the lengthy stride of the man. He stopped before the entrance to the room, ducking down to clear the doorway arch above him, his height making it difficult.

"Lady Hawise, you've a guest." The servant called to her.

"Sir Matheu!" Hawise turned quickly.

When she saw he wasn't him, her expression changed. Her eyes locked onto Gawain's.

Gawain watched her guardedly. She was a very pretty young woman, older than he'd imagined. Her rich, auburn hair trailed down her back, framing large brown eyes. He supposed more than one man had admired her unmistakable beauty. Yet, not unlike other ladies he'd met, she had a spoiled look about her. She scrutinized his dust-covered clothes.

He put his hands to his side, his weapon hugging him.

"Where's Matheu?" She appeared as if she were longing for news. Her nose turned up, and she eyed him with an eager expression.

Another admirer, he sighed. Matheu seemed to draw women to him like thieves to gold. "It's not your concern. I came to check on you."

Hawise lifted her chin. "He thought enough to send you here. He'd want you to tell me what his plan is."

"He would not care how much I impart to you."

Her eyes narrowed again. "You're merely a squire, and I'm his ward!"

"Hmm. A lowly squire, it's true. Except when Sir Matheu returns, he'll be making me a knight, and I'll inherit my own manor."

Hawise's brows knit together, and her voice softened. "I only wished to know where he went?" She lowered her lashes demurely, looking out the corner of her eye.

Gawain rolled his eyes. "Do not play games with me, miss. It will not work."

She scowled. "Then tell me, and I won't need to play games."

"It's no secret he left for London after Isabella." He let out a long, slow breath.

Hawise stalked over to where he stood, almost tripping over her long, green dress, struggling to right herself. "He didn't?"

His mouth turned up slightly on one side.

She stamped her foot. "You are jesting with me, sir."

"I've no reason to, as we've never met before this. Yet, Matheu did wish to see Isabella. And it will be good for you to know this, as it is apparent you are sweet on him and will be sorely disappointed when he returns." He snorted.

"Sweet?" She leaned in closer, poking a finger against his chest. "I am concerned for him."

Isabella's Shield

Gawain sighed. He braced himself for her reaction. "Then you will be happy to know that he is in no grave danger, and that he left for London to find Isabella and ask her to be his wife."

Hawise's voice rose an octave. "That is not the truth! He would not! You're lying!"

Gawain reached out to her. "Hawise…"

Her arm shot out and just missed slapping him in the face.

He grabbed her and held her steady. "You must stop this now and calm yourself, girl."

She railed at him. "Leave me be! Let go!" She tried to free herself from his hold.

Gawain let out a breath. Matheu would pay for leaving him to deal with this girl. "Stop, or you'll hurt yourself."

Hawise tried to wriggle out of his hold, but was unable. "Let go you idiot! You're wrong you know! He was going to make *me* his wife, not her!" She shoved at him and choked back a sob. "Matheu did not like her. I know this to be true."

Despite her tough exterior, Gawain could see the young woman was hurting. Hawise seemed to have little understanding of Matheu's intentions toward her, and it was likely she had few experiences with men. She must have confused Matheu's care for her with a suitor's love. His heart stirred at her cries. "Aw, Hawise, you cannot wish for such a thing. His attentions are elsewhere. He loves her."

She shook her head. "But, you're wrong. He does care for me! I know it." She pushed him away. "She's nothing to him!"

"I cannot let go. You are angry, and would not appreciate a fist in my face. I plan leave here intact."

She quit struggling. "Please. You've no need to worry."

He released her, taking her by the shoulders. "Isabella's a fine lady. She's done nothing to you. Matheu has had feelings for her for some time."

Her eyes began to fill with tears, and she looked up at him, as if seeing him for the first time. "But, he cannot."

"She's kind, and he had deep feelings for her from the first day they met."

181

Hawise frowned. "But, I'm kind, and I knew from the day Matheu took me from that awful place, he saw something in me. And I truly believe it was I, he intended to marry."

"Because he was kind to you, as Matheu has been, does not mean he intends marriage. I tell you, Matheu never had those intentions in regards to you. I know him. He is my friend." Gawain sighed, as if he wasn't sure what else to say.

Hawise sniffed. "Yet, I will wait for him, regardless of what you say."

Gawain shook his head. "This will change nothing."

She chose not to answer him.

"He cares for you, Hawise, but in a different way."

She turned and wiped at tears that had dropped onto her cheeks.

He reached out and smoothed back her hair, lifting her chin to look at him. "You're very pretty, and I'm sure he noticed this. But, Matheu sees more than the physical aspects. He also considers the heart."

"He saw nothing in mine?"

He sighed. "I'm sure he did, but there's more to it than that."

She cocked her head to the side, her tone less agitated. "What more?"

He suddenly looked as if he'd fallen in a moat and was searching for a way out. He rolled his eyes. "As in his beliefs, yet I do not believe you would wish to hear about them."

Hawise's eyes lit. "But I would. I want to hear what I have to say about them."

Gawain smiled wearily. "I'll help you understand these things, but you must know that Matheu's intentions will not change." He couldn't help feeling sorry for the young woman.

She turned toward him and reached out to extend a hand. "Oh, please. I'd be grateful."

Gawain took her hand in his, shaking his head slowly back and forth. He wondered how he might help her to see Matheu wasn't interested in her. How many trips to the manor might it take before she came to a realization and understanding in regards to this? What was he was getting himself into?

\*\*\*\*\*

# Chapter 16

The trip to London took weeks of traveling, yet Isabella found it was much easier to make time with good horses and agreeable accommodations. She was happy to have arrived in the city, and relieved to find an inn where they would be close to Threadneedle Street.

Standing in front of the tailor shop she hesitated, turning to Blysse and her Uncle Mauger. "Should I knock? Is this it?"

Both of them nodded.

A breath caught in her throat, as she raised her fist to the door and rapped on it.

There were footsteps inside, and a tall, thin man with graying hair opened the door, squinting at them. He bowed slightly, a wide brown, leather belt wrapped about his green tunic, sucking him in at the waist, revealing a slight paunch.

"You're Hereward Walker?" Blysse eyed him curiously.

"I am. Are you here for tailoring?"

When they didn't answer immediately, he leaned closer, inspecting the young women. Then, his eyes opened wide, as he looked from one to the other. "Blysse, Isabella, it is you! I'm sure of it!"

They nodded.

He put a thin finger to his lips and motioned for them to follow him into the back of the shop. "We must speak in another room." He stopped and turned, squinting at Mauger. "And who is this? A relation?"

Isabella nodded. "Our Uncle, Mauger of the Moors. He's been good to us."

Hereward bowed slightly to Mauger, his eyes somber. "You'll want to hear this, too. You can see to it the young lady's best interests are kept in mind."

Mauger tipped his head.

Blysse and Isabella took quick steps to keep up with Hereward's long, skinny legs. The green hose covering them made it look as if he had two long stems poking out beneath his belted tunic. He walked with a slight hunch. He took hurried strides, as if eager to impart to them the information he'd kept hidden for so long.

They entered a small room with two benches and a long table laden with scraps of fabric, patterns and scissors. A pincushion held needles of different sizes, and a glass jar containing buttons sat on the end. On the wall was attached a long, wooden dowel from which hung unfinished hose, hoods and tunics of various colors.

Hereward bowed again and extended his arm, pointing to the benches where Isabella, Blysse, and her uncle sat. They watched as he reached up under the table and pulled out a metal box.

There was a musty smell in the dark room, and the light was dim other than a thin ray of sun coming through the window. Hereward lit a candle and set it on a workman's table next to the container. He pried open the lid. The rusty hinges made a grating sound. "This is what I've kept for you, until you were seventeen." He pulled a solid brass key out of the metal container and placed it in Isabella's hand.

"The key." Isabella's voice was a whisper.

Hereward squinted, leaning closer to her. "I did not know you were aware there was one? How do you know this?"

Isabella sighed. "The last words of a dying man, Ailwin of Bedford, were 'Find Hereward...the key.' I didn't know what he meant by it."

Hereward gave her an interested look. "Ah, Ailwin, a good man. He knew this, as I did for many years. Ailwin and I were the only ones."

Hereward looked tired. "Well, it's time you learn the truth, also. But we must take a trip to Godfrey Hall. It's in the manor, where you'll find your answers."

Isabella sucked in a breath. "The manor?"

"Yes."

Blysse groaned. "If I have to lay eyes on that preposterous cousin of ours again, I'm not sure I wish to hear this. He had no right to our home."

Hereward put his hand up to dissuade her from leaving.

Isabella looked pained. "I have no desire to lay eyes on him, either, after dealing with Wolfhart."

185

"But, you must. There are four of us." Hereward leaned forward. "Hastulf will find he's not so important when he sees what this key reveals. And I would like to be there when it happens."

Blysse tilted her head. "So, this holds promise for us?"

"It does." Hereward smiled. "Hastulf may find himself in a predicament he is unaware of."

Blysse looked interested. "Maybe we *should* go. I would not mind watching our cousin deal with some troubles of his own."

Mauger smiled. "It might prove interesting."

"I suppose there is no one here who might consider this a bad idea?" Isabella's expression was one of reluctance.

All three of them looked at her with expressions that told her she'd get no further with them.

Instead, they shook their heads.

Isabella let out a breath. "Then it seems as if I will be forced to participate in this uncertain plan, and will find myself in the midst of another of your capers, Blysse, one that requires some prayer."

\*\*\*\*\*

# Chapter 17

Hawise flung the club with all her strength toward the wooden pins on the end of the worn path of grass, knocking over three of them. She jumped up and down. "I knocked some down, Gawain! I did it!" She twirled in the grass her gray silk skirt flaring out around her. Then, she lost her balance falling to the ground, laughing.

Gawain's eyes rolled back, and he shook his head. He limped over to where she was lying and offered his hand to her. "Get up."

Hawise took her hand in his. She tilted her head, studying him. "You must not be so serious, when we're playing a game."

Gawain stood there, not sure of what to say. He shook his head, eying her with reserve.

She watched his reaction and then suddenly giggled, a sparkle in her eye.

He pulled her off the ground, his mouth twitching at the corner. "I suppose you deserve some entertainment after being held captive in Mauger's manor for so long."

"It is true. All this waiting for Matheu is making me brain-sick."

"And you understand how I would answer to that."

"Well, at least when he's back, he'll see I've mended my ways."

Gawain nodded. "He will. Yet, you must give up on the idea of him as a suitor, as I believe God has other plans for you."

She tucked her hair behind her ear and looked up at him. "Are you going to set up the pins, again?"

He shook his head and smiled. "I'll do it once more."

He limped over to where the wooden pieces lay on their sides and set them back up. Then he pulled the club out of the midst of them and carried it back to her. "Here, make this one your best."

Hawise lifted the stick in her hand. Then, she thrust the club as hard as she could, catapulting it through the air toward the pins. All of them were blasted to the ground scattering across the grass.

Hawise let out a scream and tumbled into Gawain, nearly pushing him over. "I did it! I knocked all of them down! I knew it would not be long before I did."

He laughed, setting her away from him. "I suppose, you impress me at times. I must admit, it was a good toss."

Hawise smacked him on the arm playfully. "And it is good to see you laugh, which I rarely see. You might even be considered handsome, if you kept that hard look off your face."

Gawain's eyes rested on hers gently. "Laughter was uncommon in my childhood. And if I am correct, I believe your home life was not so different than mine, and you might know why I am reserved.

Hawise studied him thoughtfully. "I do. Yet, I have learned to put things in the past where they belong."

"I suppose it is a good thing." His eyes were solemn.

Hawise placed her hands on her hips. "There you are, again." She reached out and quickly poked him in the ribs, and then ran away toward the manor, giggling and half tripping over her long, leather shoes and gown.

Gawain followed her across the yard. A slight smiled tugged at the corners of his mouth as he watched her run down the path to the house. She half-floated up the steps to the manor and turned back laughing, as she opened the door and slipped through.

He let out an exasperated sound and then smiled to himself while he carried the pins with him to the house.

During the time he spent with Hawise, he was pleasantly surprised to find some admirable qualities she kept hidden beneath her spoiled exterior. Under the mask she wore, he found she possessed a penchant for others who suffered, was quick to learn, and had a considerate heart for the servants working at the manor. She was also protective of those she loved.

She revealed to him how she had good reason to look after herself as a child with the way she was treated. And from his disillusioned childhood, Gawain understood what it meant to lose trust in people.

He couldn't deny he had a penchant for this young women's soft chestnut hair and almond eyes. Yet, more often than not, Gawain began to feel something in his heart for her, after learning her vulnerable side, full of tenderness for others. It made him hope for her to see him as more than just a friend.

*****

# Chapter 18

Isabella took a seat next to her sister and her Uncle Mauger on a long bench in the Great Hall. Hereward was hunched over a table in the center of the room. He tapped his fingers on its wooden surface.

Childhood memories haunted Isabella as she eyed the massive hall. She studied the large candlelit chandelier hanging from the ceiling in the room. Despite the ornate furniture, exquisitely designed tapestries, and heavy Persian rugs spread out on the floor, the place felt empty and hollow.

A cold draft swept through the arched doorway when Roldan, the scar-faced knight who was one of the few remaining staff still guarding Godfrey Hall, entered with Hastulf. Isabella tugged her gray jacket tighter around her and shivered.

A servant man called to them. "Lord Hastulf and Sir Roldan." He bowed low and backed out of the room.

Isabella sighed. Her cousin hadn't changed. He was dressed in a fanciful velvet tunic and wearing the same smug look. He was still the young, insolent man who she'd left months ago.

He refused to look at her or Blysse, instead turning to Hereward. "It's been some time since I've seen you, sir. It's puzzling to me, as to why you're here, and why you brought my cousins."

Blysse stammered on her words. "He knows you?" She looked at Hereward, astonished.

Hereward nodded. "Hastulf was about four years of age, when I was a servant at Godfrey Hall."

"You worked here?" Isabella looked at him with surprise.

"Before you were born."

Hastulf sneered. "I remember little, yet I do recall my parents arguing with you and that I did not care much for you."

Hereward laughed. "You wouldn't have. I don't know how many times I told them you should learn your place as a child. Even Muriolda and Alward agreed with this."

Hastulf's eyes narrowed. "Yet, a server wouldn't know what's best for a lord's son, would he? My father was an important man." And then he shrugged, as if none of it mattered to him. "I do not have time for this, but must find out why you are here."

Hereward nodded. He turned to Isabella. "You have the key?"

Hastulf frowned, as Isabella pulled the key Hereward had given her, out of a leather pouch and gave it to him, and then sat back down next to her sister.

Hereward had pleased look on his face. "Years ago, I used this to lock up a great secret. Blysse and Isabella would have no knowledge of it, as it happened the day they were born. And you, Hastulf, were merely a child. You would not have remembered."

Roldan rubbed the scar on the side of his face. His eyes narrowed. "I was hired, when the old staff was told to leave. And from what I hear, they were an unworthy lot."

"It's not true, Roldan." Hereward shook his head. "The servants were greatly thought of by the former owners. It was a graven thing done to them."

He carried the key across the room and stood next to the wall nearest the fireplace. Everyone in the room watched curiously, when he pulled on a brick and pried it loose.

Blysse leaned forward, watching curiously.

The gap in the wall revealed a keyhole.

Both Hastulf and Roldan's eyes grew large.

Hastulf couldn't hide his astonishment. "You knew this and did not say anything?"

"There was no one I could trust. I hid the paper that belonged to the true owners of the manor here behind the wall."

"True?"

Hereward nodded and turned the key in the lock. He opened a small door, taking out a piece of paper, charred on the edges. "It's a will, written by the lady of the manor. She died shortly after she wrote it. Her name was Bela Godfrey."

"My Aunt?" Blysse looked surprised.

Hastulf wiped sweat off his brow and began wringing his hands. "So what has this to do with me? I am the male heir, the next descendent."

Hereward frowned. "You never knew the truth?"

"What?" Isabella questioned.

"Bela was not your aunt, but your mother."

Isabella's mouth drew open. "Mother?"

Blysse rose from her seat. "Bela?"

Hastulf started forward. "Give me that! This is the work of the devil."

"No." Hereward put up a hand. "When Bela was in childbirth and dying with the twins, she was a widow. It was her wish for the young women to inherit this place. This will was written soon after Blysse and Isabella were born. She gave it to Muriolda to keep in trust, so they would someday inherit the manor. I'm sure Muriold assumed it would pass on to a son of hers someday."

Blysse sat back down. A look of shock was on her face.

Hereward sighed. "After Bela was dead, Muriolda tossed the paper into the fire. She wanted a child of hers to inherit the place. So, when they were not looking, I took the will out and hid it in this safe built into the wall by Steward Godfrey, Blysse and Isabella's father."

Hastulf shook his head. "It makes no difference! Read the blasted thing! We'll see whether or not it changes anything!"

Hereward held the paper up to the light of the window and squinted. He began to read.

\*\*\*\*\*

25, August 1333

My dearest daughters, Isabella and Blysse,

If you're reading this, I'm sad to say, I was not able to care for you, as a mother should. It's been a very difficult childbirth. I do not believe I'll make it, as I'm also grieving the loss of your father, Stewart Godfrey. I learned very recently, that he was on his way to see me and had a horrible fall from his horse. He was not able to rally from it and died. I'm distraught to have lost him in this way.

## Isabella's Shield

My sister, Muriolda knows I'm giving this land and Godfrey Hall to both of you at the age of seventeen. No other male heir will be privy to it. It's tearing me apart to know that I'll not know you and will not be here to see you mature. I pray you'll have a happy, joyful life and that God will watch over you. You must know that both your father and I loved you very much, even before knowing you. I pray you'll both walk with the Lord. You're precious to me and will always be so. I'll wait for you both to join me one happy day.

Your loving mother,
Bela Godfrey

*****

Blysse reached out and took Isabella's hand. Both sisters were spellbound and didn't say a word.

Mauger let out a long breath. "It all makes sense. The violet eyes were Bela's. Isabella, you're so much like her. And Blysse, you've the face of my brother, Stewart, and the darkness of his hair."

Isabella looked up, her eyes soft. "They've wronged us."

"They deceived all of us, even our cousin." Blysse snorted.

Hereward smiled. "But, Bela would find pleasure knowing her prayers did not fall on deaf ears. You are believers."

Roldan's eyes narrowed. He looked down his nose. "What it says does not concern me." He reached for his lance and drew it out. "I refuse to lose everything I've gained through all this. Hastulf was going to make me his partner and confidant here."

Hastulf put his hand on Rolden's arm. "Put that away. You can't kill them. This isn't the way."

Roldan thrust his sword at the open door to a room off the main hall. He shoved Hastulf inside. "Get in! I'm taking matters into my own hands. I will do something."

When Roldan turned, Hereward slid the will into his jacket.

Hastulf shook his head. "Don't do it, Roldan. You will not get away with it, and they'll think I had something to do with it." He backed further into the room at the tip of the lance.

After Hastulf was on the other side of the door, Roldan pushed it shut and locked it. He turned, waving his lance at the others in the room. "Get down the hall, all of you!" He flashed the end of the sword at them.

Isabella got up from the chair and took her Uncle Mauger's arm. "It'll be all right. God will surely care for us."

All four of them walked slowly down an empty hallway lit by lanterns. They were led out a door in the back of the manor.

"Keep moving," Roldan said gruffly.

The night air was chilly, and the grounds were quiet. They walked toward a large fenced area with animals inside.

Roldan held the lance, ordering Mauger and Hereward to hitch a wagon. "Do it quick," he ordered them.

Blysse stamped her foot. "You have lost your mind, and will only add to Hastulf's troubles by going through with this dark deed."

Isabella tugged on her arm. "Blysse."

Blysse snorted at Rolden, ignoring Isabella. "You're a fool and will be caught for sure!"

"Cease these idle words, or you'll regret it!" Roldan sneered and flashed his lance. "Now, you must get into the wagon! Mauger take the reins. I have tethered the horse to me, also."

Mauger sat in the front of the cart and took the reins. The rest of them climbed into the back.

Roldan rode next to the cart on a large stallion.

It seemed like miles of jutting and bouncing along, before Roldan finally grabbed the reins and slowed the wagon to a halt.

"Here."

Blysse stood in the wagon and crossed her arms. "Whatever you plan to do, you'll surely be found out."

Roldan laughed. "I'll make sure everyone in London will know what happens, as it will not be by the lance you'll die, but at the hand of a cart and horse."

Isabella looked out over the fields. She could smell salt in the air and feel a cool breeze upon her face. She shivered, holding her jacket tighter around her.

"We're near the shore." Blysse's dark eyes narrowed. "And the cliffs."

Roldan laughed again. "To be sure. No one could survive such a fall."

There was a haunting silence that hung between them, save the sound of water crashing violently against rocks in the distance. Fog was moving in, thick upon their breath.

Suddenly, Mauger reached for the reigns and made a move.

Isabella cried out to him. "Uncle!"

"Get down! Hold on," he yelled.

Yet, Roldan was quicker. He screamed at the top of his lungs and charged forward with his horse. He grabbed the reigns from Mauger and threw them on the ground. The mare began pulling the wagon, spooked and lunging forward, running toward the cliffs at breakneck speed.

Roldan disappeared into the darkness and fog, his haunting laughter echoing after them. The blackness of the day was closing in on them.

Isabella screamed and fell on top of Blysse, who tumbled into the wagon bed. Hereward and Mauger tried to stop the frightened horse, but the cart bounced over the rocky terrain and sped along toward the water.

It seemed surreal, flying through the dark mist, the spooked horses charging at breakneck speed. Isabella couldn't help picturing the certain disaster that lie in front of them. She grabbed for Blysse's arm, but missed, the rocking motion of the wagon too strong.

Blysse tumbled about the wagon, taking ahold of the side of it. She groped around trying desperately to find the reigns that were most likely dragging on the ground beneath the cart.

It was then that Isabella peered into the dark. There was someone riding after them. Roldan? Did he have a change of heart?

"Matheu! Dante!" Blysse screamed. "It's them!"

Isabella blinked. It was true! She could see Matheu. The stone gate on his shield stood out on the dark background.

Both men raced past the wagon on horseback. Matheu took quick hold of the reigns and pulled, while Dante's horse ran along on the other side, guiding the frightened mare away from the cliffs. They rode for a distance alongside the cart before they slowed and finally stopped it.

In the distance, thundering hooves caught their attention, and they all watched Roldan charge off into the night.

Matheu got off his horse and pulled Isabella from the wagon and into his arms. His cool, blue eyes met hers. "Are you hurt?"

She hugged tight to his neck and held him close. "No, but I didn't think I'd ever see you again."

Blysse nodded. "I thought for sure we'd go over the cliff."

Dante stood next to the wagon. "We left Thorneton Le Dale and rode here as fast as we could, and I'm glad we did."

"There was little we could've done," Isabella agreed.

Matheu let out a breath. "M'lady, you mustn't do this, again. You must stay by my side, from now on."

Her eyes moistened, and she spoke softly. "But, I am at my uncle's manor? How can I do this?"

Mauger and Hereward got down from the wagon and stood next to her.

Mauger winked at Isabella and turned to Matheu. "Yes, how is this possible, when she lives at her uncle's home?"

Matheu smiled. "I wished for a more proper place, but this will have to do." He knelt to the ground, laying his shield aside. "I suppose it is only right that I ask for your hand in holy matrimony, so you might be at my side for all our days. Does this seem a possibility to you, M'lady?

Isabella blushed, looking up at him. "If you wish it."

He pressed his lip to her hand. "M'lady, you know I do."

"And Thorneton Le Dale will be my home." She smiled.

He wiped away tears beneath her eyes. "Yes."

Isabella threw her arms about his neck and she whispered in his ear, "Then, let us not waste a moment in this place."

He let out a whoop and turned to the others. "She's coming, with me..."

Everyone cheered.

Dante sidled his horse up next to the wagon, eying Blysse with a grin. "I believe I've been struck with the same fever as Matheu, and will be going to the church with a pretty lady soon."

Blysse stood up and put her hands on her hips. "And who do you think this might be?"

Dante got down from his horse, reached up and pulled her onto the ground next to him. He gave he a churlish grin and then laughed. "A dark-haired lass I met, who I want to take back to the Moors with me."

Her lips drew into a pout. "Hmm, dark-haired?"

"I think it might be you, miss."

She smiled. "And yet, I'm certain you'll need to make it worth my while, before I can say yes."

Dante laughed, a growing spark in his eyes. "Maybe this one will be convinced, quicker than she believes." He pulled her to him in a long stirring kiss, enveloping her in his arms. Then he whispered in her ear. "It is my belief God has put us together. I do not think it was a coincidence when I came by that day at the well. We are quite well-matched." Then, he reached up and stroked her cheek tenderly, his eyes shining. "Do you believe this is enough convincing for you, Blysse?"

She waved her hand in front of her face, as if she were out of breath and needed air. "I believe it is, sir." Her cheeks were rosy, and her eyes slanted at him. "And I've come to the conclusion that I might enjoy living in the Moors."

He grinned, and touched her cheek, again. "I'm happy to hear it, as we'll spend all our years there, together." He took her hand in his.

And then he looked out over the dark field. "Yet, there's something Matheu and I must tend to, first."

Matheu nodded, "Roldan."

Isabella looked alarmed. "But surely he's gone?"

"Until we find him, he's still a threat. Hastulf said he won't quit until the manor is his."

Blysse frowned. "Hastulf?"

"Yes, he saved your lives. He told us where you went."

"Our cousin said this?" Isabella put a hand to her mouth.

"He did not wish to be connected to Rolden's dark deeds." Dante nodded. "But, I think he's also had a change of heart, knowing so much of your family is gone."

Matheu agreed. "Yes, even though he didn't want this dark deed on his conscience, he had a measure of sympathy for you." Matheu got back onto his horse, which pranced forward, and he reined it in. "We'll take you back to the inn first, where you'll be out of harm's way."

"You'll not stay with us?" Isabella looked pained.

Matheu laid a hand on her arm. "We'll find him, and in no time he'll stand before the law."

They all got in the wagon. Matheu and Dante guided it back to the inn. Once they were settled inside, both men headed out into the night. Isabella and Blysse prayed for their safe return.

*****

# Chapter 19

Hastulf pointed a bony finger at Blysse. "Why are you doing this? I don't understand."

"We're moving to the Moors. We've no need to take this place from you. You played no part in any of it, and we hold nothing against you."

Hastulf's eyes were like slits. Either his cousins were brainless fools and had no understanding as to how much this place was worth, or they were out to wreak some plot against him in another way.

Isabella tried to make him see reason. "We mean what we say, Hastulf. We hold no ill will toward you. Truly."

Hastulf leaned forward, clearly puzzled. He shook his head. Whatever the reason, they were giving him the manor. It didn't matter. He didn't care. The new deed was drawn out, signed, and the estate was his.

"Must I worry about that morbid knight, Roldan, lurking about here?"

Blysse shook her head. "Roldan is locked up and will suffer in prison for life. He'll pay for what he's done, but maybe find his way to the cross in the end."

Isabella nodded.

Hastulf chortled, "Believers? You?"

Blysse stood up and smoothed out her green, satin skirt and then readjusted a bow. "It is not so bad. You might put your trust in God and feel his peace."

Hastulf stood up. "Spare me this. It is one thing I do not care to hear. There's enough of that in the church I attend."

Blysse's eyes gentled. "You might read the Holy Scripture, Hastulf, to understand."

There was a brief silence. The room shuddered, as the fire in the hearth burst forth, throwing sparks onto the stone floor.

A wary expression crossed Hastulf's face. "What has happened to you both?"

Blysse placed her hand on his arm. "A very good thing."

Isabella's violet eyes were gentle. "Which we are willing to disclose to you."

Hastulf put his hand up. "Maybe another time. I've things to do."

Isabella spoke softly. "God will show you the way. Just ask." She touched his shoulder, then got up from her chair and stood next to Blysse.

Hastulf eyed them both warily, not speaking.

Isabella ignored her cousin's silence. "Well, we must be leaving. It is time. We wish you well, Hastulf."

"We will visit." Blysse curtsied.

Hastulf leaned against the table. "Yes, well, someday maybe things will change between us. We have little in the way of family after these dark times."

Both sisters each nodded, turning to find their own way down the familiar halls and out of the manor.

As they stepped under the massive, arched stone gate leading outside the walls of the grounds, they turned to smile at each other.

"There are changes in Hastulf's heart already. I can sense it." Isabella clasped her hands.

Blysse nodded. "Surprisingly, I sense it, too."

Isabella breathed in the scents of summer flowers and lifted her face to the rays of sun streaming down on her. "It's time to leave him behind us now, but I'm determined to visit when I can."

"Yes, maybe Hastulf can find the peace he's been looking for."

Isabella eyed the stables where Mauger stood with Dante and Matheu, waiting for them. Four horses had been hitched to a carriage and sat at the end of the path. "We've much to be thankful for, Blysse. We have been through many trials, and yet, they have all worked out for the good in the end."

Blysse agreed with a shake of her head. "God's been good to us. He's taken from us, yet given back in full measure. Our mother's prayers were listened to even after death."

"Yes," Isabella replied, a wistful expression on her face. "He has done great things."

Blysse didn't speak. She took her sister's hand, and they made there way to the carriage that would take them to their new homes.

\*\*\*\*\*

# Chapter 20

Blysse urged her horse to race faster across the field, her hair whipping wildly behind her. She felt the thrill of the tumultuous, Moor winds against her skin and laughed when Dante's horse came rushing up beside her.

She slowed her animal and turned to him. "I believe you're regretting your decision to race. You are having trouble catching me."

Dante grinned. He got down from the animal and pulled her to the ground with him. He lifted her in his arms and carried her to a small pond nearby, threatening to drop her in.

She laughed. "You best not do this!"

One of the horses suddenly reared up, and Dante turned. He lost his balance with her in his arms and fell, both of them dropping into the lake.

When Blysse righted herself in his arms, she gasped, spitting out water and looking down at her dripping clothes. A pout threatened her lips, and then her eyes were drawn to him, grinning from ear to ear at the water dripping down his face. She began to laugh. "What will the servers at the manor say?"

He drew her to him, smiling. "I'll tell them how much trouble you are, and I'm sure they'll most likely agree."

Her eyes sparkled, and her chin lifted high. "You better not…"

But before she could finish her sentence to argue, she was drawn into a deep, contented kiss.

When he finally let her go, her dark eyes met his, and she smiled. "Well, I suppose it won't matter what you tell them."

Dante laughed and drew his new wife into his arms. Later, he'd think about what they would tell the servants. But for now, he was going to enjoy a moment with his wife.

\*\*\*\*\*

Isabella tipped her head to the side, frowning. "Hawise is coming for dinner?"

She looked up from the weaving loom she sat behind, threading the thin, wool strands through the vertical pieces stretched out and weighted with clay.

Matheu smiled. "I was at Mauger's home the other day, and she said she wished to visit."

"And you wanted her to come?" Isabella sighed. "Were you aware she told me you were going to marry her?" She let go of the thread she was working on and turned.

"No." Matheu looked surprised. A grin spread across his face. "Am I seeing a spot of jealousy in you?"

At first, Isabella frowned. Then, she couldn't help smiling, when she saw the way he was looking at her. "Maybe. But, it's for good reason, and I'd rather not have her around."

His blue eyes sparkled. "Well, I couldn't turn her away. And I know you'll be kind to her for me." He sat down on the bench beside her and took her hand, drawing it to his lips. "Hawise does understand I'm a married man now." He smiled. "And happy."

Isabella felt her cheeks grow warm. She raised her eyes to his tenderly.

He leaned down and kissed her, pulling her to him.

They both turned when one of the servants called out. "Hawise Ellis and Sir Gawain, squire to Matheu Thorneton Le Dale."

Isabella got up and straightened the folds of her skirt.

Hawise entered the room with Gawain. Her face was rosy and brown, eyes sparkling. "Sir Matheu! I'm so glad to see you again!"

Matheu smiled. "Hawise, it's good to see you in such high spirits."

Isabella clasped her hands in front of her. "Yes, Hawise, you're looking well."

Hawise turned suddenly, a solemn look in her eyes. She took quick steps across the stone floor and grasped Isabella's hand in hers, sighing deeply. "M'lady, there is something I must tell you, to make amends."

Isabella's eyes widened. "Amends? Oh, Hawise. You do not need to make amends for anything."

Hawise smiled. "But, I do. I know now, how I've wronged you sorely."

She turned to Gawain, motioning for him to stand next to her. "I've taken steps to change. Gawain's helped me to understand, through God's grace."

"God's grace?" Isabella put a hand to her mouth, her heart suddenly lighter. "Oh, Hawise. I'm so glad of it."

Hawise nodded and smiled, but then became solemn. "I wished to apologize for how I treated you."

Isabella squeezed Hawise's hand gently. "Oh, all is forgotten where it concerns me. I knew you did not understand so many things."

Hawise eyes became misty. She let go and stood next to Gawain. "I supposed you would be forgiving, and I thank you for it." She turned to Gawain. "I am glad for the changes in my life."

Gawain's eyes tenderly met Hawise's.

Isabella eyed the pair curiously. "I see there might be something else you came to tell us?" She smiled.

Gawain's brown eyes lit, and he smiled back. "Merely that Hawise and I have plans to marry very soon." He took Hawise's hand and held it tenderly.

Her eyes sparkled when she looked at him. She pulled him closer. "Before he backs out of it."

He grinned. "Not on your life. I need a partner who is able to win at pins at the tournaments."

"Gawain!" She began to laugh.

He laughed with her, and they all joined in.

Isabella turned and eyed the spread on the table. "So, we're ready to eat? It looks like a hearty meal set out for us."

The others all nodded and sat down together. It wasn't long before they were deep in conversation.

As the night grew longer, Isabella couldn't help but wonder at the changes that had taken place in their lives. Hawise and Gawain seemed so very happy, as were Matheu and herself. Blysse had found love with Dante in this wild, heather-filled country, and recently her cousin, Hastulf had sent word he was looking forward to visits from them. Things had surely changed for the better. God had done great things for all of them, and she pictured many years of happiness ahead.

She smiled, catching Matheu's tender look across the table, a considerate man, and truly the most handsome she knew. She couldn't have asked for a better match.

Thorneton Le Dale was surely a home where she would find the love and peace she had always longed for.

*****

*Any reference to scriptures is from the King James Version of the Holy Scriptures.

Made in the USA
Charleston, SC
08 October 2015